W9-CEI-322

PHANTOM WARRIOR

Center Point
Large Print

Also by Fred Grove and available from
Center Point Large Print:

The Running Horses

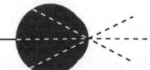

**This Large Print Book carries the
Seal of Approval of N.A.V.H.**

PHANTOM WARRIOR

Fred Grove

CENTER POINT LARGE PRINT
THORNDIKE, MAINE

This Center Point Large Print edition
is published in the year 2020 by arrangement with
Golden West Literary Agency.

Originally published in the US by Doubleday.

The text of this Large Print edition is unabridged.
In other aspects, this book may vary
from the original edition.
Printed in the United States of America
on permanent paper.
Set in 16-point Times New Roman type.

ISBN: 978-1-64358-680-9 (hardcover)
ISBN: 978-1-64358-684-7 (paperback)

The Library of Congress has cataloged this record
under Library of Congress Control Number: 2020934766

To Elza,
who knows the way to Doubtful Canyon

PHANTOM WARRIOR

CHAPTER 1

Second Lieutenant Ewing Hall Mackay moved to the edge of the camp and paused, feeling the desert's coolness rising after the stifling day's hard ride. Something was stirring among the Tonto scouts. He had sensed that something was wrong since they had left San Carlos two days ago. They were much too quiet. Normally at this hour they would be talking and smoking and indulging the Apache passion for gambling.

Watching, he saw Sergeant Archie drift across the campsite. "Santo," Archie said, referring to one of the scouts, and shook his head. "No *bueno* scout like Tontos."

"Tontos are always the best," Ewing said, displaying a dry grin. "Everybody knows that."

"Chiricahuas, Tontos hate. Tontos, Chiricahuas hate."

Ewing nodded to that, seeing demonstrated again how the fragmented nature of Apache life, combined with fierce Apache individualism and independence, worked against loyalty between tribes and bands.

"That's part of it, all right—that hate," Ewing agreed. "But he's not sulking just because he's a Chiricahua. He's sore because I jailed him at San Carlos for making *tiswin*, getting drunk on it, and

9

beating his wife with a club. Broke her arm in two places, the surgeon said. He seemed sorry for what he did and asked to enlist. Maybe he fooled me."

"Too much you trust, Nantan."

"I have to trust any Apache I enlist."

"Better kill him now, Nantan. Before you he kill. I tell you this thing, Nantan. Kill him!"

"I can't do that."

"Archie will do." He took a deliberate step away, his eyes flaring the wildness that was always close to the surface of these wild people.

Ewing did not extend a restraining hand. But when he said, "No—Archie," the Tonto stopped and slowly faced about. "Nantan, trust Archie?"

"I'm surprised you'd ask," Ewing replied, smiling.

"*Enjuh*. You watch, Nantan. Archie watch."

Archie was Ewing's chief scout, guide, and interpreter. His mixed-up "reservation English," proudly learned from a short-term eastern school-teacher when the Apaches were concentrated on the Verde Reservation, somehow carried a formal, almost ceremonious, tone. He was tall for a Tonto, nearly six feet, deep-chested, extremely strong in the legs and thighs, which enabled him to cover from sixty to seventy-five miles a day on foot, alternately dogtrotting and walking. To Ewing, Archie's black, high-crowned hat, which the scouts favored, had long ceased to seem out

10

of keeping with his moccasins and leggings, breechclout, and long-tailed calico shirt tied with a sash. Two belts of cartridges crisscrossed his chest.

Archie was proud to be an Army scout, because that way he was still a warrior and could fight other Apaches. He was proud to wear the broad-brimmed hat, proud to carry a Springfield carbine, but his proudest possession was the $5.95 mail-order watch, an American Horologe, which Ewing had presented him when Archie made sergeant. He would gaze endlessly at the leaping stag engraved on the gold-filled hunting case. He seldom wound the watch or looked at the face and its roman numerals, simply, Ewing supposed, because Archie knew where the sun stood and when the moon rose, unlike the puzzling *blancos*, who were to be pitied because they seemed not to know and, therefore, had to depend on this ticking thing. Archie's interest, Ewing decided, was purely aesthetic, as a white man might enjoy something precious.

In turn, impulsively, Archie had given him a stone-bladed hunting knife, the handle of whittled-smooth mountain oak, in a scabbard of soft buckskin.

Ewing slowly moved back to camp and sat down by his saddle and pack, thinking of Archie's warning—assassination. Every Army officer and white civilian scout working with Apaches risked it. Enlisted White Mountain Apaches, drunk on *tiswin*, the native beer, had killed old Gus Fowler not long ago in the Pinals. Three years ago Archie had been a hostile. But by now Ewing could trust these Tontos—Archie, Rowdy, and Jim in particular. He was far from sure about Santo.

With the Tontos, Ewing had shared the same hardships, the same dangers, the same Army rations, often less. They had pursued Flores and his band of runaway Chiricahuas across the Mexican border, found their sanctuary in the rugged Sierra Madre and brought them back after a stiff fight. And once, to the great delight of the scouts, they had fought a force of Mexican irregulars, or *nacionales*, some fifty of them, when the latter attacked, mistaking the Apache scouts for hostiles. Not that it made any difference to the long-suffering people below the border: to them an Apache was an Apache.

Comrades. Ewing hesitated over the word. But the four of them were that, if a *blanco* and Apaches could be.

He took a cigar from the small bale in his pack, lit it from the dying mesquite fire, and looked across at the scouts. Santo sat alone, silent, sulking. After a while, Ewing saw him turn his back to the others and reach for his blanket. Moments later a figure hunkered down some yards behind Santo . . . Archie. Archie was still there when Ewing finished his smoke and carried his blanket and carbine past the picketed horses, deeper into the greasewood to sleep.

Stretching out, he found himself dwelling again on the cryptic wording of his orders:

HEADQUARTERS DEPARTMENT
OF ARIZONA
Fort Bowie, Arizona
June 14, 1881
Second Lieutenant Ewing H. Mackay, Troop F, 6th Cavalry, San Carlos Reservation, will proceed without delay with ten enlisted Apache scouts for detached service to Fort Cummings, Territory of New Mexico, Department of New Mexico. On his arrival at Fort Cummings, Lieutenant Mackay will report to the commanding officer for further orders. The Quartermaster Department will furnish necessary transportation.
by command of
Maj. Gen. Orlando B. Willcox

That was all. Something was up, but what was it? He slept on that question.

They first sighted the smoke before midday, a grayish plume against the brass-bright sky, rising southeast of the scouts in the Peloncillo Mountains. Archie pointed and Ewing said,

"Doubtful Canyon," and hastened the detail forward.

When the San Simon Stage Station appeared ahead on the valley floor—a shrunken adobe building within an adobe corral—he untied his dark blue Army blouse, rolled and strapped to his saddle, and donned it over his blue flannel shirt. He always did so before approaching a ranch or settlement as a precaution against getting shot at. The field-service blouse and his brown canvas trousers represented his only semblance of regulation dress, canvas suits being an innovation of General George Crook for southwestern campaigning. Other times, Ewing would cut a hole in a sheet of canvas for his head and wear it like a serape. Slouch hat and moccasins completed his "field uniform." His pack held his black cavalry boots, an extra shirt, underwear, and a pair of light blue cavalry pants, unworn for months.

He rode on alone, crossed the dry creek, and called out, "Hello, Hap Sullivan! Hello, Hap Sullivan!"

Inch by inch, a head rose over the adobe wall, then the long snout of a rifle, then Ewing heard wooden bars sliding, and then the stout gate squealed open and a bib-bearded man with eyes the color of slate came out.

"Do I have to introduce myself?" Ewing mocked.

"All I could see was Apaches."

"Hostiles don't wear white-man hats."

Sullivan broke into coarse laughter. "Hell they don't! One time a war party come by here wearin' derbies ransacked from some poor freighter's outfit they'd rubbed out in Doubtful." He sobered. "Well, Lieutenant, you see the smoke. The eastbound went through late yesterday. I figure they made it on to Stein's, but that wagon train sure didn't."

"Wagon train?"

"Went through here this morning. Three wagons. Everybody in a big hurry to get rich. Just couldn't wait. Prospectors bound for the Hillsboro gold mines over in New Mexico. The firin' went on for an hour or more. Pretty quick after that, I saw smoke." He gritted his teeth. "I wanted to go up there, but what could I do?"

"Just got yourself killed."

"By God, the Army oughta keep troops posted here."

"There was a detail at Stein's."

"You mean a month ago."

"We'll take a look."

"You know what you'll find," Sullivan predicted gloomily and turned back to his adobe fortress. Suddenly he wheeled. "There was one woman—a young woman."

Ewing groaned. Why in the name of common sense did people travel through Indian country in small parties? He took the scouts on at a gallop.

15

Reaching the mouth of Doubtful Canyon, he spoke an order to Archie and flankers cut away. The smoke was a mere feather of thinning gray by now, drifting eastward. Watching about, Ewing spotted Santo delaying instead of prowling the left-hand slope. Ewing yelled the Indian's name. Santo did not seem to hear. Ewing yelled again. At last Santo turned.

Ewing, eyes kindling, motioned emphatically for him to move out.

Santo sent back an inscrutable look which he held until Ewing motioned again. Only then did the Chiricahua heel his mount away.

It's coming to a head, Ewing boiled. *Just a matter of time and place.*

Twisting, the pass narrowed and its walls rose higher, ribbed with brush and boulders. The flankers advanced more warily.

About a mile onward, where the pass made a sharp bend, Ewing saw the wagons, or rather, what was left of them. One, a Shuttler, was still smoking. The fire had gone out in the nearest blackened vehicle, leaving the box and running gear intact; the cover was gone and exposed the skeleton ribs of the bows. Everything was a strewn mess—tools, bedding, utensils, flour.

Drawing nearer, he froze at sight of a figure tied between the Shuttler's front and rear wheels. The fire beneath the man, naked except for his boots, was down to embers. Rushing over, Ewing dismounted and ran to the wagon, kicked and scattered the coals and cut the man down. He was dead. Other bodies lay under and beside the wagons. Two downed mules still struggled in the harness of the lead wagon. Ewing put them out of their misery with his carbine and walked over the site, reading the signs of an old story. Hostiles, posted above the trail, shooting the lead mules first, then gradually closing in. A sudden charge, fiendish yells that paralyzed the few remaining defenders, and it was all over except for the torture and looting. The seven prospectors had been mutilated, but not scalped. Apaches didn't scalp. There was no woman, so she had been taken, which was worse for her.

Archie galloped back. "Chiricahuas," he said and pointed south, the direction they had gone.

"No sign of the woman?"

None, he signed.

"Maybe she's farther upcanyon," Ewing said, "though I doubt it."

Archie was staring beyond Ewing, his eyes widening. Ewing jerked and saw an apparition rising from behind a boulder—a woman. She stumbled toward them, arms outstretched, hair streaming below her shoulders, her taut face a carving of utter disbelief and appeal.

"My God—" breathed Ewing and ran to her.

She stumbled. Ewing caught her before she could fall. She looked up at him with that sprung-eyed expression of unreality. "I thought they'd come back," she mumbled, "till I heard your voices." She kept shaking her head.

"You're all right now. These are Army scouts. I'm Lieutenant Mackay."

She held on to him fiercely, her hands digging clawlike into his shoulders. Her rigid body shook. But when after several moments she let go, she managed a kind of forced calm, as if she must not show her feelings, her pained eyes boring into his. He led her to the road. As they came to the wagons, her hands flew to her mouth. Her pallid face drained to an even more ashen hue. He hurried her on by. Below the wagons he sat her on a rock, uncapped his canteen, and handed it to her. She drank like an obedient child.

Watching her, he thought of matters that had to be done. The detail would have to return to San Simon, closer than Stein's by some miles. He turned.

"Don't go. Please!" She flung out an appealing hand, caught herself, and looked down, ashamed. "I'm sorry. I was thinking only of myself, while those poor men . . ."

"I promise you we won't be far away."

He called Archie. Shortly, two unwilling cavalry mounts were hitched to one usable wagon, the victims loaded thereon, and the procession started down the pass to San Simon, the young woman on the driver's horse, the two dismounted scouts dogtrotting ahead.

Sullivan and a Mexican hostler were waiting outside the corral. A Mexican woman stood in the gateway, wringing her hands, moaning, "*Indios! Indios!*"

"Got any whiskey, Hap?" Ewing called. "The young lady's in shock, but she's all right."

"Got more whiskey than water. Bring her in."

Sullivan scowled at the burdened wagon. "There's a nice little place we've been usin' now for some time, upslope from the creek. Show 'em where, Francisco."

Afterward, Ewing returned to the station to find the young woman sitting in the shade of the brush-roofed *ramada*, hands clasped on her lap. She was slim, and he remembered that she had come to his shoulder. Her face—sunbrowned skin over high cheekbones, hazel eyes long-lashed and set wide, a full mouth, pensive at the moment—showed an acceptance of what had happened, yet minus any self-pity. She had gathered her dark hair behind her neck. Her dress of sober gray, torn above the hem, was obviously of the plainest material; still, even here, she gave it a certain grace. He decided she was in her early twenties, perhaps younger, though her maturity made her appear older. For the briefest instant, Elinor crossed his mind, causing him to wonder whether she would have pulled through something like this years ago, and immediately struck aside the comparison as unfair and of no meaning.

"You're looking much better," he said.

She smiled a little.

He said, "We have to go on to Stein's Station. That's just on the other side of the mountains. Now, the eastbound stage comes through twice a week. You could wait for it here . . . or I could borrow a mount from Hap Sullivan . . . escort you on to Stein's, if you feel up to it? Accommodations are better there. It's a meal-and-change station. You could wait there for the stage."

She did not hesitate. "I'll ride horseback."

He had to grin. "You don't take the easy way. However, it's only thirteen miles or so, Miss . . ."

"Ivy Shaw," she said in a small voice.

He took off his hat. "Mind telling me how you happened to make it behind that boulder?"

"Mr. Clark . . . the man in charge of wagons . . . told me to run there just before the Indians made their charge. They all came out of the rocks on one side of the wagons. When they did, I ran across the road and hid." She gazed at her hands, her expression kindred to guilt. "Mr. Clark was very kind to me. He was the one they—" She couldn't finish.

"May I ask where you started from?"

"Prescott."

"I can send word back to your people by the next westbound—that is, if you like?"

She hesitated. "I have no people back there. My brother is working in a gold mine near Hillsboro. That's where we were all headed. I was cooking for them."

"I'll need their names for my report."

"I can help that much."

That completed, with Sullivan promising to send the report by the next westbound to Fort Bowie at Apache Pass, Ewing said cheerfully, "Well, then, Miss Shaw, we had best get you along to Stein's."

Before he could assist her, she mounted and seated herself sidesaddle. Coming to the ambush site, Ewing halted the scouts and turned to her, riding without complaint on Sullivan's battered stock saddle.

"We might look for your baggage," he said.

"I'll look," she replied, dismounting quickly. Hurrying past the Shuttler, she went to the lead wagon and climbed inside the partially burned hulk. She came back carrying a small carpetbag of old-fashioned vintage. "The rest of my things were burned," she told him, her head going up.

Wordlessly, Ewing took the bag from her, thinking, *She's a brave one and independent as hell.*

Five o'clock had come when Ewing led the detail through the eastern end of the canyon,

Stein's Peak a treeless landmark towering on their right, Stein's Station a short distance beyond on a gentle rise south of the mail road: a rectangular bastion of flat rocks stacked higher than a horseman's head, its only entrance a stout gate on the north side, built before the Civil War as a relay station on the Butterfield Trail. Far to the east Ewing's eyes met a broad alkali plain, its sterile face glaring under the late sun. An empty stage waited on the farther side of the gate.

As the scouts clattered up, the gate swung open and Rip Carr, the station agent, stepped out to meet them. His experienced eyes moved in recognition to Ewing, switched to Ivy Shaw, and back to Ewing. "We heard the shootin'," he muttered. He was a tired-looking man, long-haired, beak-nosed, calm, and decisive.

Ewing told him concisely, skipping the gory details, adding, "Miss Shaw will need a seat on the eastbound for Fort Cummings."

"Well, there it is, Lieutenant," Carr said, jogging his head. "Bitter Creek Bill's on the box. He wanted to go on—that's Bitter Creek. But I made him hold up. Everything's busted loose east of here. War party took a swipe at Barney's Station day before yesterday, only the boys happened to be ready. About daybreak this morning, we had company. Same bunch, I figure. Rushed us, but the gate was closed. Daybreak's when you want to stay put—that's when they like to rush you. I never water stock that early. Well, they pulled back, hung around an hour or so, wasted some shots on us, then tore out for Doubtful."

"How many you figure in the war party?"

"Fifteen or so."

"Sergeant Archie, here, says they were Chiricahuas. Says they went south. That should leave it quiet around here for a spell. Since we're on orders to Fort Cummings, we can furnish escort that far. We were over the route two years ago."

"Lieutenant," sighed Carr, a slow-breaking relief creasing his long face, "that will sure take a load off my mind more ways than one."

"How many passengers?"

"Four." Carr's voice dropped a notch, guarded. He glanced toward the gate. "One is the wife of the Cummings commander—Mrs. Thorn. Complains about the meals, when ever'body knows you can't beat sowbelly, beans, raw onions, sourdough bread, and black coffee to stick to the ribs. Why, sometimes I even throw in a little deer meat and green chiles. If it ain't the meals, she complains about her bunk last night. Claims bedbugs wouldn't let her sleep. Why, I change the blankets ever' few weeks, an' last month I went over the whole shebang with coal oil to get the bugs."

23

"How about the men?" Ewing asked, smiling. "Would they be any help if we get jumped?"

The station agent made a face. "One's a whiskey drummer . . . carries a little pea-sized derringer. One's a mining engineer, interested in purty rocks. Other's a gambler headed for El Paso. They got rifles and six-shooters. Both talk a big fight, but they look like green hands to me." He brightened, regarding Ivy Shaw with sympathy. "Be plenty of room for you aboard, miss. Now, if you'll come in, we'll make you right at home."

The scouts watered at the spring northwest of the station in the wide wash that extended on through the canyon, picketed the horses across the road, and bivouacked.

Twilight was a gossamer veil hiding the starkness of the Peloncillos. A repentant breeze purred through bloody Doubtful Canyon, bent for the alkali flat. The faintest sounds became magnified at this hour: mounts cropping the short grama grass, distant voices seeming near and unusually distinct. Someone was banging on metal inside the stone station, each stroke like a summons.

Ewing eased down and took his evening smoke, his weariness not so much of the body as of the mind, seeing the same cycle of senseless killings repeated over and over. General Crook had been correct from the beginning: it took

24

Apaches to catch Apaches, if you caught them at all. A wiser Washington would have left him in command. After Crook, Colonel August Kautz; after him, Major General Willcox. Both capable officers, but the situation had not improved; in fact, it had worsened. Rumors were flying again that Crook—Nantan Lupan, the Gray Wolf Chief, whom the Apaches feared the most, yet respected and relied on for protection because he kept his word—would be reassigned to Arizona.

Ewing could look back on considerable frustration. He had been posted to Fort Bowie after graduation from West Point as a second lieutenant and newly married. But promotions were slow in the postwar Army. He was still a second lieutenant after eight years, also a graying one. However, he felt no bitterness, just a heavy discouragement, relieved by the knowledge that others like him shared the same gut-busting duty and bleak prospects.

He had a sudden burst of impatience, thinking of the great breadth of land northeast of the Peloncillos, in fancy picturing it as he had ridden over it after bountiful summer rains: land as level as a floor, the carpeting of dark green grama grass up to a horse's belly. Land that waited for cattle. With windmills and earthen tanks, a man could lead a good life there when this ugly game was finished. But that, he realized, could take years.

He shunted the dream aside and trailed his

attention over the camp, his eyes fixing on Santo. As usual, the Chiricahua sat apart, nursing his surly dislike for all *blancos* and Tontos alike, and Ewing remembered how Santo had lagged going back to San Simon until Archie spoke to him. Something would have to be done about Santo before long. If Ewing discharged him now, he would run for the Sierra Madre. If Ewing did nothing, what then?

Archie strayed over, as if seconding Ewing's thoughts.

Ewing asked, "What did Santo say when you ordered him to close up on the way back to San Simon?"

"He say his horse sore feet horse had."

"Was he telling the truth?"

Archie threw him an incredulous stare.

"Well," Ewing chuckled, "that wasn't a bad excuse."

"Santo also say sick him was. Devil in belly."

"That's still better."

"When Santo like three wolfs eat?"

"I'll discharge him when we get back to San Carlos."

"Maybe too late. You watch, Nantan. Watch."

Ewing didn't reply, his eyes drawn to a woman coming to the gate. The lucky young woman. Hesitantly, she looked right and left, her gaze settling on the camp.

"Nantan, good wife needs," Archie said.

26

"An Army post out here is no place for a wife," Ewing said, shaking his head. "I found that out long ago."

"That *blanco* woman there good wife would make."

"How can you tell?" Ewing asked, sounding amused.

"Not one time complain, that *blanco* woman."

"You're a keen observer, Archie. I noticed that, too."

"She is like Apache woman, that *blanco* woman."

"There's one big difference, Archie. An Apache woman dares not complain for fear she'll get a beating. That *blanco* woman doesn't complain of her own free will. But if she wanted to, she would. You could bet on that."

"Nantan, you are learn little bit about women, you are," Archie said, making certain Ewing caught his superior smile, and walked away as Ivy Shaw left the gate and strolled down the road toward the scouts' camp.

Ewing went out to meet her. "Good evening, Miss Shaw. Though I should remind you not to leave the station, even to venture this short distance."

"My head has finally cleared a little. I came out to make up for my lack of manners. I haven't thanked you or the scouts."

"Not necessary at all."

27

"But it is, and I thank you now. All of you. I wish you would tell them for me."

Seeing her in the half light, he was struck by the freshness of her face and her hair, brushed gleaming.

"I'll do that," he said, and wishing to encourage her, he said further, "We'll make Soldier's Farewell by tomorrow evening. That's the second station from here. Next day as far as the station on the Mimbres River, then Fort Cummings."

"Somehow, when I think of Mr. Clark and the others, I feel guilty that I survived."

"Don't. If there was a choice, they wanted you to be the one who got out."

"We would all be camped here now, the men smoking and talking. I would be fixing their supper."

He was silent. *Let her talk about it. Let her get it out.*

To his dismay, she suddenly put both hands to her face and began weeping. He considered stopping her; on second thought, he threw an arm around her shoulders, sensing that she had not yet let down and needed to shed tears.

It wasn't long before she wiped her eyes with a forefinger, saying, "I guess it's weak to cry," and straightened herself.

"No, you need to. It's good." As he spoke, the insight went through him again how she guarded her innermost feelings.

28

She was still distraught and not doing a very thorough job of clearing away the tears. And so, awkward at best, using his bandanna, he brushed at her cheeks and eyes. That embarrassed her and she drew back, murmuring, "I'm all right now, Mr. Mackay. Thank you."

Of a sudden, knowing more about her became important. At the same time he discovered himself wishing to please her, to make up for what she had gone through. "You said you have a brother around Hillsboro."

"Yes. My brother Eddie. He's three years older than I am."

"No other kin?"

"An uncle back in Missouri. Indians killed our folks in the Bradshaw Mountains."

He shook his head deploringly. "You didn't want to go back and live with your uncle?"

"He didn't ask us. He was poor. He's still poor. We'd have been more burdens to him."

"What did you do?"

"Just earned our keep wherever we could. Stuck together. When I was discouraged, Eddie made me go on. When he felt like giving up, I made him go on. We're mighty close."

"I can understand why."

In apology, she said, "Here I am talking about myself, when that wasn't my aim, when other folks have had harder times—well, good-night," and turned to go.

He caught up with her and took her arm. Touching her, feeling her lightness, he was reminded of his long absence from feminine company. They walked in silence to the gate. She thanked him and would have gone in had he not held on to her arm.

"Miss Shaw," he said, on impulse, "I want to say something. You're a very brave young lady and I admire you very much. Now, good-night."

She was startled, left motionless; one moment more and she hurried inside the station.

Thoughtfully, a little surprised at himself, he retraced his steps to camp, aware of an appreciation he had not felt for a woman in a long, long time. Glad that he had said it. Many times an approval was left unsaid that ought to have been said. Maybe if he and Elinor . . . Maybe. He shook off the useless supposition.

Ewing looked about, inspecting the bivouac. Twilight was giving way to purpling darkness. He did not see Santo and he did not see Archie. Unconcerned at this early hour and restless, Ivy Shaw still occupying his mind, he meandered on to the broad path from the road to the wash, following the descent toward the spring, his moccasined feet softly treading gravel and sand.

He did not know when he first caught the rustle of sound, so faint it was, a just audible slither coming from the dark bank to his left. It ceased, it picked up again. More curious than alarmed, he stopped and turned his head, the sound growing.

The onrushing crunch of gravel galvanized him into action, instinctively leaping aside as a figure charged out of the wash's darkness, knife upraised, pure hatred snarling from the man's throat. As Ewing dodged, he heard the swish of the blade slashing past his face. At the same instant he struck downward at the greasy shine of the broad face amid the tangle of long hair.

Ewing felt his fist strike bone, heard the man's astonished grunt, heard him go down. Closing, Ewing kicked with all his strength. The kick smashed the man's shoulder, spun him. His knife flew loose, clattering. Catlike the man sprang up. They collided, grappled, swayed, grunted, Ewing breathing the rank stink of sweat and woodsmoke. Ewing rammed his knee into his attacker's mid-section, felt the knot-hard muscles there give.

The man sprawled. With a wild cry, he scrambled to his feet and fled up the dark mouth of the wash.

Next, swift footsteps from the camp. Archie's voice calling, "Nantan! Nantan!"

"I'm all right," Ewing hacked. "It was Santo. Lost his knife—ran. Guess he thought I had a side arm. I didn't."

Without another word, Archie ran up the path. Ewing began to sense his purpose. And within moments Ewing heard a horse going hard on the old mail road in the direction Santo had run.

31

CHAPTER 2

When Archie had not returned soon after breakfast, Ewing sought out Rowdy and Jim. "We can't wait much longer," he told them. "We're escorting the stage to Fort Cummings."

"Archie come," Private Rowdy said and glanced up at the climbing sun. "By'em by, Archie come." He possessed the muscled body of a natural wrestler, packed with primitive energy. But instead of the hot, fierce eyes of an Archie, his were temperate and cool, dark pools recessed in the cliff of a strong and chiseled face. There were times when he reminded Ewing of a large child, unaware of his strength, and like a child too young to know fear, he had yet to show Ewing panic or to hold back when to do so would have been human.

Private Jim looked undersized beside him: proportioned like a deer, quick, intense, tireless, not a soft line or feature on his lean face, his intelligent eyes wary and suspicious. The two were always together. Members of the same clan, Archie had explained to Ewing. Other Apaches, look out.

"Archie knows where we're going," Ewing said. "Maybe he'll catch up before we reach Fort Cummings."

Rowdy and Jim merely nodded. To them, Ewing knew, Archie's chase after Santo was nothing more than a lark. "By'em by" could mean at any moment or days later. Time meant little or nothing to an Apache, so long as he got what he went after, beast or man, today, tomorrow, eventually. *Blancos* worried too much about time, the Tontos said, and Ewing was inclined to agree.

There came a jingling and stir of hooves at the station gate as Rip Carr and a Mexican lad led forth six lively mules and began hitching them to the stage, while the bearded Bitter Creek Bill and the guard, the latter packing two six-guns, rifle, and sawed-off shotgun, warily craned their heads about on the mountains, alert for trouble. A husky young white man started loading baggage into the leather-hooded rear boot.

An unusual amount of baggage, it seemed to Ewing. The sleepy-eyed passengers emerged from their stone bastion, walking stiffly—three men, Ivy Shaw in the same gray dress, and Mrs. Thorn, stylishly attired for travel in a blue serge suit. On her pretty head a ridiculously tiny hat topped with jaunty feathers. When the young man dropped a small leather-covered trunk, she rushed there, scolding, "Young man, you must be more careful."

"Yes, ma'am," he said, cowed, and carefully

lifted the trunk to the hinged platform and secured the hood's straps.

Appeased, Mrs. Thorn stepped to the side of the stage to await boarding. Spying Ewing, she called, "Lieutenant, may I speak to you, please?"

Ewing, recognizing the positive tone of a superior officer's wife accustomed to deference from a junior officer, felt the familiar grip of resistance before he nodded and crossed over, hat in hand.

"I am Mrs. Theophilus Thorn," she said in an assertive but not unpleasant voice, extending a gloved hand, her eyes critical of his field garb. "My husband is post commander at Fort Cummings."

Ewing spoke his own name and inclined his head, saying, "It is an honor to make your acquaintance, Mrs. Thorn," aware of Ivy Shaw's close attention to all this.

Mrs. Thorn was, he judged, in her late thirties. A fashionably dressed woman, an eastern woman, a genteel woman from a genteel family of means, the sort he had not conversed with in years. A perfect oval face of smooth whiteness, unmarked by the harsh sun. A perfect mouth. Great violet eyes. About her the faint scent of jasmine. So much beauty there it almost took his breath away. She was saying:

"Mr. Carr informs me that you and your scouts will provide escort to Cummings?"

"That is correct, ma'am."

"And indeed fortunate for all of us, I'm delighted to add," she said, releasing a little sigh.

"In fact, I have orders to report there."

"That is even more fortunate, Lieutenant," she said, interested, and in the gracious voice of the garrison hostess, "Major Thorn and I shall look forward to seeing you at dinner."

He bowed his head. "By the way, are you acquainted with Miss Ivy Shaw, your fellow passenger?"

"Indeed I am, Lieutenant," and her voice carried. "Poor child. She's been through so much. Poor child."

At her words, Ewing barely had time to see Ivy Shaw's head snap up, her proud eyes resenting the patronizing tone—that and no more, before a shout that was Rowdy's wheeled him about. "Nantan! Archie come! Archie come!"

Archie clattered up, an expression of justifiable satisfaction filling his triumphant face. He clutched a brown sack across his saddle.

Ewing shot out on the double to intercept him, knowing. There wasn't time. Archie dropped the sack at Ewing's feet, a grisly head rolled out, and Archie announced, "Santo, Nantan."

A woman shrieked.

Ewing looked. It was Mrs. Thorn, a hand pressed to her throat, her lovely face contorted, frozen in ashen horror. Her knees buckled. She was about to go down when Ivy Shaw ran over and caught her and, supporting her, helped her inside the station.

With a backward glance, Ewing toed the gruesome trophy into the sack and carried it to the wash. Well below the spring, he plunked it behind a boulder and strode back to the station.

Archie was waiting, an Apache warrior who had killed an enemy and brought back the proof.

Ewing looked up at the proud face, grunted an emphatic *"Enjuh,"* and snapped his sergeant a snappy salute of further commendation. Not to approve would cause his friend to lose face. Archie had brought in the head much as a small boy might bring an apple to his teacher. A farfetched parallel, and repugnant to be sure, Ewing realized, but the head also backed up Archie's warning that Santo was not to be trusted.

Once across the big wash, the scouts fanned out on both sides of the stage, and Ewing and Archie took the point, following the rutted trace across a series of lesser dry washes, skirting the dreaded alkali plain glimmering far to their right. Miles on, they left the gravelly land and came out on an expanse of dark green prairie where sickle-headed grama grass ranked high and rich. Cow country, Ewing mused. Gazing back at the buff-colored Peloncillos, which the Mexicans called the Sugar Loaf Mountains, he knew a certainty.

When the senseless killing finally stopped, and it would, no matter how unlikely that seemed now, he was coming back here to put down roots. By God, he was. And gradually a scene formed in his mind, piece by piece: an adobe or rock ranch house, corrals, a windmill, tanks, horses, whiteface cattle. It stayed there, growing, it turned him thoughtful.

Archie's voice interrupted. "Nantan sick in belly?"

"Just dreaming," Ewing said.

The sun's brassy eye soon burned away the early coolness. At intervals Ewing caught Bitter Creek Bill's strident voice yowling at the mules. In the distance a band of antelope ran free, their white rump patches bobbing. For a lark, one scout clapped heels to his mount as if to run them down. Alarmed, they bounded away with effortless ease, swift and graceful.

The morning lengthened into boredom. Everywhere Ewing saw emptiness. No dust whorls. No movement. Solitude. The broad humps of the Burro Mountains bulged beyond the heat haze. Fortunately, the stage road didn't go through the Burros. His concern was what might come helling out of them.

Five hours from Stein's they dusted up to Barney's Station, an adobe house and wall corral on the sloping plain below the Burros. No meals here; this was only a change station.

The stationmaster came out, the stage rolled up and stopped, and Bitter Creek Bill called down, "Where the hell's all the 'Paches?"

"Mean you didn't see any between here and Stein's?"

"Nary a one."

"Wish I could guarantee the same luck on to Soldier's Farewell."

All the passengers got out and stretched and walked around. Ivy Shaw and Mrs. Thorn together. The gambler and the drummer shared a bottle of whiskey. The mining engineer picked up pebbles and studied them for color. Hostlers hurried up fresh mule teams; before long Bitter Creek Bill called, "Git in, folks. This stage is leavin'."

As the gambler climbed aboard, Ewing heard him ask, "How far's the next station?"

"About nineteen miles, mister. I'll get you there. Just hang on."

"Watch the mountains," the stationmaster cautioned as the stage rolled out.

The road took them northeast, upgrade. The afternoon wore on and the heat waves danced. Archie pulled up and pointed. Ewing saw it also, a streak of dust spurting out of a canyon in the Burros. He threw up a hand, halting the stage, and signaled the scouts, who closed in.

Archie, studying the dust streak, held up three fingers.

As the riders continued to approach the stage, Ewing observed them through field glasses. Three young bucks with rifles. Young bucks stripped for battle. Just beyond carbine range, they pulled up. One stood on his pony and shook his breechclout at the scouts, the supreme Apache insult, daring them to fight. Ewing passed the glasses to Archie, asking, "What are they?"

"Warm Springs," Archie said after a moment.

"A little far west for them, but they've always been close to the Chiricahuas."

When the three hostiles cut a taunting circle and drew away for the mountains, yelling insults as they went, not riding fast, Archie let out a giant guffaw of disdain. "Tontos no fools there go. Tontos no fools."

"You Tontos are just smart," Ewing said, grimly humorous.

They were witnessing one of the oldest ploys in a deadly game. If the scouts took the bait and gave chase, a withering fire would greet them when they reached a canyon or deep wash. Even so, the worn ruse often worked on greenhorn Indian fighters, such as posses of liquored-up townsmen riding hell-bent or ranchers reckless over the loss of horses.

Archie made a chopping motion. "Warm Springs cowards. Come out and fight, to Big Sleep them all we send."

Ewing, reining back to the stage, told the driver,

"Some young bucks. They want us to chase 'em into the mountains where their ambush is set. It's all right to come ahead. We'll keep a sharp lookout." He was already thinking about the pass this side of Soldier's Farewell. He kept the scouts in tighter.

Hours later, they rode up to an adobe ranch house, no sign of life about. A dead horse lay in the front yard, a pincushion of arrows. Riding slowly around the house, Ewing found an empty stone corral and sheds. Going inside the house, he dreaded what he expected to find. The place was in shambles. Ripped bedding. Dishes and glassware in bits. Tables smashed. Chairs like kindling. Coming out, he told Archie, "Looks like everybody got out in time."

A mile or so later the old trail began climbing steadily, winding toward the foothills of the Burros, toward the wide mouth of a low, wooded pass. Ewing halted the coach again, rode on a way with Archie and uncased the glasses. Observing the quiet slopes, dotted with piñons, junipers, and dwarf evergreen oaks, he saw nothing amiss and handed the glasses to Archie, who took a lengthy look.

"If Warm Springs there, Archie don' see 'em. Don' feel 'em. But Archie go see will. If time for Archie Big Sleep go, Archie still go see his time is it."

"You're not going to Big Sleep," Ewing

growled, "and you're not going in there alone. We're all going to scout out the slopes. Take Rowdy and Jim with you." Archie was a fatalist, and often Ewing felt the necessity of negating the Tonto's talk about going to the Apaches' hereafter.

At the familiar order the scouts fanned out, Archie's detail on the right, Ewing's on the left; methodically, they began combing through the timber and brush. A gray squirrel scampered ahead of Ewing, stopped, glanced back at the intruders, then disappeared within a clutter of rock. Jays, likewise disturbed, swooped low from bushy juniper to juniper, always scolding. Good signs, Ewing knew.

There were no Warm Springs.

By late afternoon he made out Soldier's Farewell, huddled below the mountain of that name, a faulted peak on an irregular ridge. This relay station was somewhat larger than Stein's, another of the stone-barricaded type that provided meals as well as fresh stock. He could see parked wagons and people moving about. Pulling on his rumpled cavalry blouse, he rode ahead of the scouts.

The station's host, a roly-poly man seeming to enjoy the influx of company, said, "Some ranch families are forted up with us. Afraid not everybody got in."

"What's the situation on east of here?"

41

"All I can tell you is there's been no westbound through in a week. I figure they're markin' time at Fort Cummings till this blows over."

"That won't be till it's all over," Ewing said. They rode to the little dam that impounded water from the spring in the ravine and set up camp for the night.

With the coming of evening, he went to the station. Bitter Creek Bill and the ranchers talked and smoked by the gate. A man looked accusingly at Ewing, his voice hot with ill feeling. "Say, soldier, when's the Army gonna corral these goddamned Apaches?"

A worn civilian complaint, to be sympathized with. "I understand how you feel," Ewing answered. "However, most of the Apaches are on the San Carlos Reservation. It's a handful of hostiles causing the trouble."

Another man spoke up. "I don't feel easy with Apache scouts camped close to the station. Hostiles or scouts, they all come from the same litter. I don't trust 'em."

"These Apache scouts," Ewing replied distinctly, "enlisted of their own choosing. They're as loyal as any white trooper. The Army needs them because it takes an Apache to catch an Apache. They can follow tracks over rocks and through brush that a white man can't. When a horse or mule plays out, they go on afoot. When rations are gone, they live off the land or do without. They're damned good fighting men."

"You didn't answer my question," the first man grumbled.

"I can't because I honestly don't know," Ewing replied, and left them to go inside the station. He ached to say more, but held his tongue, knowing they wouldn't believe him. That the "Tucson Ring" of contractors and others, even some Federal officials, were responsible for removing the Apaches from their Verde Reservation to sickly San Carlos, "Hell's Forty Acres," it was called, a denuded hellhole, hot, dry, dusty, at the confluence of the Gila and San Carlos rivers—a move that had led directly to the Victorio war and other outbreaks. Add the crooked agents— all political appointees—selling Apache rations to mining camps and neighboring towns and unscrupulous contractors wanting to keep the war going so they could rob the government on bay and beef contracts. The Army caught between, trying to keep peace.

Ivy Shaw was visiting with the ranch women, while Mrs. Thorn, nearby, gazed off at the Burros, removed from the small talk. Ewing saw Ivy Shaw's hazel eyes find him and realized that she was his main reason for coming here, to see how she fared. He needn't have concerned himself, for she was at ease among these frontier women. She was a frontier woman herself and would, he knew, make do whatever the conditions.

He turned to leave. As he did, Mrs. Thorn noticed him. Before he could go out, she called, "Oh, Lieutenant," and stepped across, plucking at his arm. "May I speak to you in private, please?"

"Certainly."

"Private" meant outside. Taking her by the arm, he escorted her past the men at the gate, out of earshot to the corner of the station. "It's been a long day for you," he said conversationally. "With an early start and good luck, we'll make Cummings by tomorrow evening."

"Oh, it isn't that," she said, as if the post commander's wife would not deign to admit discomfort. "I'm just bored, after visiting old friends at Fort Lowell this past month. Friends we knew in the East."

"How did you find Tucson?"

"Unchanged—dusty and indescribably dull. At times so hot I actually longed for Cummings, if that's possible."

"Cummings is cooler this time of year. I don't suppose you dined at the celebrated Shoo-Fly?"

"You must be joking," she said, her reserve fading.

"Would I slur the cuisine of Tucson's finest restaurant, where the flies are big enough to carry off dinner plates?"

"We only went out a few times, once to see 'Elena and Jorge' performed out of doors."

He gave an exaggerated bow. "In Tucson's

44

elegant quartermaster's corral under the stars. The audience seated on cottonwood saplings. The stage set atop wagons. Elena—young, beautiful, rich, yearning for her lover. Her uncle—mean, mercenary, traitorous, anxious to sell the lovely heiress for gold. Jorge—young, brave, handsome, kept from Elena's side by her wicked uncle. The French officer—liar, coward, scoundrel, a despot over the fair land of Mexico, eager to wed the lovely Elena for her money alone."

"And," Mrs. Thorn said, taking the cue, "the crowd shouting '*Muera! Muera!* May he die!' "

They were both laughing, and she said, "I can see that we both know Tucson and its arts."

"Tucson—the flower of all Arizona Territory," he said, further caught up in the gaiety of the moment, aware that she was holding on to his arm, in her face the loneliness of an Army wife transported from comfortable posts, buzzing with social life, to the isolation and arid dreariness of the desert forts. "To be honest," he said, "I like Tucson. I like the desert Southwest."

"I detest it. I pray for the day when Major Thorn will be stationed far away from this godforsaken wasteland."

He understood. She missed the advantages of a long-established post, the pleasant rides, off bounds in Apache country, the garrison hops, the card parties, the charades, the picnics. He said, almost before he thought, "My wife didn't like it out here either. She went back East after a few months. We were divorced, eventually. She has since remarried, comfortably, I understand, to a well-to-do Connecticut harness maker."

"When was that?" she asked softly, her hand yet resting on his arm.

"About eight years ago."

"How terrible for you, a young officer."

"A shock at first—but for the best in the long run. I doubt that it would have worked out had we been stationed elsewhere. I didn't blame her."

"I'm sorry."

"You needn't be. It was for the best."

"You are generous to say that."

"Just the truth, is all."

The twilight had deepened to filmy darkness, and for a moment he saw only the pale oval of her finely etched face, quite near as he looked down at her. In that moment he discerned more than loneliness, he sensed her need as a woman, naked and appealing, a perception that startled him, that also reminded him of propriety. In another moment she freed her hand, and her face altered, formal again, in control, so quickly that his insight might have been something imagined, and she was saying, "Thank you, Lieutenant, for allowing me to escape back there. I think I can bear the rest of the journey. That drummer and gambler—both crude and profane—nipping from their bottle along the way. That mining engineer—staring at his rock samples like some idle schoolboy playing with marbles. And that poor child of a girl, Ivy Shaw."

"She's quite self-reliant, I assure you."

"No doubt, to survive as she has." Her expression changed back almost as before, her voice brushing the edge of intimacy, yet formal and correct, the voice of the post commander's lady as she said, "You may call me Josephine. Now, if you will escort me back to the station."

He did so. The men outside the station had gone, and when he said good-night and glanced inside, Ivy Shaw was not in sight.

As he made for camp, an old truth came to mind: that the frontier either brought out the best or the worst in a man. Well, to that he would add that sometimes it also bared long-denied needs for both man and woman.

He kicked at a rock, sent it flying.

The scouts were waiting before dawn when the passengers filed stiffly out to the stage, the two women hugging themselves against the chill of the foothills. A fresh driver mounted the box. He yowled, "Ha-aww—Rube! Ha-aww—Babe! Roll—damn yuh!" and the stage lurched into motion.

Leaving the humping Burros, the road struck across rolling grama prairie. The morning was not spent when a stand of green cottonwoods rose

47

out of the plain, as beckoning as an oasis: Ojo de la Vaca—Cow Spring—another rock station and also a junction of trails.

"Was a big fight yesterday at Mimbres Station," the agent reported. "A Mexican brought word. Was comin' down from Santa Rita on his way to Janos in Chihuahua."

Ewing frowned. "Did the station go under?"

"Hadn't when he slipped by. It was afternoon."

"Been minor brushes at Barney's and Stein's Peak," Ewing filled him in, and considered him a moment. "My orders are to report to Fort Cummings without delay, but I don't want to leave this stage without an escort. If you agree, we'll proceed ahead, since it's open country on to the Mimbres."

The agent mulled that over. He was middle-aged, black eyes lively and resourceful, a man wholly in charge of himself, not easily turned back, Ewing sensed, accustomed to such a day as this. The man said, "Don't forget you've got Cooke's Canyon between the Mimbres and Cummings."

"I'll worry about that when we get to the station."

"What if it went under?"

"You're forgetting they may need help."

"That's true. Well, go ahead."

Ewing rode to the spring, his mind on the station at the Mimbres River. It wasn't like

Apaches to attack a fortified stage station in daylight. The odds simply weren't in their favor. Canyon ambushes were more their style. Furthermore, Mimbres Station was the only dependable watering place between Cow Spring and Cummings. Feminine voices cut short his thinking.

Looking, he became aware of the contrast between the two women. Mrs. Thorn had changed to a stylish, tan-colored traveling suit. Ivy Shaw still in the gray dress, the tear above the hem now mended. That worn, gray dress continued to bother him, and he doubted there had been another burned with "the rest of my things" in Doubtful Canyon.

"Well, Lieutenant," Mrs. Thorn said, "what are we going to do? I dread to think of an overnight stop in this place."

"Going on. Open country all the way to the Mimbres River." Why tell them about the attack on the station? And reversed himself a moment later and told them in a few words.

Neither woman looked surprised. Josephine Thorn taking it like an Army wife, composed, resolved; Ivy Shaw like a frontier woman, accepting, facing.

"Very well," Mrs. Thorn said. Momentarily, her eyes on him possibly suggested many things, or possibly none, before she left them to walk to the stage.

"Mrs. Thorn is quite a lady," Ivy Shaw said, following her with impressed eyes.

Ewing nodded. "And so are you."

He caught her immediate confusion as her face flushed. "You say things," she said uncertainly, "I'm not used to hearing, Mr. Mackay."

"My given name is Ewing. Look," he said, pointing eastward, hoping to encourage her. "See that peak way off there, the one that stands out like a landmark, higher than all the others? That's Cooke's Peak, named after crusty old Colonel Philip St. George Cooke, who led the Mormon Battalion from Santa Fe to California in eighteen forty-six. Cooke's Peak is where we're going. Fort Cummings isn't far from there."

"It seems a long way."

"It is—but not as far as it seems. We'll get there."

He walked her to the stage.

Thereafter, he led off across a world vast and still, deceptively tranquil, the cloudless sky all turquoise. Now and again he swept the emptiness with the glasses, searching for suspicious dust whorls and sighting none.

Some four hours later he marked the curving course of the river, gradually broadening as it came down from the northeast. He recalled that the Mimbres, rising in the Black Range, had a good surface flow down its lovely valley, then sank into sand, surfacing here and there in the rainy season. This far south it was treeless and dry. Mimbres Station was farther up, where the river's course was timbered.

Archie swung over. "Nantan hear that?"

"What?"

"Guns." He pointed upstream.

Ewing cocked an ear. "I don't hear guns."

"Archie guns heard."

"I believe you. Still hear 'em?"

"Archie don' hear now."

Ewing peered through the glasses, along both sides of the winding river, seeing cottonwoods and willows in the upper distance. Only that. As he started to lower the glasses, something moving on a grassy swell pinned his eye. Quickly, he sighted again, but whatever it was did not reappear. He continued to watch. Within moments, a thin streak of dust smoked up beyond the low rise, dust that a running horse could make, unseen because of the swell of land.

He rode ahead, wanting to know.

Well past the rise, the Mimbres Station came into focus, a walled, rectangular adobe structure crouched on a broad flat extending from the wooded river to the nearby hills. Ewing scowled when his glasses picked up a stage between the river and the station, two mules dead in harness. Relief washed over him when he saw the closed gate. Moving the glasses, he found three dead

Indian ponies littering the flat. Yesterday's, he thought, or a while ago.

He drew the flankers in tighter still and went slowly on, halting on a terraced bluff that overlooked a long flat which let down to the flowing river. Across the flat the rutted stage road angled to the crossing, disappeared into the packed willows and cottonwoods, to emerge straight for the station's gate.

He studied the thick timber, up and down the river. Seeing no Indian ponies, he handed the glasses to Archie. After an interval, he said, "Apaches, Archie don' see," and shrugged.

Ewing reined back to the stage driver. "What's the crossing like, Jake?"

Yuma Jake, lank and long-haired, whose big hands made him look bigger than he was, wallowed a lump of tobacco around, spat thoughtfully, and said, "This time of year it's low. Good gravel bottom. No trouble."

"One of my scouts heard shots as we came up from the southwest. So there may be Indians in the timber along the river. You don't have to take your stage across if it's against your judgment. You can go back to Cow Spring. If you go on, we'll ride a scout alongside each mule. That will lessen chances of getting a team knocked down. What do you think?"

"My wife an' kids are over there, Lieutenant. She cooks for the station. I've got to know how

52

they are. Let's go. Believe Andy, here, is willin'."

The young guard nodded and patted his rifle.

"Don't stop for anything. If any of us go down, you keep on going." And turning to the faces watching him from the coach's windows, Mrs. Thorn's pale and tight, Ivy Shaw's beside her, brown and somber, the men very still, a white paste of fear on the drummer's round face, "When we start our run, you ladies get down on the floor. You men watch out for my scouts when you're firing."

He took the scouts down the bluff road, behind them came the squeal and rasp of the coach's brake blocks. Nothing stirred along the river. When within accurate carbine range, Ewing halted the detail and told Archie, "Fire two volleys into the trees on each side of the crossing."

Archie barked an order in Apache. The scouts spread out, their single-shot Springfields banged, then banged again, again, again. If there was anything the Tontos enjoyed more than hand-to-hand combat, it was a frenzy of shooting, the noise, the smoke, the action.

Then Ewing formed the detail, a scout siding each mule, and with screeching yells they charged for the crossing, Yuma Jake howling at his leaders. "Ha-aww—Rube! Ha-aww—Babe! Goddamn yuhr mean hides—roll!"

The first shot cracked just as the coach dropped

down to the sandy footing of the riverbed. It sounded from above, in the trees. At the same instant Ewing heard a cry from the box. Before him, in the shadows, a figure darted from behind a big cottonwood, rifle swinging. Ewing aimed his mount straight at the surprised rifleman a moment before the man fired. Ewing heard horseflesh strike bone, saw the Indian pitch sideways with a cry, ridden under. Summer-low water gleamed ahead, dappled by sunlight. Ewing's horse hit it galloping. All about them now the unbroken din of firing. Powder smoke bloomed like puffballs, bitter on Ewing's tongue, in his nostrils.

Whipping around, he saw the mules tearing headlong into the stream, water flying in sheets, the coach swaying on leather thoroughbraces, Yuma Jake lashing his leaders. "Ha-aww—Rube! Ha-aww—Babe! Roll—goddamn yuh—roll!" His voice higher even than the continuous yelling of the Apaches and the scouts. Andy the guard lolled, head down, on the box.

Abruptly they were across the Mimbres and the coach slamming up the rutted grade of the east bank, Yuma Jake ever cursing his game leaders and laying on the leather, the mules walleyed, with ears laid back. They lurched out, running upon the dusty flat, the station dead ahead, behind the stage the fading cries of Apaches in the timber.

Ewing swung back with Archie and the others to cover any pursuit. None came, just a scattering of shots and yells. Ahead, two men were struggling open the heavy gate.

Inside, Yuma Jake hauled in his lathered teams, still full of run, the two men slammed the gate shut and slid home the long bar. There followed a kind of lull, a kind of inertia, until Yuma Jake said, "It was short and sweet, but I'm afraid Andy's a goner."

Helping hands lowered Andy to the ground. He was gone, Ewing saw. Yuma Jake climbed down and a Mexican woman ran out to him. The mining engineer, first out of the stage, assisted Mrs. Thorn and Ivy Shaw, the women standing numbly by, as if emerging from an unreal world. The gambler stepped down, smiling broadly at their luck. The drummer, jaunty now, sure of himself, said around, "Some were in the trees. Like monkeys. Guess we showed 'em."

Suddenly everyone was talking at once, including the usually taciturn scouts, and the station agent, heavy and red of face, out of wind after his labor with the gate, hurried up to Ewing and gabbled, "This started yesterday, when they caught the westbound comin' in out there. Everybody ran for it. Two didn't make it. We've been under siege. Don't know how you got through."

"Over there," Ewing said, indicating the

55

Tontos, "and maybe we did some things they didn't expect."

A man called down from the adobe wall, "They're pullin' out. Headed east. Had their ponies hid upriver."

"You can lay over now and rest," the agent said to Ewing.

"For a little while. To get through Cooke's Canyon we have to make it tonight. Wait till daylight, they'll be there, ready for us."

CHAPTER 3

The road ran dimly on under a last-quarter moon, climbing gradually in the beginning, then sharply as they reached the rocky foothills toward the black-hooded mountains, Cooke's Peak a vague and brooding presence to the east.

Around midnight Ewing called a halt and waited for the stage to catch up. On Yuma Jake's left the mining engineer now rode as guard. "The canyon is not far ahead," Ewing said. "Let's rest ten minutes. I'll drop a couple of scouts behind you when we go in."

"Just git outa my way if we have to roll," Yuma Jake said.

The minutes dragged. Presently, Ewing took the scouts ahead into the inky darkness of the canyon's mouth. Everyone rode at a steady trot, the stage rumbling, trace chains rattling, wheels crunching gravel, at times banging on rocks. Shod hoofs rang. Dust smell rose on the chill air. As the grade grew steeper, the road became increasingly broken. When the escort came to some fallen rocks, Ewing sent Archie back to halt the stage while he and the scouts cleared the way.

Then they were going downgrade, the road no better, no worse than coming up, about halfway through, Ewing figured. His hopes began to build. Usually, Apaches did not fight at night, but that didn't rule out the exception. He halted once more, conversed with Yuma Jake, closed the detail again, and swung back to the head of the escort.

They were going through without trouble. Yes, they were, Ewing had decided, when a single shot shattered the calm. Immediately, he heard Yuma Jake yowl and lash the teams, the stage's wheels grinding faster. There came a splatter of gunfire, the darkness virtually winking to Ewing's right, high up. He gave the order to fire. For a space, as if surprised, the hostiles up there did not answer the volley. When they did, that side of the canyon erupted with flashes and cries.

"Ha-aww—Rube!   Ha-aww—Babe!   Roll—goddamn yuh!"

By this time Yuma Jake had the stage under way. It struck a large rock and bounced high, swaying, rocking, teetering, settled heavily on thoroughbraces and rolled on, drawing a burr of bullets, other shots, farther off target, making whistling and frying sounds. Downgrade, faster, still faster, almost out of control, brake blocks screaming, the scouts racing ahead of the careening coach, until Yuma Jake cursed and fought his leaders to slow down.

Back in the canyon the firing slackened, died.

Indeed, they were through the canyon, and Ewing shouted for the scouts, strung out during the long dash, to close up. The road eased down into low foothills. Ewing halted a short way onward, to account for the passengers and the detail, then went on. They crossed a wide wash, passed south of Cooke's Spring, and rolled on to Fort Cummings, its walled shape standing high and dark.

When the stage pulled up in front of the sally port on the south wall and, after some moments, there was no challenge from within, Ewing called, "Hello, the fort!" and repeated the call.

That brought a sentry's sleep-dulled voice, bawling, "Sergeant of the guard! Sergeant of the guard!"

Another delay, after which a voice called down from the guard tower, "Who is it? What d'you want?"

"I'm Lieutenant Mackay from San Carlos with a detail of Apache scouts with orders to report here. We're escort for the Mimbres stage. Major Thorn's wife is among the passengers."

Lanternlight flared in the tower. Ewing spotted a face peering owlishly down at them; boots pounded on stairs, the gate opened, and a voice from among four sentries challenged, "Lieutenant, advance and be recognized." The man was swinging a lantern.

Ewing rode forward, his patience strained. "I'm Mackay. I suggest that you get these people inside at once. They've had a rough time—fired

59

on in Cooke's Canyon. I'll report to the adjutant in the morning. My detail will bivouac at the spring."

He reined aside for the stage to pass and led the scouts away.

The post adjutant was usually a wearied individual beset by a multitude of varied complaints, besides handling the post commander's official correspondence, issuing all orders, running the post in the Old Man's name, and seeing that all matters were conducted through proper channels.

Lieutenant Wirt Cooley was no exception, Ewing soon saw when he reported next morning after mounted drill. Cooley wore that particular look of harassment, a lanky man about Ewing's age, nervous and conscientious and imposed on, yet undaunted, sociable and tactful. Behind him a morose clerk scribbled away, now and then scowling at the pile of paperwork by his elbow.

Cooley shook hands warmly, curiously regarding Ewing's appearance, and Ewing grinned and said, "Arizona field dress—General Crook's idea for campaigning. Canvas wears much better than wool and, in addition, takes a beautiful shine on the seat."

"Of course. Good idea." Cooley pulled at the chin of his rust-colored beard. "I'm thinking how I can squeeze you in at Bachelor Officers' Quarters. We're full up. Let's see . . ."

"Never mind. I always quarter with the scouts. We bivouacked last night at the spring."

Cooley raised an eyebrow. "Somewhat unusual, isn't it? Sleeping with Indians?"

"In this case, no. Works better this way. We eat the same rations, share the same ground. I'm used to it."

"At least you won't be bothered with the invasion of centipedes and tarantulas we're suffering. They drop in platoons from the ceilings of these 'dobes. I suggested tacking muslin overhead, to which the quartermaster agreed. But at last report I hear we've been outflanked again. No fewer than three complaints this morning from Officers' Row. Mrs.—no, I'd better not give the lady's name—informs me that she's had to place the legs of her bed in cans of water to keep red ants from crawling into bed with her and the lieutenant. Furthermore, when she opened her kitchen cabinet door this morning, there was a big fat rattler coiled and waiting for his breakfast."

"I know how that is," Ewing commiserated. "I was adjutant at Fort Bowie. We had the same problem, plus being overstaffed with gnats and flies. Rubber sheets tacked to the ceilings worked pretty well."

"Rubber sheets!" Cooley pounced on the suggestion, only to reject it immediately. "Everything here has to come from Fort Union, east of Santa

Fe. We might get them within a year, then likely not at all. Last week we received galvanized washtubs meant for Fort Concho over in Texas. It's a thought, however. You're a kindred soul, Lieutenant."

"I believe I can qualify even further," said Ewing, enjoying the exchange. "Another high honor bestowed on me, one in which, I might add, I served with distinction, was that of post engineer. My main duties were disposing of tons of horse manure and never-ending heaps of post garbage."

"A true cavalryman you are, Mackay. Well, if you don't need quarters, is there anything I can do for you?"

"There is one thing," Ewing remembered. "We're out of rations."

"That's a request I can pass on for you with some assurance. Meantime, I suggest that you report to the Old Man. He's on the prod. Matters haven't gone exactly well of late with our Navajo scouts. And there's the main problem."

"What problem?"

"He'll have to tell you. Out of my province, you know." Cooley's face lost its harried imprint, became intrigued, secretive. As Ewing turned on his heel to go, the adjutant's voice came again. "There's one little custom here I ought to mention. Call it courtesy or smoothing official fur, whatever. Major Thorn was a brigadier in the

War. He still prefers to be addressed as 'General,' if you get what I mean?" And he winked.

"Believe I do," Ewing replied, thinking, *More of the nonsense of postwar protocol, of bowing and scraping to inflated egos still feeding on brevet promotions of the past,* and went outside.

Going next door to the commanding officer's sanctum, he noticed a civilian slouched against the adobe wall, a flamboyant man: fringed buckskins, gun belt hanging loose on his hips, a revolver on each side, gray sombrero pulled low over a watchful face whose quick eyes followed him inside.

A minute later Major Theophilus Thorn returned Ewing's salute with a snap of his wrist, stood, and reached across the desk to shake hands. "I commend you and the Apache scouts for the effective manner in which you escorted the stage through from Stein's Peak. Mrs. Thorn gave me the full details, with some added flourishes, since she likes to extol my junior officers."

"Thank you, General," Ewing said and saw the address register.

Major Thorn was a bear of a man, his face heavily jowled, a shock of black hair to go with his close-cropped beard, shaggy brows that shaded eyes as gray as gravel pits, somewhat bloodshot at the moment, and a bearing that suggested the self-portrait of a superior intellect, buttressed by the determined set of the heavy mouth and the flattened nose, possibly a token from his pugnacious younger days. He was older than Ewing had expected, around fifty, and was picking up substantial girth. His drillmaster's voice hinted of brooking little disagreement, a professional judgment that sent warning signals flying through Ewing, and not a modicum of dread.

"First," Thorn continued, "I want a verbal report from the time your detail provided escort from Stein's Station." Ewing complied briefly, adding, "I've never known Apaches to attack at night before," upon which Thorn nodded and said, "When you are dismissed here, I want a complete written report." He steepled his big hands and leaned back, the gravel-pit eyes busy. "At ease, Mr. Mackay. You may be seated. Somehow I was expecting a grizzled veteran of the Arizona desert. A man in his fading forties. You are turning gray, all right, but your face is young behind your beard. You look lean and hard and ready. Not a particle of fat on you," the last said with a trace of an older man's envy.

"You don't get fat on field rations, sir."

"There are times, many times, when I wish I were back in the field, this aggravating hernia of mine be damned, with the entire command on the move. But we shall come to that certainty in due time, I trust. Right now we could use a victory to quiet the territorial press. The Army has been accused of everything except collaboration with the enemy. We are constantly criticized, with complaints reaching back as far as President Hayes and now President Garfield, when the real problem lies with the Indian Bureau. If that collection of rump-sprung geniuses in Washington had left the Warm Springs at Ojo Caliente, instead of removing them to San Carlos among their tribal enemies, we would be at peace now."

Ewing mustered a tired smile of agreement.

"I understand you have served mostly with Apache scouts. How long?"

"Seven and a half years, sir."

"That's a long time. Tell me how it came about."

"I volunteered to take charge of the enlisted scout unit at Fort Bowie. Not, however, from a sense of devotion to duty. Frankly, I saw it as a chance to get away from desk work, having just served as post adjutant for four months, then as post engineer. For me, an Easterner, it was quite an education. My attitude . . . that the Apaches were little better than animals, that we had no common ground, man to man . . . began to change. I learned to respect them, and they respect me, I believe. I never lie to them, always tell them the truth—no matter how hard it is sometimes. We share the same dangers, eat the same rations, which seem pretty good to an Apache, who will dine on rodents if he has to. . . . When General Crook was in command, our orders were quite flexible"—he felt his face turning wry—"so long as we followed a trail to its bitter end, never giving up, even after our mounts played out and our rations were gone, our moccasins and boots worn out."

Thorn's knowing nod said he was familiar with that policy. "General Crook's concept of fighting Apaches works up to a certain point, Mr. Mackay. A number of small commands in the field using pack trains, constantly keeping the hostiles stirred up, crossing and crisscrossing their range for tracks, tends to wear them down. True—but such a plan has one obvious weakness." Pausing to bring the full force of his opinion to bear on Ewing, he said, "It leaves out any chance for a single smashing blow. That, Mr. Mackay, is the way campaigns are won."

Ah, Ewing thought, *a book campaign is shaping up. The command moving unhurriedly, halting ten minutes of each hour, nooning for a comfortable hour, camping early, tents in neat rows, picket lines just so, a long supply train in tow—the command kicking up clouds of dust that keen Apache eyes can see forty miles away.* He said nothing.

"I must inform you, Mr. Mackay, that I have well-founded doubts about the effectiveness of

Indian scouts in the field. We were using Navajos here until a short time ago, when I sent them home in disgust. They proved useful as trackers, I admit, but would not close with the Warm Springs or Mescaleros. When a fight seemed imminent, they always found some excuse to make medicine until all danger had passed. We've had that happen on the upper Mimbres and in the foothills of the Black Range."

"You won't have that with Tonto Apaches. If anything, the problem will be holding them back."

"When junior officers couldn't make the Navajos move, we hired a civilian scout, Luke Tisdale, who had the same results, though he claimed they were improving under his command. 'Getting their brave up,' as he called it. Tisdale is still employed as post scout, but will be so in a secondary or advisory capacity until— and if—your Apaches convince me they are what you say they are."

"I am confident they will, sir."

"Which brings me to why you have been assigned here at my request," Thorn said, with self-satisfaction. "I'm sure you have pondered why."

Ewing nodded.

"Even Major General Willcox doesn't know of this one particular matter, which I have not disclosed publicly for fear of causing panic over southern New Mexico, particularly in the mining communities of Silver City, Pinos Altos, Georgetown, Santa Rita, and Hillsboro, not to mention east across the Rio Grande."

Ewing waited in puzzled silence.

"You see," Major Thorn resumed, "I have irrefutable evidence that Victorio is back raiding," and left off, awaiting Ewing's reaction.

"Victorio?" Ewing said, his voice rising. "Mexican troops killed him and most of his Warm Springs band last year in Chihuahua."

"To be precise, on October fifteenth at a place the Mexicans call Tres Castillos—that's the accepted tale. On the contrary, there is one very curious countering fact: nobody from this side, no white man, no officer, no one in authority, no Apache scouts who knew what Victorio looked like, visited the battle site, which is a misnomer, because it was more of a massacre. Nobody from our side was allowed there, mind you, though Americans had been in hot pursuit. Four troops of cavalry from here led by myself . . . some Chiricahua scouts, under a white officer, and some Texas Rangers. Mexicans get very nervous when American troops are on sainted Mexican soil. In addition to that, throw in the political difficulties and ambitions south of the border, the usual revolutionary outbreaks, and the fact that the Mexicans do not trust Apache scouts with our troops."

He paused and spread his hands, a sardonic gesture of the inevitable. "So, General Joaquín Terrazas . . . seeing that Victorio's people were bottled up and low on ammunition, which Terrazas could determine from the manner in which the Warm Springs returned fire . . . and no doubt seeing the opportunity to gain popularity and influence in Chihuahua . . . bluntly ordered all Americans and Apache scouts to get the hell out of Mexico." Thorn's heavy lips curled. "Terrazas said it would be objectionable to the Mexican government if we didn't vamoose. What government, I say? That was Terrazas alone wanting to hog the glory, when if it hadn't been for the Americans, Victorio would have slipped back north across the border, out of the Mexicans' grasp. Of course, we had to pull out— no choice. International incident, had we not. Next day Terrazas virtually wiped out the Warm Springs in a 'terrific battle'—so he claimed. Said he had killed Victorio, though how Terrazas could identify Victorio from any other Indian is highly questionable."

"Warm Springs captives could have identified Victorio's body, sir."

"A frightened survivor would say anything to spare his own life. Can you imagine the fury of Terrazas if a captive had told him that Victorio had escaped? A death sentence for certain." Major Thorn assumed a dramatic stance, pointing.

"No. There is Chief Victorio. He died fighting."
Thorn crossed his arms and affected an amused
expression of further contradiction. "There is yet
another version of Victorio's alleged death. That
he was wounded in a battle with prospectors in
the Florida Mountains, died at Palomas Lake,
and was buried nearby. That a subchief took his
war trophies and it was he who was killed at Tres
Castillos. I put no stock in either story."

"Why not, sir?"

"Because of the outbreak of recent raids—
Victorio style. Ranches hit, lonely prospectors
ambushed, stages and small cavalry details
boldly attacked in daylight. The road from El
Paso to Silver City is not safe without strong
military escort."

"That could be Nana, sir," Ewing said. "Our
scouts in Arizona heard that he and about thirty
warriors were gone on a raid for supplies and
ammunition when Terrazas attacked."

"Nana is more of a quick-hitting raider.
Here today, a hundred miles away tomorrow.
The attacks I'm telling you about are fairly
concentrated in southern New Mexico, from here
to the Arizona border. East to the Rio Grande.
From here to the Black Range and northwest to
Silver City and beyond. There's almost a pattern
to them, as if they're planned."

"Sir, there hasn't been the slightest rumor in
Arizona that Victorio is still alive."

"There are other contradictions to the contrary, Mr. Mackay. Furthermore, the Black Range is Victorio's old stomping ground. He loves his old haunts in that high country. For instance, several Navajos said they saw Victorio at a distance. He had a favorite war-horse, a paint stud. The Navajos saw that horse—not once, but three or four times. I happen to know the original owner, a rancher named Juan Montoya, who lives south of Hillsboro. His ranch has been hit many times, always for horses and mules."

"Another Apache could ride that paint stud."

"I did some checking on that point. I messaged General Terrazas at Chihuahua City. His men saw a paint stud early in the fight, but not later, dead or alive. I believe Victorio escaped on that stud before the band was overrun."

"That's possible. Else another Apache could have."

"You are hard to convince, Mr. Mackay. But there is even stronger evidence." The major had a bent for histrionics, Ewing saw again, as Thorn paused significantly. "Here is the clincher. A Mexican—a captive of the Warm Springs—showed up in Hillsboro a few weeks ago. Said he was at Tres Castillos and escaped with Victorio and others. Said they hid out in the Sierra Madre for some months. When the band returned to its Black Range haunts, he left them. Said he was tired of war."

"He is still in Hillsboro, sir?"

"We don't know."

"I was thinking he could lead us to Victorio."

"At any rate, this is where you come on stage, Mr. Mackay. You and your Tonto scouts. Your objective is to locate Victorio and his band . . . to move when he moves, always dropping a courier back to me in the field. At the proper time to attack, I shall come up with the entire command."

Ewing sat back in stunned silence, feeling the old dread of the hard days, weighing the improbabilities. Before he could speak, Major Thorn called sharply, "Orderly! Bring Mr. Tisdale in here."

CHAPTER 4

Soon the civilian Ewing had noticed outside headquarters entered the room and, nodding to Major Thorn, stood at slouched ease, a detached expression on his craggy face.

Thorn introduced them. Tisdale shook hands and sat down, but in that moment Ewing caught the gauging rake of the man's light eyes. Tisdale looked somewhere in his forties, of stringy muscle and long bone. There was a deliberate air about him, a square-shouldered erectness, as if nothing could ever shake his calm, a studied posture that went with his fringed buckskins and gun belt and the large-roweled Mexican spurs on his shiny black boots. His yellowish-brown hair hung to his shoulders, and his sweeping moustache, of a darker ginger color, was likewise carefully groomed. The man was almost a dandy.

Ewing could not escape the contrast between Tisdale and veteran civilian scouts in Arizona—sun-blackened men, hair uncut for months, beards straggling, ragged flannel shirts and canvas trousers, and sweat-soaked slouch hats, Tonto leggings, and moccasins—and already felt his bias take root.

"Lieutenant Mackay is in charge of the detail of Tonto scouts from San Carlos I was telling you about," Thorn explained to Tisdale. "You will assist Lieutenant Mackay in every way possible, particularly in reference to guiding him and acquainting him with the mountain country."

Tisdale's noncommittal face switched immediately to amiability. "You bet, Gen'ral. Any way I can help."

"I don't think it necessary for me to repeat why Mr. Mackay and the Tontos have been assigned here. Nor to stress the need for absolute secrecy as to his mission. You understand that, Mr. Tisdale?"

"You know I do, Gen'ral."

"Mr. Tisdale," Thorn said, turning to Ewing, "is the best-informed man hereabouts on the country north and northwest of here, the Mimbres Mountains and the Black Range."

"Yes, sir," Tisdale took up when Thorn paused, "prospected all through there. Fought Indians at the same time. Learned their ways. Finally had to give up huntin' gold and silver, go to huntin' 'Paches."

"Tomorrow," Thorn said, "a woodcutting detail will be going out. Mr. Mackay, you and the scouts will provide escort. Mr. Tisdale will serve as guide. I scarcely need to remind you that our woodcutters seem to be special targets of the Warm Springs. That is all, Mr. Mackay."

Ewing rose, saluted, and left, behind him Tisdale's voice picking up, low, droning, close, confidential. The man apparently had unusual access to headquarters, and he had all but fawned on the major. Ewing didn't like him. Tucson and Prescott were full of such Daniel Boone poseurs. They had helped fuel the Camp Grant massacre of more than one hundred Apache women and children ten years before.

At the adjutant's office Ewing wrote out the requested report and handed it to Cooley, who scanned it rapidly, filed it in an overflowing box marked FIELD REPORTS, and said, "By the way, Mackay, my wife, Evelyn, and I would like you to come to dinner this evening. I don't know what's on the menu, but whatever it will be a change from field rations. Hope you can make it." When Ewing did not reply, hesitant at the thought of proper dress, Cooley puckered his lips and said airily, "We have a house guest . . . a Miss Ivy Shaw. Thought you might be interested."

"I'd be delighted. Thanks very much. Only I won't be much more presentable than this. I've been wondering about her."

"There was quite a commotion last night when the stage pulled in here. I got up and went out to see what was up. Saw this young woman standing there, alone. Just then the O.D. asked me if Evelyn and I would put her up for the night. We were glad to, of course."

"You mean Mrs. Thorn didn't ask her in?"

"I don't know," Cooley said, thoroughly loyal. "There was a great deal of confusion about then. Evelyn is starved for company. Somebody to visit with. Miss Shaw had breakfast with us. I seldom got a word in. Those two were chattering like magpies when I left, with Evelyn doing most of the talking. Now, step outside and I'll show you where our quarters are."

Coming out, Ewing saw a dark-haired woman and Ivy leave an adobe and go along Officers' Row, chatting like schoolgirls.

"There they are," Cooley said, amused and pleased. "Haven't stopped talking yet."

Ivy looked happy and relaxed. For the first time, Ewing realized that he was seeing her outside threatening surroundings, for the first time seeing her truly smiling. She still wore the gray dress, that symbol of hard times and make do and a young woman's pride. He was, he found, beginning to loathe it.

He took his leave of Cooley and headed for the post trader's store next to the sally port. A decision was firming as he walked.

The trader was the customary sort: genial, alert for prospects, his eye catching Ewing the moment he entered. Within the cramped confines was a general merchandise store, plus a bar for enlisted men and the public, and a club room for officers.

"What can I do for you, Lieutenant?"

"Do you carry dresses?"

"Not ready-made, sir. But we have a pleasing line of dress goods and the latest Butterick patterns."

"Dress goods?" Ewing mulled, discouraged.

"Yes. Most of the ladies on the post make their own dresses."

"I see. Well, show me something."

Casting him a sidelong glance, the man pulled out a bolt of gray cloth and laid it on the counter.

Ewing stopped him instantly. "No gray."

"Then perhaps something in imported China silk?"

"Silk? That sounds better."

"Here, sir, is a black brocaded silk of very fine quality at only ninety cents a yard."

"No black. I want something light and cheerful. Something bright."

"I believe there is some blue silk here somewhere." He searched behind the counter. "Here it is. Brocaded, too. Of very fine quality. Very stylish."

When the trader unfurled the bolt, it was like a shaft of bright blue sky to Ewing. He said at once, sensing, knowing, "That's what I want. I'll take it."

"How many yards would you like, sir?"

Ewing chewed his lower lip, stumped. "How many yards does it take to make a dress?"

"That depends somewhat on the lady's . . .

measurements," the man replied, putting it delicately.

"She comes to my shoulder and she's quite slim."

The trader bent a measuring eye. "I would say . . . four or five yards."

"Make it six."

"That should be ample, sir, with some left over."

When the trader had cut the cloth and folded it, Ewing said, "You mentioned the latest Butterick patterns. Give me two of your most stylish." He wasn't finished, he discovered; once started, he was feeling a surge of enthusiasm and confidence in his selections. He moved to the jewelry case. Something took his eye, but he went on, looking, rejecting. He turned back to the object. It was delicate, intricate, alien among its cheap counterparts.

"That pink cameo brooch there, with the gold filigree mounting?" he asked.

"The only one in the store," the man said. "Little demand out here. Too expensive."

"How much?"

The keen eyes met Ewing's. "For you, Lieutenant, to move the merchandise—just twenty dollars."

Outrageous, Ewing knew, but he said, "I'll take it."

"Very well, Lieutenant."

"In a box, please."

"Yes, sir!"

"I would like everything neatly wrapped, with the brooch on top of the dress goods. Can you deliver that to Officers' Row this morning?"

"I'll send it over at once."

"Please address it to Ivy Shaw—Miss Ivy Shaw—in care of Mrs. Wirt Cooley."

"Oh, yes. Mrs. Cooley. Charming lady. Would you like to sign a card? I keep such on hand."

"Why, yes. I'd almost forgotten such proprieties existed." On the plain white card, Ewing signed: *To Miss Ivy Shaw, from Lt. Ewing Mackay.* He didn't like that; too formal. He asked for another card and wrote: *To Ivy—from Ewing.*

But, still, he wasn't quite finished. Spying the bar, he selected a bottle of French brandy, had it wrapped, paid for his purchases, and with the brandy under one arm went to his mount and rode to the scouts' camp at the spring.

The rations had arrived, true to Cooley's word, and the camp, now that Santo had passed, was like of old, the Tontos cooking and joking.

That afternoon he bathed and trimmed his beard with care, brushed his blouse, shook out the rumpled light blue trousers, eyeing the wrinkles in dismay, and set to polishing his boots with a rag.

Archie observed these careful preparations in silence; at last, as if he could not restrain his curiosity, he sidled over and said, smiling, "Soon Nantan wife have will."

"Wife? I'm just going to the fort this evening. Going to see the Nantan adjutant and his family."

"No *blanco* woman?"

"I understand she will be there."

"*Enjuh*! Nantan, that *blanco* woman you take. Good wife she make. Archie know."

"Just because she didn't complain?"

"*Enjuh*! Take her."

"Maybe she wouldn't like that."

"Take her anyway, that *blanco* woman."

"Then I would end up in a *blanco* jail."

"You *blancos*, strange your ways are," Archie said. He walked off, shaking his head.

At sunset Ewing heard the precision sounds of the evening parade and the bugles blowing retreat. Listening, he knew that such ceremonies, the barked commands, the marching, the music, the lowering of the flag, close to the hearts of those who loved the service, helped compensate for the severity of frontier existence. That the orderliness of the day, from reveille to taps, gave lonely women an added sense of protection and of life going forward, the garrison like a valiant shield around them. Fort Cummings, said to be the only walled post in New Mexico Territory, fulfilled the image of a remote bastion standing alone.

A little later he rode that way.

Evelyn Cooley was as sociable as her husband, a true Army wife, gracious and quick to make a guest feel at ease. Her face round and full, laughing eyes of soft brown, chestnut-brown hair beginning to show gray, done in tight curls. Her low-necked dress revealing an ivory skin.

"Welcome to Hacienda Cooley," she said, greeting Ewing with a kiss on the cheek. "Ivy will be out in a minute."

Ewing presented her the bottle of brandy. Delighted, she thanked him and gave it to her husband, who shook hands and said mockingly, "You've disappointed Evelyn. I told her you'd come in your field-dress canvas pants, which are quite an oddity here."

"Sorry," Ewing smiled.

"I think I like him much better this way," Evelyn said defensively. "Please sit down, Ewing."

He did so, taking note of the quarters. As a first lieutenant, Cooley was entitled to two rooms and a kitchen. As a second lieutenant assigned to Fort Bowie, Ewing recalled, he and Elinor had one room and a shed for a kitchen. Two iron cots and straw mattresses. One pine table. Two rawhide chairs. One lantern. ("I won't live like this, Ewing. I won't!")

An old problem, quarters. A new officer arriving on post could bump a junior officer, who in turn could do the same to another lower in grade, creating a domino effect down the line, causing no end of resentment and upheaval. Somehow Evelyn Cooley had managed wallpaper of a rose pattern and a scattering of frame prints, all eastern scenes, wooded and green, even a waterfall, likely chosen from nostalgia. And an oblong piece of worn green carpet on the rammed-earth floor, a battered parlor suite that showed the carelessness of soldier packers, a prim little wooden bookcase, and two kerosene lamps with decorated shades. Besides her somewhat plump attractiveness, Evelyn Cooley was a resourceful Army wife. Already Ewing liked her tremendously.

Hearing a rustling, he turned his head to see Ivy Shaw, a self-conscious flush on her fine-boned face, coming from the bedroom. She was clad in high-necked blue silk, with puff sleeves, the brooch pinned near her throat.

"Good evening," she said, ill at ease.

Ewing stood. "You look very nice."

Ivy flushed deeper, said no word.

"Yes," said Evelyn Cooley, breaking the silence, "Ivy looks very nice, and she's easy to fit—so slim." She sighed. "Reminds me of when I was sixteen or so."

"You couldn't have squeezed into *that*," Cooley twitted her.

His wife whirled on him. "Wirt Cooley! And

you used to say that you could circle my waist with two hands."

Ivy, finding her voice, said, "I want to thank you, Ewing, for everything."

"You are more than welcome." He felt stiff and overmannerly, and wondered whether his lengthy field service had left him unfit for polite company.

"Evelyn did all the sewing. She and Mr. Cooley have been so good to me."

"It's Wirt, remember?" Cooley interrupted, simulating sternness.

"We've tried to persuade Ivy to stay with us and rest up," Evelyn said, a faint worry knitting her brows, "but she insists she has to go on to Hillsboro."

"The stage will be under strong escort," her husband assured her.

Suddenly his wife said, "Why don't you get Ewing a drink, while I take a peek at our dinner."

"I'll help," Ivy offered.

"You have already," the hostess said, fixing her a look to stay.

Ivy seated herself, hands clasped in that now-familiar posture of self-containment. Ewing smiled at her, silently admiring her, while the adjutant served him whiskey, and turning to Ivy, "Would you like a glass of wine?"

Ivy shook her head. "I believe not. Thank you. I feel wonderful. Everything is so nice."

"Yes," Evelyn called from the kitchen, "that would be good for her. She needs building up after all she's been through."

Cooley, with a roll of his eyes, brought Ivy a glass of wine and sat down, saying, "Cummings can't rate with posts like Stanton, where the quarters are built of stone, and Fort Clark, down in Texas, which has deep, cool porches and there's room enough that you don't run over each other. However, hunting is first-rate here and the climate is exceptional, the water is good and we have a garrison garden so we won't all come down with the scurvy." He raised his glass. "Here's good luck to you, Ivy, and to you, Ewing." They drank, even Ivy sipped tentatively, and the whiskey smacked of smooth Kentucky to Ewing. "Another thing," Cooley went on. "The post is wet, thanks to Major—that is, *General* Thorn, who likes his toddy; in fact, more than a matutinal eye-opener," he added, with a broad wink. "I dare say the desertion rate here, which is bad enough, would double if he decreed the post dry. Now, up at Fort Bayard, when the post commander determined the post should be dry, the trader got around the order by selling Peruna as a flavoring for plum puddings. Happened it's mostly alcohol, a tonic, shall we say. Troopers bought it by the case, and the post was saved from abandonment."

They sat down to a candlelight dinner of

antelope steaks and gravy, green beans from the garrison's garden, dried peas, prunes, tinned butter and sourdough biscuits, followed by custard for dessert. When Ewing marveled at the food, Evelyn said, "I'll let you in on a secret. The custard is made without eggs. Its base is cornstarch."

"I still tasted eggs," he swore.

"You are just being gallant."

"Her apple pie is a real fooler," Cooley said. "Soda crackers flavored with cinnamon and lemon extract. You even think you can taste the peel."

"Wirt, you are revealing all my secrets."

"I dare not mention them all," he said, suggestively, continuing the constant teasing between them.

Afterward, Evelyn Cooley played the guitar while the men had brandies; resting, she deftly rolled a cigarette of black Mexican tobacco and calmly touched a match to it. "Only in the privacy of my quarters," she said, laughing.

"I put my foot down when she asked for a plug of Brown Mule," Cooley teased.

When tattoo sounded, Ewing rose to go and paid his respects.

"Good luck tomorrow," Cooley said, extending his hand, and when his wife glanced at him in inquiry, he explained, "Ewing and the Tonto scouts are riding escort tomorrow for a woodcutting detail into the mountains. Luke Tisdale's going along as guide."

"I can't stand that man," she blurted. "He's no scout. He belongs in a Wild West show."

"He does know the mountains. That's why he was hired."

She started to say more, then held out a warm hand. "We enjoyed having you, Ewing. It was good for all of us."

"It took me back. A wonderful evening, Evelyn."

Ivy accompanied him to the *ramada*. For a while they gazed out at the moon-bathed parade ground, neither speaking. The sergeant of the guard stepped from the guardhouse and called to the sentry on Post Number One, "Nine o'clock and all's well!" and the call, picked up, went around the garrison from post to post. A reassuring sound, Ewing thought.

"Thank you again for everything," she said, after a long pause. "That's the nicest thing that ever happened to me."

He touched a hand to her shoulder in silent response. Thoughtfully, he said, "Did your brother say what camp he's in?"

"Bonanza—the Bonanza Mine. I believe it's north of Hillsboro."

"Maybe I'll be up that way on a scout. I know I'll be assigned here, in and out, for some time. Maybe a long time."

"You sound troubled."

"Not really. I'm used to it. Only there's much in the wind. The campaigns are far from over."

"I'm afraid—afraid I'll never see you again."

He turned to her. "You will. That's one thing that's going to be. Write me here in care of Wirt. Tell me where you are."

"I will."

"Is that a promise?"

For reply, she leaned in and kissed him quickly on the mouth, a sweet, fleeting kiss, and left him as quickly. He was shaken. His eyes followed her into the dimness of the room.

The woodcutting detail formed as fatigue call sounded, a gray-haired sergeant in charge of eight bored troopers half-heartedly loading a grindstone, axes, saws, sledges, wedges, and water jugs on three mule-drawn wagons.

This morning Luke Tisdale wore a buckskin jacket, black doeskin pants, trimmed with silver lace, Spanish style, and leather gloves with beaded cuffs. He carried a Henry rifle across the pommel of his saddle, the two low-slung revolvers, and a long knife at his belt.

He nodded to Ewing alone, ignoring the scouts. A trooper turned to Tisdale, a muscular man of medium height, straw-colored hair thick below his forage cap, his broken nose left crooked, scar tissue around his washed-out yellow eyes and more around his rock chin—the troop brawler, Ewing decided. There was always at least one. The darker blue patches on the man's faded shirt sleeves told that once he wore corporal's chevrons.

"If it ain't ol' Hawk Eye Tisdale, himself," the trooper mocked. "You gonna watch for bad 'Paches today while us poor peons bust our butts?"

"Don't I always, Wexler? Don't I always?"

Wexler spat tobacco. "You've got it rough, Hawk Eye. Ride around all day or sit in the shade. Meantime, the rest of us hit the grit." He spat again, deliberately.

"If I didn't, you gold bricks wouldn't be around to bellyache. You'd be out in the post cemetery, pushin' up grama grass."

"Like hell," Wexler growled, trailing a jeering grin.

Despite the ridicule, Ewing gathered, there seemed to be a rough alliance between the two.

"Cut out the chin music, Wexler, and take the first wagon," the sergeant ordered.

"What's the rush, Larkin? We got all day."

"Move!"

Wexler drilled him a look and, laggardly, climbed to the wagon seat and took up the reins. His hands were almost square.

The detail swung out of the fort and headed into the foothills on a well-defined trail, Cooke's Peak to the northwest, a towering landmark. Ewing took the point with Tisdale, the scouts strung out on the flanks. The sky was cool and cloudless; by afternoon the heat would be intense.

About four miles onward Sergeant Larkin halted the detail by a grove of scrubby, evergreen oaks. The troopers, loath to begin, milled around the wagons, dawdling at unloading, delaying, until Larkin barked at them. Wexler was the last to pick up an ax.

Ewing posted the scouts on higher ground beyond the troopers and rode back, whereupon Tisdale muttered, "If I'se you, Lieutenant, believe I'd pull in my scouts a little tighter."

"They're where they can see a long way off."

"Looks peaceful enough, but don't let it fool you. Just thought I'd tell you."

"That's why I posted them there. If trouble comes, they'll see it."

Tisdale pulled out a twist of black tobacco, bit off a chew with even, brown teeth, settled it between his lean jaws, and chewed reflectively. "That's what Lieutenant Avery said."

"Lieutenant Avery?"

"Young fellow. Mighty likable. Fresh out of West Point. Lost him and two troopers that afternoon. Had his Navajos too spread out. After that, the gen'ral had me take over the scouts."

"I see."

"Just thought I'd tell you."

Ewing let the exchange pass. If a man took offense at every intrusion or slight, he would be in a state of constant war. Yet Tisdale, he sensed, would be no friend in the hard days ahead. A person of his obvious conceit would harbor ill feelings over being relegated to an advisory status, as Thorn himself had put it, after commanding the fort's Indian scout unit.

Voices cut across Ewing's thoughts.

Wexler was saying, "Watch where you're swingin' that ax, Boyle. You just missed my foot."

"Too bad I did. And the name is O'Boyle—not Boyle."

"I said Boyle, you Mick!"

At once they were swinging at each other. Wexler the older and far more powerful of the two, O'Boyle slim and hardly out of his teens, yet unafraid, his fury blinding him to his disadvantage.

Sergeant Larkin tore across, prying them apart with both hands. They stepped back, panting.

"You're on report, Wexler!" Larkin snapped.

"What! When little Sonny Boy tried to cut off my foot."

"You started it with your name-calling. Now, you work at the farther end of the grove. O'Boyle, you can help load."

Wexler picked up his ax and idled off.

O'Boyle, his young face contorted, breathed

after him, "He's been raggin' me ever since I came out here a month ago. I'll bash his thick Dutchy head in, I will!"

"You'd better think twice about that, Tim. He could break you in two. Now, give a hand with the loading."

The tedious morning wore on to noon. Ewing made another round of the outposts, rode in, and ate cold rations with Archie. "Let's take a look up around that big peak," Ewing said, pointing toward the landmark. "As a matter of courtesy, guess I'd better tell Tisdale."

"That *blanco* man," Archie said, shaking his head. His thin Apache lips curled. "Him scout, him say. Archie don' like him."

The detail was resting in the meager shade of the oaks. As Ewing rode by a group of troopers, he caught a voice, low but clear, muttering, "Injun lover."

He reined in sharply. Wexler and three others sat there. "Who said that?" Ewing demanded.

No one answered. All faces wore masks of innocence.

He said, "I'd better get an answer or you'll all be bound and gagged for one man's remark," and saw their faces stiffen.

Wexler's broken features became forthright. "I said it to Private Hoch here, sir. He was just sayin' he liked Tontos better than Navajos, and I said as many times as I'd been shot at, I didn't like any kind of Injuns. Ain't that right, Hoch?"

Hoch looked down and up, silent. Obviously another recruit, he had farm boy stamped all over him. Big hands. Big feet. Awkward. Unsure of himself. His red face peeling from the harsh southwestern sun. His Adam's apple bobbed.

When the boy didn't speak, Ewing asked, "Is that correct, Hoch?"

Hoch swallowed again. "Yes, sir."

"That will do for now," Ewing said and rode on. Wexler was lying, and Hoch, afraid of Wexler, had lied for the troublemaker. Best cure for troop bullies was a good thrashing, though no man in this detail looked capable of administering it. Sergeant Larkin, an old soldier, no doubt would relish somebody who could.

The reconnaissance to Cooke's Peak turned up no fresh signs of hostiles, only a distant view of the incredibly rough country farther north that rose into the fabled Black Range. A forewarning, Ewing reflected, of the scouting and campaigning to come over murderous terrain that would kill horses and loosen a trooper's cartridge belt five or six holes.

An orderly was waiting for Ewing when the woodcutters pulled into the post an hour before retreat. "Lieutenant Cooley presents his compliments to Lieutenant Mackay and says report to the adjutant's office immediately."

There Ewing found Cooley brooding over a

stack of reports. He seemed to put routine matters behind him as he waved Ewing over, saying amicably, "How did the woodcutting go?"

"Uneventful, except for observing how one Private Wexler can disrupt a detail."

"Ah . . . Kirk Wexler. Been busted so many times from corporal he puts chevrons on with hooks and eyes. Even made sergeant once. Gets drunk and fights, the bane of the cavalry. But no man is better in the field."

"A constant troublemaker. Hasn't anybody taken him down?"

"Several men have tried. He's in C Troop."

"Well, if he jumps a Tonto, he'll get a knife between his ribs. He baited young O'Boyle today. Sergeant Larkin broke it up."

"Routine, friend Ewing, routine. Now . . . the Old Man's getting impatient. His orders are for you and the Tontos to draw five days' rations and work out the country from here to Juan Montoya's ranch, some miles south of Hillsboro. From there you will strike west on a scout through the foothills of the Black Range to the Mimbres River, carefully cutting for sign down it on both sides, then looping back here. The major thinks possibly war parties are using the Mimbres Valley as a passageway to hit the stage stations, the lower trails, and ranches. You are to engage any small party you can." A small crease ran across Cooley's forehead. "The major wants a prisoner, preferably a woman. A prisoner might give us a clue to Old Vic's whereabouts, even lead us there. Another purpose of this scout is to familiarize you and the Tontos with the country. Tisdale will serve as guide. You are to move fast. There will be no troopers to encumber you. You'll make Montoya's by tomorrow."

"I understand that's where the paint stud came from."

"Exactly. Old Vic's favorite war-horse. The Old Man doesn't trust Montoya. Thinks it strange that despite the many horse-and-mule raids on Montoya's ranch, nobody's ever been hurt or carried off up there—that is, to our knowledge. Maybe the *señor* is more than a handy source for replacing stock. Maybe he's peddling ammunition and rifles and other supplies, in keeping with a common practice up and down the Rio Grande. In return, Montoya survives. The Old Man wants you to talk with him . . . feel him out."

Ewing listened with a doubtful smile. "You don't think he'd confess, do you?"

"Hardly. Point is, the hostiles never clean him out. You know—take some, leave some. If they took all the horses, there wouldn't be any left for next time. Find out what you can. You might pick up something from Montoya. Also, I think back in the Old Man's mind is the hope that you might cut Old Vic's trail up that way."

"That's out of the Black Range."

"Not far. And Old Vic seems to be everywhere. The one place we know he's not is in Chihuahua. The Mexican authorities tell us it's quiet down there. After all, they say, didn't their great General Terrazas kill Chief Victorio?"

"So you honestly believe Victorio is back in the Black Range?"

"I have no reason not to, in view of what's happening. Remember—and it always seems to come back to this—nobody from this side of the border identified Victorio among the dead at Tres Castillos."

"His trail would look the same as any Indian's."

"You're forgetting the paint stud, sighted not long ago by the erstwhile Navajos."

"In the event we do, I am to drop a courier back and Major Thorn then brings up the entire command?"

"That's it, Lieutenant. Also if you strike a broad trail leading into the Blacks or locate a big *ranchería*. Old Vic will be with what's left of his band. And likely some Mescaleros off their reservation. He has strong connections there." He held out his hand. "I wish you luck, Ewing."

"I'm beginning to see I'll need a great deal of it."

CHAPTER 5

In the afternoon of the second day, as the Tontos cut for sign through a huddle of stony hills, Luke Tisdale halted and swept a downward arm. "There's Juan Montoya's ranch. Told you I'd guide you here pronto."

"How well do you know Montoya?" Ewing asked, ignoring the pomposity. Tisdale was a bore and a blowhard. En route here, he had talked constantly, besides holding himself aloof from the Tontos. In turn, Apache-like, they had acted as if he did not exist.

"Enough that I don't trust him."

"Some particular reason?" As usual, Tisdale was quick to echo Major Thorn's opinions. Good garrison politics. Also helped keep a civilian employed.

"Any rancher that survives in Apache country just about has to trade with Apaches."

"A strong man might not. You survived as a prospector."

"That was different," Tisdale said, drawing himself up. "I lived by my wits, knowin' when to show myself, when to hole up an' play possum. You can bet your boots, Lieutenant, I never put my rifle down that I didn't take a sharp look-see around first. It didn't take the Warm Springs long

96

to learn when they tangled with me, they had a bobcat on their hands."

Ewing, stomaching the bombast, thought of the old Army saying that you never really knew a man until after you had gone on a long scout with him. A bad-weather scout was a particular revelation.

Swinging down the slope, Ewing saw a tangle of pole corrals and sheds, therein many horses and mules. Nearby, an elongated adobe house, made so by the addition of rooms, a cluttered *ramada* extending its length. Beyond, he saw the dust of three riders driving beeves toward the main corral.

"Better let me break the ice for you," Tisdale said importantly.

"I will do the talking," Ewing said.

By the time they rode up, the beeves were corraled and the three riders waited, a man and two boys of about fourteen and ten years of age, Ewing judged.

Head high, Tisdale said in a loud voice, "Remember me? I'm Luke Tisdale, in charge of scouts at Fort Cummings."

"I remember you, señor," the other said, his voice sharp.

Juan Montoya was a short but straight-bodied man whose piercing eyes held no welcome for Tisdale beyond mere courtesy. Seeing that, Ewing rode past Tisdale and held out his hand to Montoya, saying, "*Buenas tardes*, señor. I'm Lieutenant Mackay. These are Tonto Army scouts from Arizona. Needless to say, we are looking for Apaches. So far we've cut no fresh sign between here and Fort Cummings. I hope you've had no trouble lately."

Montoya, visibly surprised at the friendly greeting, held out his hand and smiled. "Not since they took some horses."

"When was that?"

"Two months ago."

"How did it happen?"

"Lieutenant, this day has been long," Montoya said and in a tone that pointedly excluded Tisdale, "Come to my house and we will talk." He called to the older boy. "Manuel, take the lieutenant's horse."

At the house Montoya poured mescal and, with apology, said, "You must pardon me, Lieutenant. But I will not explain to Tisdale or invite him into my house. He came here with Navajo scouts and accused me of selling rifles and mescal to the Warm Springs. I have never sold rifles and mescal to the Warm Springs, but I have given them food and I cannot stop them from taking what is mine. The cattle you saw us driving up, my sons and I will drive tomorrow to sell to the miners around Hillsboro. When the Warm Springs come here, I always offer them a beef. Sometimes they take more than one. But they have never harmed my family. Tisdale does not understand that. He says because the Montoyas are alive they are guilty. If we were all dead—my two sons, Manuel and Luis, my little daughter, Maria, my wife, Rosa—Tisdale would say we are innocent."

Montoya spoke with convincing emotion, now and then brushing at his dark moustache. As Ewing took his drink, nodding his thanks, he became the object of luminous, coal-black eyes in a small, brown face peeking shyly at him from a doorway. When he smiled back, she fled at once.

"The Navajos are gone," he said. "Sent back to their reservation. I'm in charge of the Tontos. Tisdale has no authority over them. He's a guide for the post. No more."

"That is good. Tisdale thinks all Apaches are alike. He laughed when I told him Victorio does not drink mescal, opposes it, refuses to let his young men go into the Mexican villages and get drunk, because that is when the Mexicans kill them. Gerónimo is different. He likes mescal."

"Has Gerónimo come here?"

"No. That is only what Victorio has told me. Victorio is my friend. Sometimes we talk."

"I've been told that Victorio was not killed at Tres Castillos, that he is back raiding from his old haunts in the Black Range. Do you believe that?"

Montoya's reply was to shrug and refill the glasses.

"May I ask if you have seen Victorio since Tres Castillos?"

Montoya delayed but an instant, but the hesitation was there. "I have not."

"By chance, did you see the Indians who took your horses?"

"They came at night."

"Since you didn't see them, they could have been white outlaws. They are active around the mining camps."

"There were signs. It was Apaches. Outlaws would have taken all the horses. Some were left. It is like an old game the Warm Springs play with me. I will be glad when it is finished."

"I hope you will excuse so many questions, señor."

"You are not Tisdale. Ask what you like."

Ewing thanked him with a smile and said, "When was the last time you saw Victorio?"

"Before Tres Castillos he came by here."

"Then likely he was killed there."

Montoya went to a wooden cabinet, opened a drawer, took something out, and turned to Ewing. "I had fenced off a box canyon to hold my *caballada*, my extra saddle horses, thinking they would be safe there. Luckily, Manuel's favorite, a three-year-old dark chestnut gelding with Steel Dust blood, is always stabled here.

One morning when I rode out there, I found some of the horses were missing. On a post by the gate where I could not fail to see it, I found this." In the palm of his hand he displayed an American silver dollar, punched through and strung like a pendant on a long strand of minutely braided leather. "I gave this to Victorio years ago as a token of friendship, before the fool gringo government tried to force all Apaches onto the San Carlos hell. Times were better until then. Victorio was still wearing this when he last came here."

Montoya replaced the ornament in the drawer and said, "So, Lieutenant, you will have to decide for yourself whether Victorio is alive."

After a thoughtful pause, Ewing said, "I've also been told that his favorite mount is a paint stud taken from here."

"Not taken. I gave him the stud two years ago. Call it a bribe if you prefer, but my family is still unharmed. I told Tisdale the stud was stolen. I am under enough suspicion as it is without telling the truth."

"I would have done the same to protect my family."

"*Gracias*, Lieutenant. It is a new experience for me to hear understanding from your Army. In dealing with Apaches, remember this: Always give them something, but never give them mescal. Do, they will get drunk and demand more. If you refuse to give more or have none to give them, they will kill you."

"Tobacco is much better," Ewing said, smiling.

"Tobacco or beef or calico—or your best horse," Montoya said, his dark face rueful. "There is a price for all things in life, Lieutenant, especially peace. I have learned that."

"Speaking of the need of peace, could you tell me where Victorio's *ranchería* might be?"

"My friend," Montoya said, smiling as only he could, disarmingly, "could I tell you where an eagle nests?" He waved a vague hand northwest. "Somewhere up there. In the Black Range, in the Sierra Diablo."

Ewing reflected a moment. "Then perhaps you can verify the report at Fort Cummings of the Mexican captive who escaped the Tres Castillos massacre with Victorio?"

Montoya nodded. "His name is Gómez. I know him. He was captured as a child at Janos and raised as a Warm Springs. He is like a Warm Springs, he is no longer a Mexican like me."

"You have seen him lately?" Ewing asked, leaning forward.

"No, Lieutenant. It has been a long time."

Montoya's reply was casual, almost too much so, and Ewing said, "He was reported seen in the vicinity of Hillsboro, telling his story and saying he was tired of the warpath and desirous of peace."

"I know nothing new of Gómez," Montoya said, a sort of weary resistance dulling his voice.

"Do you know where I could find him?"

"No, Lieutenant. No more than you know."

Ewing, sensing that Montoya would tell him no more, rose and thanked his host. On the porch Montoya said, "I hope you understand my position, Lieutenant. I must think of my family. We live by the thinnest of threads. I cannot take sides at this time. If the Warm Springs suspected that I had betrayed them to the Army, they would wipe us out. I mean," he amended hastily, "if I could betray them. I know nothing. Nothing. Absolutely nothing about them."

Ewing held out his hand. "I understand. If the time comes when you feel you can help us, or if we can help you, send me word at Fort Cummings."

Tisdale sidled up as Ewing led the scouts away. "What did the noble *señor* have to say?"

"Nothing that we don't know already."

"I could have told you that."

"However, I don't think he's selling rifles and mescal to the Apaches."

"He denied it?"

"He did and I believed him."

Tisdale's lips framed disgust. "He sure pulled the wool over your eyes, Lieutenant. If he's not sellin' to the Apaches, how come he manages to make out here?"

"Like you, when prospecting," Ewing said, his voice turning brittle, "he lives by his wits."

They bivouacked that night at a spring in the foothills and next day saddled down to the shining ribbon of the Mimbres River, winding through a gentle but strange valley of curious rock formations eroded by wind and time that resembled turrets guarding this unspoiled wilderness. A generous valley sharing its bounty of mule and whitetail deer, and sweet, running water, and pines, junipers, and oaks, and rustling grama grass and soft blue sky.

While they watered the horses, the superstitious Archie kept glancing at the chiseled cliffs, some like giant idols. "Forgotten Ones," he whispered to Ewing, "long time ago here live, my people say. Gone now. Don' know why."

"They lived here long before the Warm Springs came," Ewing said, looking. "The Apaches were intruders. Now, the *blancos* are.

"Forgotten Ones, their spirits near," Archie said, uneasy, wide eyes gleaming. "I feel them, Nantan."

"Guess I feel them, too," Ewing admitted, sensitive to the timeless surroundings. Because he had ridden with the Tontos so long, he sometimes wondered whether he was becoming more like them, closer to their primitiveness; understanding them, he saw through their eyes and felt what they felt. At the same time, a white officer did not ridicule an Apache scout's beliefs, not if he wanted his loyalty.

"Let's look for pony tracks," he said after a moment.

"You and your Tontos," Tisdale sneered, when Archie set the scouts in motion. "You'll be wearin' a breechclout next."

"Which," Ewing said, "is a most sensible piece of apparel in desert country. Another example of the Apache's adaptation to his arid environment. Beats wool a mile, or buckskin."

They fanned out downriver, the scouts criss-crossing the grassy strips and prowling through the timber like game dogs sniffing for scent. The afternoon began to slip by. The valley changed, broadening, leaving the stands of cool pines, the flanking foothills, dropping lower, denuded, reduced to cloaks of scattered junipers.

Ewing rode relaxed, his thoughts turning now and again to Major Thorn's ambitious campaign, to Juan Montoya, not without sympathy for his precarious situation, and to Ivy Shaw. She had touched him. A natural young woman, unaware of her warmth and appeal. Also a realist, born of childhood's heartache and hard times. Somehow he would see her again, because the main thrust of Thorn's battle plan pointed past Hillsboro and into the Black Range.

Archie, unexpectedly turning his horse and motioning, broke Ewing's musing. When Ewing galloped ahead, Tisdale grumped, "Reckon he's found himself a turkey track to ponder over."

Archie was pointing to a broad pattern of horse prints emerging from a southwest canyon and continuing to the river. Both shod and unshod tracks. Ewing dismounted for a closer look and knelt down. The grains of sandy dirt flung up around the tracks were still as cast, nodular and distinct, not fallen in or dried by the sun, and horse droppings looked fresh.

"About how long since they passed here?" Ewing asked Archie.

With his nose and pursed lips, Archie indicated the hills across the river.

"You mean they've just crossed?"

Archie nodded, his smile wolfish, and Ewing read the familiar expression: Archie ached to fight.

"Are they watching us now?"

Archie nodded again.

"How many Warm Springs?"

Archie held up both hands, adding, "Maybe more." The teeth-baring, wolfish smile again. How many didn't bother him.

"From the looks of these tracks," Ewing said, considering the trail again, "they raided a mining camp or helped themselves to Fort Bayard's mounts. We'll go on a way as if in a big hurry. It may confuse them." When he galloped off, the scouts falling in behind, Tisdale spurred up beside him, grunting, "This close and you're gonna let 'em get away?"

"Not if I can help it. They're sitting across the river in ambush, hoping we'll charge over there. We'd accomplish nothing by doing that, just get cut up. We'll make cold camp below, pull back on them later. Better expect a long, hard night."

"Helluva way to fight Indians, if you ask me."

"That's it, Tisdale. I'm not asking you. This is how we fight hostiles in Arizona. General Crook's style. Move at night. You may come along as an observer. Might learn something to pass along to the major. If not, stay behind."

Several miles on, where the river made a gradual bend to the southwest, Ewing drew up in the shade of ancient, massive cottonwoods. The Tontos unsaddled and watered, then, picketing their mounts, rested and smoked. Some started gambling. Toward evening they ate cold rations and waited.

Tisdale, still miffed, had said no word to Ewing since discovery of the tracks.

When darkness fell, Ewing led the scouts back up the valley where they had found the tracks. Across the stream, he sent Archie and Rowdy working in advance. The detail was soon climbing, turning up the mouth of a rocky wash slanting down from the foothills. Ewing figured they had covered several miles, up and down, over rocks, through scrubby brush, when, alarmed at the clatter the stumbling horses were making, he dismounted the scouts and left the mounts with a guard and proceeded on foot. In the muddy light, the little line of bobbing figures looked not unlike a caterpillar humping along.

Archie dropped back. There was no sign yet of the hostiles' camp, he said, and left.

Once, not finding Tisdale, Ewing retracked and found the guide, blowing and grunting, paces behind the tail end of the detail. "Better close up," Ewing told him quietly. "It's easy to get lost in mountains at night."

"Me?" came the scoffing reply. "I could follow this trail blindfolded, and a damned sight faster."

Ewing left him there, his doubts renewed concerning Tisdale's competence as a field guide and scout. Maybe Evelyn Cooley was right. Maybe the man was all show and blow.

Up. Up. The advance crawling like stalking cats. Stopping at times to make certain ahead, the others holding up until they heard the come-on signals, the calls of a whippoorwill or a screech owl or the chirrup of a cricket.

Ewing lost track of time. It was past midnight, he guessed. Deeper into the night he got his first whiff of woodsmoke, the sweet smell of juniper. At the same moment a whippoorwill's call came. Soon after, Archie loomed up before Ewing. "Wait," he whispered, and disappeared.

An hour must have passed before he returned,

Rowdy with him. The Warm Springs, he said, were camped on the crest of a wooded ridge, their horses held in a side canyon close to the camp. A strong camp. There was only one way to approach close without alarming them.

"How?" Ewing asked, sensing greater difficulty.

Archie seemed to think on that a bit, then said, "Around, where ridge breaks off, away from their horses. Rough trail. Long way. Hard way. Steep. Big drop. But that is good, away from their horses. Their horses nervous are, like sentinels."

"We'll take it," Ewing told him.

Single file, the detail followed the two scouts, hugging the right side of the trail. Off and on, Ewing heard the whippoorwill calls. Step by step the ascent narrowed and twisted, growing steeper, made slippery by loose gravel and rock. To Ewing's left he could feel the breathless emptiness below. Coming to a boulder jutting out onto the trail, he shifted his carbine into its sling across his back and slowly, hand by hand, began easing around. His chest was slick with sweat by the time he felt broader footing. Archie paused often. Time was suspended. Up. Up. Now on hands and knees. Behind Ewing a rock slithered loose and dropped. Much later, it seemed, he heard a faint *pink* when it hit, a series of fainter *pinks* as it skipped, until the sounds faded, lost, died. All this time Ewing was conscious of the figures ahead and behind him freezing as he froze, tensed, head cocked. But nothing changed higher on. He breathed easier.

It was even longer before Archie touched him, the signal to creep ahead. The smell of juniper smoke reached Ewing much stronger, like incense on the cool night.

When next Archie halted, Ewing, peering across, made out the glow of campfires burned low. Beyond the camp a horse snuffled. Rising, feeling each step through his moccasins, Ewing deployed the scouts and Tisdale as skirmishers, placing Tisdale purposely on the right flank, out of the way. No firing until daybreak; that was always understood. Slipping back, Ewing lay down to wait until shooting light. The rocky ground felt cold. He shivered a little. Time hung as it always did like this. He had no particular thoughts, his concentration solely on the formless shapes around the low-burning campfires under the pines. Now and again he heard the horses move in the side canyon. The camp was still silent.

When a shaft of dull light pierced the eastern sky, Ewing quickened. Not yet. Not enough light. Beside him Archie shifted without sound and brought up his carbine to make ready.

Just then a shot slammed prematurely off to Ewing's right. He jerked that way in astonishment, in anger. The camp erupted into yells. Feet pounded toward the side canyon. With a curse, Ewing fired toward the yells. On both sides of him the scouts were firing rapidly. Powder smoke roiled. A pause to reload and they charged with whoops, drawing a scatter of rifle flashes. Hastening forward with the Tontos into the murk of the timber, Ewing heard horses clattering down the canyon. When he ran there, the sounds were already receding. The Warm Springs were gone.

Walking over the campsite in daylight with Archie, Ewing found only a few blankets and food pouches. He kicked at a pouch and told Archie, "Find out who fired that shot."

Archie was back in a short time. "No Tontos," he said, shaking his head.

"So it was Tisdale?"

Archie's reply was a shrug, but the fierce eyes held a mixture of amusement and disgust.

Ewing went straight to the guide, who was watching a loose horse stirring in the timber below the ridge. "Tisdale," he said, "your shot ruined our surprise attack. Set it off. Why did you fire?"

"I saw an Indian slipping down and around to sneak in behind us on the trail. The instant I spotted him I let go. It was instinct."

"That's funny. None of the Tontos saw him, and there's no dead Apache down there."

"Guess I missed him."

"Guess you did. And we missed bagging the whole war party, plus taking a valuable prisoner the major wanted to interrogate. Archie thinks there were several women in the bunch. We wanted a woman prisoner, particularly. Sometimes they'll talk."

"Sorry, Lieutenant. It just happened that way."

Ewing, turning away, swung back on a stabbing suspicion. "You wouldn't try to make us look bad, would you?"

Tisdale's jaw fell. He wore the guileless, hurt look of one falsely accused. "Look bad? You know better than that, Lieutenant."

If Tisdale was covering up, he was quite an actor. Still, Ewing's insight persisted. He flung away, rigid with dull anger, thinking of all the night's gut-busting work for nothing.

CHAPTER 6

"In view of the fact that the general is . . . ah . . . somewhat indisposed this morning," Adjutant Cooley explained, straight-faced, "a verbal report of your scout will not be needed. Your written report will suffice."

At Cooley's words the eavesdropping clerk ceased his steady scribbling and looked up at the ceiling with a what-again expression.

Ewing wrote his report in detailed length, including Tisdale's untimely shot, and handed it to Cooley. After a close perusal, the adjutant said, "So Montoya had nothing to contribute?"

"That doesn't rule out the chance he won't later," Ewing said, conscious of wanting to defend the man. "You will notice there that he did give me the name of the Mexican captive, one Gómez, captured as a child at Janos, who could be the key to Victorio's location in the Black Range."

"Except," Cooley replied, "as you noted, that Montoya did not say where this Gómez can be found. You're also rather hard on Tisdale."

"He's a blunderer. Hereafter, I'll leave him with the horses. I don't want him along."

"I fear the Old Man won't like your appraisal."

"I'll stand behind it as a factual field report."

Frowning at the listening clerk, who, caught, quickly took up his pen, Cooley inclined his head and Ewing rose and followed him outside to the *ramada*.

"Tisdale," Cooley confided, "is a privileged character around here. He goes back to the Old Man's heyday early in the War . . . was attached to the headquarters staff as a courier. Went roaming west after the War, prospected when he wasn't hanging around Army posts on the Rio Grande. Hearing the general was in command here, he presented himself and was promptly made chief of scouts. He's a clever man, a flatterer. Don't underestimate him. Also an informer on what's going on around the post and off the post. For that, he draws a sweet one hundred and twenty-five dollars a month."

"My God! Him . . . drawing a second lieutenant's pay."

"I remind you, friend Ewing, it is all quite proper, the going rate for a guide."

"Proper, if deserved. Just keep the man out of my hair, and sight, if you can."

"Not my province. That's the Old Man's. You have to admit, however, that Tisdale does know the country."

"I'll admit that and no more."

"There is another matter I ought to fill you in on," Cooley said and glanced about before he spoke again, his voice lower. "Before long you'll very likely be getting an invitation to dinner at the Thorns'." He compressed his lips and frowned his adjutant's frown, a crease that furrowed his forehead. His skin grew pink above his reddish-brown beard. "I don't know how to say this, Ewing. But here goes. It is customary for young bachelor officers new on the post to go to dinner at the C.O.'s. The major . . . that is, the general . . . is a great host. Tells a good story. Serves the best whiskey. None of that belly-wash the sutler sells enlisted men. . . . Mrs. Thorn is a gracious hostess. . . . Their striker-cook, Private Labonte, is an exceptional chef. He would be at the finest New York hotel today were it not for his one great failing—drink, which, I repeat, is the bane of the cavalry, and which has followed him here. One thing about Labonte, he can cook, drunk or sober, so he fulfills his duties, regardless."

"Wirt, you are beating around the bush."

"So I am. I don't like telling this."

"What are you trying to say?"

Cooley ranged his glance around again. "Simply this. That some young officers, after going to the general's for dinner a time or two, have been reassigned elsewhere, or, worse, have resigned."

Lips tight, as if too much had escaped them, he went directly inside.

Well, Ewing thought, that wasn't too hard to figure. The young bachelors, unable to hold their liquor, had made fools of themselves, possibly for "conduct unbecoming an officer and gentleman," that familiar catchall for any variety of situations, including habitual drunkenness, which could lead to dismissal.

Cooley's reticent words crossed his mind next afternoon when an orderly rode up to the Tontos' camp, flourished a salute, and said in a singsong voice, "Major Thorn presents his compliments to Lieutenant Mackay. The major and Mrs. Thorn request Lieutenant Mackay's company at dinner tonight. Six o'clock."

Was that the suggestion of a smirk behind the orderly's bushy mustachio? Ewing did not speak for a moment.

"Any return message, sir?"

"My thanks to Major and Mrs. Thorn. I'll be there," Ewing answered, feeling a vague reluctance. But this was the sort of invitation a junior officer could not decline.

Josephine Thorn, looking lovely in green, greeted Ewing when he arrived promptly at six o'clock. Her dark brown hair fell in long, glistening waves to her shoulders. A pearl lavaliere on a gold chain laced her pretty neck. Her dress, cut quite low, accented the V of her breasts and the rounded whiteness of her shoulders. In the amber lamplight the perfection of her fine features seemed sculpted. There was the faint

116

scent of jasmine about her that he remembered.

"So pleased you could come, Lieutenant. The general has a deplorable habit, unnecessary many times, of assigning his ablest junior officers on the longest scouts."

"I do without apology to you ladies of the post," Major Thorn said, rising from his chair to shake hands. "You forget that we are fighting a war out here. Glad to see you, Mackay. This damnable hernia of mine has had me under siege, but I think I've got it on the run this evening." Although his fleshy face looked bloated and the flinty eyes bloodshot, his voice was firm and affable. "I should like you to have a drink with me, sir. I can offer you some passable sour-mash whiskey."

"Whatever you're having, sir."

The striker served the drinks. A dark-skinned, graying man of obvious good manners, he turned to Mrs. Thorn. "Would Madame care for something?"

"Just a glass of wine, please."

"Yes, madame."

"How!" Thorn exclaimed, raising his glass in the traditional cavalry toast.

"How!" Ewing echoed.

While Thorn downed his drink, Ewing was taking a swallow. The whiskey was smooth, very smooth, as Cooley had said it would be. Josephine Thorn sipped her red wine, her violet eyes liquid in the soft light. The parlor was a tasteful blending of rugs, hanging tapestries, decorated lamps, one glass-fronted bookcase, and, wonder of wonders, a handsome piano which bore the scars of Army freighting.

"I have gone over your report," Thorn began, his voice taking on an official tone. "What is your appraisal of Montoya after talking to him?"

"I think he is walking a very tight rope up there in order to survive, sir."

"Any rancher is in southern New Mexico. What I mean is, do you think he can be trusted?"

"Yes, sir, I do."

"Hmmm. Will he pass on information to us of any Warm Springs movements?"

"He says he knows nothing now, sir. Later, I think, he will be of some help."

"Later? Damnation, do you realize it's been almost a year since Tres Castillos? We can't wait. I'm going to force the issue some way. I want to wind this up by fall. I may send you into the Blacks."

"That would be interesting. From a distance it looks like mighty rough campaigning, but beautiful country just the same."

"It is both—the worst sort of terrain for cavalry. But rough country is where you flush the best game." He called for Labonte to fill the whiskey glasses. Ewing, glancing down, was surprised to see his own likewise empty. Once again the major downed his drink. He now moved his bulky proportions with greater ease. "This kind of campaigning galls a fighting man, young sir. We are constantly reacting instead of acting, instead of taking the initiative, because we cannot locate the enemy before he strikes. We are chasing dust devils riding bareback who can switch to fresh mounts by the simple means of stealing more horses from ranchers, while a laden trooper labors after them on a horse toting a hundred pounds of equipment. Seldom do we get the enemy within our grasp." He smashed his right fist into the palm of his left. "And the one chance we had was taken from us by a self-styled generalissimo, though unknown to him the main quarry escaped back across the border. God, how it must gripe Terrazas to admit, secretly, that Victorio slipped away from him! When this campaign is over, and we either have Victorio dead or alive, I intend to message Terrazas to that effect. If dead, I might even send him Victorio's head." Thorn slapped his thigh and roared with laughter. Then, gradually, a faraway look entered his eyes. He straightened. "Believe me, young sir, there is nothing to compare with the sight of an army moving up by brigades. . . . Skirmishers ahead, bearing their arms like quail hunters. . . . Boys in the ranks carrying their muskets at right-shoulder shift."

When, pausing, he called for another drink, his wife murmured, "We're having wine for dinner, Theo, and you know you always like whiskey or brandy after dinner."

"And whiskey before dinner," he replied, quieting her with a gray look. When the drinks were brought, he let his glass stand, momentarily forgotten, while he seemed to gaze beyond her and Ewing upon a vast field. "I am thinking of Fort Donelson, early in the War, when hopes were high."

"It was at Donelson that Theo was made colonel," his wife interposed, smiling on her husband.

"As a matter of fact," Thorn went on, nodding at the memory, "the Confederates need not have surrendered. They broke out after our gunboats were driven back. The door was open, but General Pillow ordered them back into their trenches, deciding they could hold the fort. . . . General Buckner knew they couldn't then, but he wasn't in command. Pillow and Floyd pulled out and Buckner was left to assume the blame for surrendering. . . . I knew Buckner before the War, thought highly of him as a man." Thorn's face hardened. "Pillow and Floyd weren't the only ones who left Buckner holding the bag. N. B. Forrest also fled. I have never entertained the regard for the man that some bleeding hearts have. . . . A Memphis slave trader before the War, without the indispensable training and well-bred qualities of a regular."

"Theo's regiment closed the gap that hemmed in the Confederates," his wife put in. "He is too modest to say that, himself."

Her husband's face smoothed. Thus encouraged, he talked on, rambling, mentioning personalities he liked and did not like, the latter either politically appointed officers or others who had come up through the ranks, "untutored in the fine art of war, sir." Between drinks he spoke of tactics, of "smashing blows," his favorite military axiom, the behavior of green troops under fire, of atrocious weather and clay-yellow roads turned to mire, and of faulty weapons. He talked of bloody Shiloh, of the Sunken Road and the littered, cocklebur meadow across which the Confederates charged again and again, of Sherman, four horses shot from under him, pulling shattered regiments together, of Sherman drawing back grudgingly, yet holding the right wing.

"It was after Shiloh," his wife remarked dutifully, "that Theo was made brigadier for bringing order out of disorder."

Thorn finished his drink. "The Confederates made the tactical error," he said, and seemed to lose his train of thought, "—of attacking in long lines on a broken front. . . . Couldn't smash through us to the river. Couldn't do it." He stared reminiscently at his glass, called for Labonte to fill it.

"In your opinion, sir," Ewing asked, recalling his military history, "would the Confederates have won if General Beauregard had ordered another final charge that first day?"

"Doubt it . . . doubt it vereee much," Thorn slurred. "They . . . were too disorganized . . . too exhausted an' hungry." Labonte set Thorn's glass down before him. "We . . . we," Thorn started over, "were scarcely better off. But Grant . . . Grant and Sherman . . . got busy patchin' up our front."

"Would you say that General Buell's arrival from Savannah saved the day?"

"Buell!" Thorn thundered, pounding the arm of his chair. "Buell was derelict . . . not comin' up till afternoon!"

"Theo, please."

He was, Ewing saw, sinking deeper into his cups when Labonte, at a signal from Mrs. Thorn, entered the room and announced, "Dinner is served, madame."

Thorn blinked, heaved heavily to his feet, staggered, caught himself, and made an exaggerated gesture for his wife and Ewing to precede him. Ewing held out his arm and escorted her to the candlelit dining room, while Labonte hovered in the shadows like an officiating majordomo. Ewing seated Mrs.

Thorn, and Labonte, ever watchful, assisted the major. Labonte poured the wine. Thorn glowered at his long-stemmed glass, pushed it away, demanded whiskey and got it. He pecked at his dinner, meanwhile conversing with Ewing about cadet days at West Point, his vibrant voice rising on "Duty—Honor—Country—," pounding the table until the dishes rattled, upon which his wife suggested tactfully, "Do try the chicken, Theo. It's baked in your favorite sauce. Labonte managed it through the commissary, the commissary through the Mexican settlements on the Rio Grande."

"Labonte," the major cackled, "is an instinctive forager. Wish I'd had 'im in Tennessee."

"Everything is quite a treat," Ewing assured his hostess.

From that point Josephine Thorn carried the brunt of the conversation, from garrison talk to provisions. "As you well know, Lieutenant, the food problem is appalling, though the commissary is getting in a few more staples. Bombay duck, for one, it is called, but Theo doesn't like dried fish, and neither do I, coming from New England, where the seafood is always fresh. . . . Sometimes we get corned willie, which is too salty, and sometimes we get what the commissary calls 'gold fish,' but canned salmon is hardly better than Bombay duck. . . . Thankfully, the canned fruits are a delectable change, and last month we began getting some chocolate, macaroni, and prunes. . . . Theo likes antelope steaks, but I don't care for the wild taste. We get eggs once a month, if we're lucky, and the garrison gardens help. So we should be thankful for green beans, onions, and squash. I fear that I'm a bit spoiled after living in the East for so long."

"I doubt that very much, Mrs. Thorn. Too, I should say that provisions for women and children are no better on the Arizona posts, maybe worse. I might add that, thanks to time and out of self-survival, I've developed a taste for Mexican cuisine. Chiles, for example, help cover up a great many deficiencies."

"Chiles," she said, wrinkling her perfect nose. "I avoid them like the plague."

She made him laugh, and he said, "It takes time to cultivate their appreciation—that and a hardy constitution, urged on by near starvation."

She turned. "Some more wine, please, Labonte."

The major, head down, engrossed with the particulars of his dinner, had not spoken for some minutes.

After dinner, Josephine Thorn sat at the piano and played and sang "Kathleen Mavourneen," which Ewing knew had been sung often on the eve of the War, when officers who had served together in the old Army met for the last time as comrades, drank, embraced, wept, and set out on their irreversible ways, North and South. A sad song, a good-by song. She played well and her soprano was clear and rich with feeling.

Major Thorn had another whiskey on that, after which she played and sang "Lorena," which she said was all too sad for this evening, and forthwith she swung into "Oh, You New York Girls," which she performed vivaciously to Ewing's applause. Rising, with a glance at her husband nodding on the settee, she excused herself and went to the kitchen and Ewing heard her say, "You may go now, Labonte," and Labonte's questioning, "But the dishes, madame?"

"I'll do them later. You may go. It's been a long evening for you. The dinner was delightful."

"Very well, madame."

She brought whiskies for her husband and Ewing, who looked askance at the glass. His head was spinning. He had no idea how many drinks he'd had. The room appeared bathed in a euphoric haze. He bowed and took the glass. Josephine Thorn sipped wine.

They chatted awhile. He would have taken his leave then, but something held him here. An exaggerated sense of unaccustomed well-being after the grueling days piled end on end. But soon he must go.

When next he looked, Major Thorn's head was

on his chest, his body slumped lengthwise on the settee. His glass was empty.

"Let me help you put him to bed," Ewing offered, rising.

She put out her hand. "No. Let him rest. He is comfortable. He often naps there in the evening."

"I must go."

Her hand again on his arm. "Not until you have told me more about your Tontos. Theo says that together you captured the raider Flores and his band of Chiricahuas in the Sierra Madre and brought them back to San Carlos."

She proved to be an eager listener, and he talked on and on, flattered by her interest, unused to an audience. When he came to the forthcoming campaign, she glanced at her husband, an almost calculating look, rose and said, her voice barely above a whisper, "There is something you need to know. We can talk better in the study while Theo rests."

The major, Ewing saw, had stretched out fully by now, and he was snoring.

She led the way to a smaller room, dimly lit by the parlor lamps. He saw a desk and chairs, bookcase, military mementos on the walls, and a small sofa. She drew him down beside her, saying, "Perhaps you've heard what happened long ago, late in the War, after Theo had risen so rapidly in those early years at Donelson and Shiloh? It's common gossip."

126

"Not in Arizona, Mrs. Thorn. I've heard nothing."

"Please call me Josephine." She laid her hand on his. "Then I must tell you. In June of sixty-four, Theo suffered an ignominious defeat by Nathan Bedford Forrest at Brice's Cross Roads, in Mississippi, though he had a superior force—eight thousand cavalrymen to Forrest's thirty-five hundred. General Sherman never forgave the defeat. At the time he was pressing toward Atlanta and fearful that Forrest would cut his supply lines. Sherman did admit, however, that Theo was encumbered with a train of wagons, which Forrest was not." She stepped to the doorway, looked in on her husband, came back, and sat down, trailing the jasmine scent. "There was a board of investigation," she said, speaking faster, resting her hand on his again. "It met and sat without making any recommendations. In that respect, it was an acquittal. Even so, Theo's reputation was ruined. He was not again assigned to active duty during the War . . . not until the summer of sixty-five, when he was sent on frontier duty to Fort Stockton, Texas—just a collection of 'dobes with stone foundations . . . what the Confederates hadn't burned. It was like being banished to the end of the world. Except for a few leaves back East, he has been on the frontier ever since . . . virtually forgotten."

"A great many fine officers go unnoticed and

unrewarded," Ewing agreed. "That old saying, 'Forty years a file closer,' was never more true."

"Now, you understand why this campaign is so important to him. It's his last chance to regain a part of what he lost in the War. You and your Tontos hold the key."

"If Victorio is still alive, and if we can locate him, and if we bag him once we do find him. There is no more difficult terrain for cavalry than the Black Range."

She was silent. Her eyes, fixed on his face, seemed to grow in intensity.

He said, "I should go. It's late."

"Wait. It's so seldom I can speak as candidly as I have tonight with anyone on the post. I could never tolerate the prattle of women. Now you wait, Ewing." Rising, she went to the kitchen and soon returned, bearing whiskey for him and wine for herself. Another glance into the parlor, and she handed him his drink and sat down beside him. He drank his whiskey like water. The moment he did the realization struck him that he was drunk tonight, had been for some time, and was becoming more drunk. He looked at Mrs. Thorn, increasingly aware of her proximity and of the fact that she was a very attractive woman.

She was murmuring, "I do not make a pretense of marital humility, Ewing. I have been Theo's main support for years. He's a proud man. His disgrace has been a heavy cross for him to bear. He drinks too much. That is evident to you tonight. His health is broken. He was seriously wounded at Shiloh, you know. He is . . . not a whole man anymore." Her voice trailed off. "These years have been difficult for me as well, as a woman." She paused again. Her breath came unevenly. She was staring straight into his face. She said, "You are a gentleman. A true gentleman of discretion. I perceive that."

They could be standing in the twilight at Soldier's Farewell, he glimpsing her naked need, yet only momentarily. He saw it now, except this time it was not imagined and did not go away, controlled by propriety. He got up suddenly.

She stood and raised her face to him and kissed him, her open lips giving and impatient, and said, "I believe you understand what I am trying to tell you."

He felt frozen. He caught his breath. He kissed her, hesitant about it, unsure, a reservation she sensed, whispering, "You need not be afraid. Theo will sleep until morning. I put a little something in his last drink."

She began unbuttoning his blouse, slipped her hands inside and ran them over him. Her eyes seemed to ignite.

Everything took on an air of unreality: this room, his presence here in this stranger's immobile body, her too-perfect face seen through the dimness, the length of her body rotating against him. Inconceivable. Yet not.

She said, "Do I have to beg, Ewing? Leave me some particle of pride."

All at once he found himself kissing her mouth, her eyes, her hair, her breasts, and being drawn out of the study's twilight into an even dimmer room of perfumed scents. His unreality returned. He heard rustlings, quick rustlings. Standing frozen again, he felt helping hands with his clothing. Soon he was naked and impelling hands went around him and he had the sensation of being swept down into a warm velvet pool. After that, he lost all sense of time and place.

When they stood in the study once more, Josephine Thorn said, "You will come here again," her eyes boring into his.

He didn't know what to say.

"And again and again," she assured him, stroking his arm.

CHAPTER 7

Tattoo was only minutes away when Private Tim O'Boyle, slipping through the moonlit darkness to the fort's gate, hissed softly, "Hey, Duffy. It's me . . . Tim O'Boyle."

A burly figure loomed. An older trooper's voice answered. "Just you. When I thought it was the Old Man come to personally inspect me post as a model of soldierly efficiency."

"Let me pass. I'll be back in an hour or two."

"In a pig's eye. Last time it was close to reveille. You're stretchin' your luck too thin, lad. Mine, too, when Corporal Patrick Duffy's post happens to be the only way out. I could face summary court-martial, if you don't make it back in time."

"I'll be earlier tonight. Come on."

"Stuck on one o' them Mexican girls from Mesilla, are you?"

"I know one. She's mighty pretty."

"A lot you know about women. Listen! Such as they be is not for you. No good can come o' that associatin'. Keep it up, you'll be on sick call to the surgeon for somethin' that quinine an' whiskey can't cure."

"I know all about that. Just let me pass."

"On two conditions. Just remember the O.D. runs a check ever' now and then, an' be back by midnight."

"I will. Thanks, Pat."

"How well I know I can depend on that," Duffy said, his voice dripping sarcasm. And sternly, "Another thing. Got your fightin' jewelry on?"

"Huh?"

"Your fightin' jewelry."

"What's that?"

"Mean nobody's told you? Lad, you are a green John. What you do is take horseshoe nails and bend 'em into rings, with the heads worn on top. Two or three on each fist. Best weapon there is in a knock-down-drag-out place, such as this Little Chihuahua, where you insist on goin'."

"I'll make some tomorrow."

"Now, get back before daylight."

Tim checked himself, aware of a disturbing reminder. "Has Wexler been through?"

"Not yet. Which calls somethin' to mind. Take it from an old soldier, you're gonna have to whip Wexler before long."

"Him? He's bigger and stronger than I am."

Duffy snorted disgust. "You carryin' a good Irish name fore an' aft an' you let such as that bother you? Listen! A smaller man can always kick an' gouge. Use the knee. A smash to the groin has stopped many a big bully in his tracks. Then finish him off with a kick. Or lay your hands on a rock or club. Every man has the God-given right to defend himself."

"Sure. You make it sound easy."

"I didn't say that. But look to your natural advantages. You are quicker than Wexler, you can slip inside his blows. He's a roundhouse swinger, the brawlin' type." Duffy leaned his carbine against the gate and went into a crouch. "Stay low, like this. When he swings, duck under and move inside. Hit him in the gut, then lift the knee. If the opening ain't there, back off, retreat. Let him wear himself out pursuin' you. Footwork, lad. Footwork. Like this. Forget his chin, it's like rock. You'll break your hand." Tattoo began sounding. He straightened and said, "We'll start workin' out on the sly at the stables. I'll fix up a heavy bag. You'll need to develop a punch. You've got to get ready, lad. You've got to whip him good. If you don't, he'll make your life so miserable you can't look a man in the face."

"All right," Tim said, without enthusiasm.

He walked fast, inhaling deeply of the cool night air. Beneath the bright moonlight the desert landscape spreading before him had the illusory appearance of a swaying sea of silver lapping at the low hills east and west. The path he followed was well-beaten, taken nightly by troopers who chanced to have money in their pockets, troopers bored by the isolation and routine of Army life, seeking recreation at Little Chihuahua. There was another name for it and other places like it, in cavalry terminology, and that was "hog ranch," a series of shacks set up just outside the reservation lines of the post, devoted to wine, women, song, gambling, and, frequently, fighting. Post commanders had no legal jurisdiction over these places, but sometimes hog ranches went up in flames, to the regret of the enlisted men. Thus far, Little Chihuahua had escaped such deserved destruction. Tim knew the whiskey was rotgut, the games crooked, the music ordinary, and the women, as Duffy had warned, were degenerate— with one exception. He lengthened stride.

Half a mile onward he caught the first notes of listless music. A guitar. And, soon, the first dim lights. Like yellow eyes below the next fold of desert. Shacks and tents materialized, grayish under the moon's glare. He experienced a surge of anticipation. The music issued from the largest shack—an oblong shed, it was. He went in.

Two men from his C Troop sat drinking at a rough table. They waved. Another cavalryman danced with a woman to music played by an elderly Mexican man. A card game was going in the next room. The proprietor, a swarthy, keg-bellied Anglo with bull shoulders who called himself Ace Gannon, stood watchfully behind the plank bar, behind him a barrel of whiskey and a clutter of smeary glasses.

Teresa stood at the end of the bar. She smiled when Tim entered. "Señor Tim," she greeted him, high heels clicking as she met him.

He liked the tone of her voice, which seemed just for him. He was learning that the Spanish-speaking people had pleasing ways of their own.

"You sure do look nice," he told her.

She smiled. She was always smiling, it seemed, because that was her nature. She led him to a table. Teresa couldn't be more than sixteen, Tim figured. In time she would grow heavy around her waist and breasts, but now she was slim, her big eyes wonderfully smoky and rich, her hair long and blue-black, piled high on the back of her head, held in place with a pretty red comb, her rose-tinted complexion quite fair for a Mexican, her lips full, her teeth even and white. Never had he known a girl like her. Mature for her age. Those eyes, wise and haunting, told her story—her eyes and what little she had confided in snatches of conversation when he had asked: a child of Chihuahua, an orphan, her entire family massacred by Apaches. *Señor* Gannon, a border trader, had generously taken her in as his very own, reared her as his daughter, cared for her. But for him she would be dead or nothing, living in a poor village.

Despite Teresa's earnestly told story, Gannon did not fit the munificent paternal role which she attributed to him. His voice was rough when

135

speaking to her. He was not generous. When Tim bought drinks, Gannon allowed her no share of the overcharge for bad whiskey. When Tim told her that in other saloons the girls drew commissions each time they sold a drink, she replied that one did not receive pay working for one's father.

It was plain to Tim that she feared her foster father, a discernment that deepened Tim's feelings for her. He wanted to take her out of this life. She was his first love, but so far he could not find the courage to tell her.

"Like to dance?" he asked, wanting to hold her.

Smiling, she slipped into his arms and he held her close. She felt like silk, moving in perfect time with the music. He liked the clean scent of her hair. They had danced but a few steps when Gannon charged from behind the bar and out to them, grabbing Tim's arm. "You know the rule, soldier. No dancin' unless you buy drinks first for you and the girl."

"I aimed to after the dance," Tim replied.

"You buy the drinks first or you don't dance." Gannon's hard eyes questioned Teresa. "You know better than that."

She stood very still, saying nothing.

Tim wanted no trouble. "All right," he said, "bring the drinks."

"Pay in advance."

Tim dug into his pocket for two dollars—two

dollars, he figured silently, out of his pay of thirteen dollars a month.

Just then the music ended. The guitarist rose and strolled outside. Tim looked at Teresa. "There's my two dollars."

"You still have your dance coming," she said, smiling. "I will see to that." She brought the drinks and sat down across from him.

She was fair-minded and cheerful, only some of the many qualities he liked about this girl whose tragic eyes revealed what her lips would not. She left her drink untouched. Tim tasted his, made a face, and put it down. They chatted animatedly. She missed her village, she said, the people, the fiestas. Did Tim miss his home? Not as much as he did when he first came out here, Tim replied, beaming at her until she lowered her eyes and looked away.

They were still chatting when Kirk Wexler arrived. At that moment an aging Anglo woman, her face slack and painted, powdered pouches under her eyes, was coming from the gambling room. Seeing Wexler, she ran over and hugged him, exclaiming, "Look who's here, everybody!" and tried to lead him to a table. Roughly, he handed her aside and strode to the table where Tim and the girl sat.

Looking down in amusement, Wexler said, "Well, if it ain't little Sonny Boy. Did you come all by yourself in the dark? Or did Sarge Larkin send a wet nurse along to see that you got back to the post? Somebody to tuck you in nice and comfy in your bunk?"

Tim could feel his face flaming. "Go find your own table," he said. "You're not welcome here."

"That's no way to talk to a fellow trooper," Wexler said, feigning hurt feelings, and sat between them and motioned for Gannon to bring a drink. He paid with a flourish and tossed down the whiskey without batting an eye, showing off, Tim thought. Then, regarding Teresa, Wexler said, "I have to say this, Sonny Boy. You know how to pick 'em."

Teresa had put on her expressionless face reserved for when trouble was pending.

The musician strayed in, started playing the same listless tune as before.

"Why don't you leave us alone?" Tim said. "There are other girls."

"Girls?" Wexler mocked, guffawing. "Them old battle-axes! Teresa's the only girl here. Let's dance, young lady."

Tim said, "She has the next dance with me."

Teresa's eyes flicked tactfully from Wexler to Tim and back to Wexler. She did not move for a bit. Then she cut her glance to the bar, and Tim saw Gannon jog his chin, indicating Wexler, before she said, appeasingly, "It is wrong you fight. Both from the same fort. So there will be no fight, Señor Tim, I will dance with Señor Kirk, then you. *Sí?*"

"Thanks, Teresa—but you stay out of this. If he wants a fight, he can have it."

Wexler, grinning, bounced to his feet and ran an appropriating arm around her waist. When he did that something flashed through Tim. He tore at Wexler's thick arm and Wexler swung on him and Teresa screamed. Ducking inside the roundhouse swing, Tim smashed his right into Wexler's middle and heard the man grunt, giving to the blow, and then laugh. "Why, Boyle, you Mick, damned if you ain't learned to spar just a little."

"You dirty Dutchy," Tim snarled, outraged, "come on and fight!"

An expression akin to mere annoyance sliding across his battered face, Wexler pivoted and came straight at Tim, leading with his left. He feinted with the left, and when Tim dodged the other way, Wexler let go a right-hand punch that took Tim fully on the jaw.

Tim's head seemed to explode as he felt himself propelled backward. He landed on the flat of his back, the packed earthen floor as hard as rock, the wind knocked from him. For moments the room spun round and round. When it righted itself, he saw Teresa start toward him and Wexler draw her back. The sight kindled his anger anew, and he rolled to his right, pushed up, and wobbled

139

to his feet, the room spinning on its axis again.

Suddenly, Gannon was blocking him off. "You've caused enough trouble here tonight, soldier. Better head back for the fort."

"He started it. You saw him!"

"You leave peaceful or I'll throw you out."

The music had resumed and across the way Wexler was dancing with Teresa. For an instant Tim saw her face, her eyes on him, hurting for him, before he walked out, head hanging in humiliation.

Bitter tears coursed down his cheeks. Wexler had made a fool of him in front of Teresa, in front of everybody. Walking gradually cleared his head and Duffy's old soldier's advice pushed into his mind: fightin' jewelry. But that alone wouldn't whip Wexler. *I'm green,* Tim admitted to himself. *Lordy, I'm green.* He walked on, submerged in thought, forced to see himself in additional discouraging light. He could see it again: Wexler's simple feint. Tim had reacted like an awkward schoolboy. A conclusion formed, hardened. Winning required more than angry purpose, no matter how right. He was untrained. Duffy would show him how. He had to fight Wexler again, and next time he had to win. If he didn't, he wasn't a man.

Wirt Cooley gave Ewing a brief, searching look, no more, when he came to the adjutant's office the morning after dinner with the Thorns. The Old Man was still "indisposed," Cooley said, sighing—an incapacitation, Ewing gathered, that happened frequently and placed more official burdens on Cooley's loyal shoulders.

"I just talked to the major," the adjutant said. "He still wants that prisoner."

"He might have one now if Tisdale hadn't flushed the game."

"Aren't you being extra severe on him? At a time like that . . . just before dawn, nerves on edge . . . any man might fire too soon."

"Except none of the Tontos saw the 'threatening hostile' that Tisdale said he saw. Guess what rankled me most was coming up empty-handed after all the punishment of getting into position." Ewing smiled thinly. "But, as you say, Tisdale does know the country."

"Makes me eat a little crow, doesn't it?" Cooley said. "By the way, here's a letter for you, from Hillsboro, I believe."

Ewing's anticipation quickened when he took it, noting the address in fine, girlish handwriting, each letter carefully drawn. Anticipation, followed by creeping guilt, as he opened it and read:

Dear Ewing—You asked me to write you. I promised you I would. I am staying in Hillsboro. Brother Eddie says it is too dangerous at the mine because of the

141

Indian scare. A man was killed the other day in sight of camp. I fear for Eddie. I hope your duties will bring you this way soon. I live in the second adobe west of the Post Office. Thank you again for the nice things. I wear the brooch every day, but I won't wear the dress until I see you again. I pray you are safe.

Love,
Ivy

"It's from Ivy," Ewing said, somewhat lamely. "She's in Hillsboro. Too dangerous at the mine. Another Indian scare."

"We have a letter from her, too. Nice young lady."

"Yes," Ewing agreed soberly.

"Evelyn has taken a special interest in her. She's going to write her. Invite her to come back, be our guest until things blow over."

"She won't. She and her brother are very close. Went through a great deal as children. Apaches killed their parents in the Bradshaw Mountains years ago."

"Don't believe she told Evelyn about her people."

Ewing's face was reminiscent. "She's not one to complain, I tell you. Does a good job of covering up her feelings. Maybe too much. She's seen too much violence for one her age, or any age."

A shout racketed across the quadrangle.

"Now, what?" Cooley growled, jerking about.

More shouts and a voice calling, "Sergeant of the guard! Sergeant of the guard!" The officer of the day, sashed and carrying his saber as he ran, made for the gate. A mule-drawn stage swayed through the gateway, arrows sticking in the coach's paneling. The right lead mule, its rump an array of arrows, hobbled in on three good legs.

As Ewing and Cooley sprinted to the stage, troopers were lifting the wounded driver down. Ewing recognized Yuma Jake of the Mimbres River fight. Three men, all civilians, got out of the stage. A beefy, red-faced man, dressed like a rancher and puffed out with anger, appeared to look around for someone in authority. Spotting the officer of the day, he stomped over. "Where the hell you soldier boys been? They jumped us in Cooke's Canyon. There's a dead man in the stage and we lost the guard back yonder in the canyon."

The officer of the day turned for assistance to Cooley, who said patiently, "We have the same concern you do, sir, but we can't escort every stage from Arizona through to Mesilla. We'll send out a detail at once. In fact, a troop." He looked at Ewing. "The Apaches can't be very far away. Maybe we can come up with that prisoner yet."

Boots and saddles was blowing when Ewing

ran to horse. To his impatience, he and the Tontos had been ready for minutes before the troop swung out of the fort. Tisdale was riding at point with the commanding officer, who somewhat formally introduced himself as Captain B. B. Kinman of Troop A. A veteran about Major Thorn's age, very official in bearing, very old Army, very correct, yet not pompous, who to all appearances did not relish the inconvenience of chasing Apaches through the mountains. His left sleeve was empty, pinned to his shoulder like a badge of honor won on gallant ground. Not a complete man, yet not disabled by present Army standards, considered fit for duty if he could ride or fire a weapon. In the War, probably a brevet lieutenant colonel or a colonel, commanding a regiment, Ewing thought. Not unusual in the frontier cavalry. A first lieutenant at Fort Bowie had an artificial leg. A captain at Fort Apache only one good eye. Some enlisted men had missing fingers and toes.

With the Tontos in advance, they cantered into Cooke's Canyon. Where the road wound about the foothills at the base of the peak, they found the body of the guard. Kinman dropped off a burying detail, with orders to return to the post.

The scenting Tontos coursed back and forth over the rocky ground, chattering among themselves. When Archie pointed northwest, along the road, Ewing waved the scouts on.

"What have they found?" Captain Kinman asked of Ewing.

"The sign goes on toward the Mimbres River, sir. Maybe we can catch up."

The pursuit carried into the afternoon without sight of the hostiles, Captain Kinman rigidly maintaining the regulation cavalry walk of four miles an hour, no faster, to Ewing's chafing disgust. Meanwhile, the Tontos ranged far in advance. They reached the Mimbres Station, where the agent said the war party had passed upriver an hour or so ago, helping themselves to a loose mule while about it, an appropriation, he said wryly, which he had not contested. How many in the war party? A dozen or more, all well-mounted.

True, the trail led along the river on the right side. After a short distance, however, it vanished at the stream's edge and did not reappear on the other side. Grinning, hugely amused, Archie pointed to the water, made an ongoing motion, crossed back to the right-hand side and galloped hard ahead.

Ewing found him half a mile on, waiting, pointing, exulting, to tracks climbing the low bank as they left the stream and returned as before on the right side. Another minute, Ewing saw, and Archie would be rolling with laughter in the river sand.

"Why, that was an easy one," Ewing jested. "Anybody could figure that out."

"Tisdale?" Archie asked, shoulders squared, nose stuck high, in imitation of the scout.

"If he can't, he'd better go back to prospecting, but I've yet to hear of any gold he's found."

Archie still couldn't get over the ruse. "Warm Springs think Tontos they fool," he said, shaking his head.

"I know. Tontos are always the best. But maybe Warm Springs are laughing about Tontos thinking they can catch Warm Springs. Now, quit gloating," Ewing said, relishing the histrionics, "and bring them in sight." *Blancos*, himself formerly included, said Apaches had no sense of humor as primitive people. They just didn't know Apaches. One form of Indian humor was seeing a man, high on himself, being brought down to size.

Less than an hour of light remained when the trail, switching abruptly from river valley to mountains, vanished on the backbone of a rock-cluttered ridge among cloaking junipers and piñons. The Tontos stooped down, their faces close to the rocks, prowling back and forth on scent.

"We find, you see," Archie promised Ewing and drifted away. A trifle later he bent down and held up a piece of rawhide moccasin sole. "Warm Springs close now. I tell you this thing, Nantan."

But when the sun plunged behind the mountains and darkness spread through the forest with high-country suddenness, and the Tontos had not found the trail, Ewing called them back and they rode down where Kinman had bivouacked.

"About how far ahead do you estimate they are, Lieutenant?" the captain asked when Ewing reported.

"An hour's ride, more or less. We'll start tracking again at first light. They've been clever at hiding their trail since late afternoon. It's up there not too far and the Tontos will find it."

Tisdale, squatted down for another cup of coffee, said over his shoulder, "There was plenty of daylight left when the Tontos lost the trail. Odd to me, they couldn't pick it up before dark."

"The problem," Ewing clipped, "is time. Likely, they will pick it up below the ridge on the other side. But it takes time. It's like reading a deep book, but you have to be able to read."

Kinman spoke up, his measured military tone surprisingly understanding. "I must agree it's a craft all its own, Lieutenant. An occult lore, you might say, concealed from most white men, unless born in the mountains or on the plains, therefore inscrutable. To an Apache, no doubt, it is elementary because of his harmony with nature. The basic elements. Even so, as you say, Mr. Mackay, it requires time." With that, he rose several notches above the rigid classification in which Ewing had placed him at first impression, and further when Kinman said, "I know you were puzzled, even annoyed, at my slow pace today. However, I learned long ago never to come upon a field of battle with exhausted cavalry mounts. Had you signaled me, we could have supported you rather quickly, in good strength. I do not profess to be a student of Apache warfare, but I do know there is one tactic they do not like, and that is the cavalry charge, when you catch them in the open. They will wilt and fade away . . . break off, I believe is the western term."

Ewing made a guess. "By the way, sir, were you at Brandy Station or Gettysburg?"

Kinman's austere face permitted a faint smile. "Brandy Station."

"The biggest cavalry fight of the war. So I've read."

Kinman nodded. "An unforgettable experience. Squadrons smashing headlong into one another, sabers swinging. Intense excitement. . . . Dust so thick sometimes you couldn't tell friend from foe. The idea was to slash at the nearest rebel and dash on. Then reform and charge again. We came within a hair of capturing Jeb Stuart's headquarters at Fleetwood Hill. That day we proved we could stand up to rebel cavalry, man to man, horse to horse. Our morale zoomed. . . . I should like to be in an honest-to-God cavalry charge just once more. Oh, I've chased Comanches and Cheyennes and Kiowas a few times on the plains, but never caught up with them, possibly to my good fortune. I mean a charge where you can come to grips with the enemy."

Ewing chose his next words carefully. "I believe Major Thorn is somewhat of the same preference."

Again the dim smile. "His 'smashing-blow' campaign? Yes. We are products of the same school of war, the same mass tactics. In that respect, I consider it a mistake to have relegated sabers for use only in dress parades. Cold steel at close quarters is a terrifying thing."

Except, Ewing said to himself, *how could you get close enough to use sabers, when Apaches either flee like desert quail or hide among rocks and lay for you?*

"Just once more I should like that," Captain Kinman said, his voice remembering, "although I comprehend that the rules of war are different out here. This is a guerrilla war. We are chasing phantoms, Lieutenant."

Before dawn the Tontos were climbing the ridge, eager to pick up the trail. As light broke, they spread out, methodical wraiths stooping low in the streaky glow. Watching them, following on foot, Ewing thought, *It's a game to them. A puzzle to be solved piece by piece.* It was broad daylight when they stopped, gesturing, talking low, after

149

which they changed directions, moving down the flank of a dry canyon that zigzagged deeper into the mountains.

Not many minutes had passed when Rowdy raised up and signaled, "Here." The others gathered around him as he pointed down. They nodded. To Ewing, the point of discovery was nothing more than a long scratch on the slanting flat rock. Archie said it was the mark left by the shod mule taken on the Mimbres. They had found the trail.

In the canyon's sharp bends, past summer rains had heaped up rocks and, straightening, left stretches of sand and gravel. Here the Tontos struck a broad pocking of unshod horses and the mule's telltale prints. At this, the scouts moved at a steady dogtrot. When the canyon played out, they followed the tracks upward to an abandoned campsite sheltered beneath a cliff. Here the hostiles had dined on mule meat. The ashes of the fires were still warm.

Departing, the war party had seemed undecided, hesitant about going farther into the mountains, their tracks circling the heads of small canyons, always swinging back toward lower country. Coming to a broader canyon that dropped toward the Mimbres River, they turned abruptly down it. When the trail came out on the valley floor, Ewing figured Kinman's camp lay within two or three miles downstream. He sent Rowdy and Jim back to bring up the scouts' horses and the troop.

"They're getting real foxy, Captain, hiding their trail, then doubling back on us," Ewing said, after reporting what the scouts had found. "Wish they hadn't butchered that mule. If they hive off into the mountains again, they'll be harder to track over rough ground."

"About how far behind them are we, Lieutenant?"

"I'd say two hours or more. They've gained on us."

"I'll stick closer to you today. If they stay in the valley, we might catch them in the open. You sight something, I'll come on the gallop."

"Mighty good, Captain." Ewing was beginning to like this Brandy Station cavalryman. In addition, the captain wasn't telling him how the Tontos should go about their trailing.

The miles fell away without change. By afternoon the trailers, past where the Mimbres tumbled out of the Blacks to its valley, were following the broad course of a creek singing between rising canyon walls. At four o'clock Archie reported three hostiles had fallen behind the main war party, apparently because their horses were lame. Ewing promptly detailed Jim to summon Captain Kinman on the jump.

"Remember," Ewing told Archie, "we want a prisoner out of this bunch if possible."

"Archie savvy."

"A prisoner that's still able to talk," Ewing emphasized.

"Archie get."

Kinman, coming up in a column of fours, was elated at the news and took the troopers on at a fast trot. Within half a mile the three Apaches drew into view, riding slowly.

"How do you assess the situation, Mr. Mackay?" Kinman asked, throwing up a halting hand.

"Their mounts could be lame or played out, or it's the old decoy game. I'm inclined to think it's the latter, sir."

Tisdale shifted in his saddle to pin his disagreement on Ewing. "Came to fight 'Paches, didn't we?"

"On our terms, not theirs."

"You are both correct," Kinman said, uncasing his field glasses. After a look, he said cheerfully, "Let's make a run at them. What do you say, Mr. Mackay?"

"I'm agreeable. But if they head for a side canyon, I'd suggest that we not rush in. I've told the scouts their first priority is to take a prisoner."

"Agreeable, in turn, Mr. Mackay." Turning, Kinman bellowed, "Gallop, ho!" and the troop surged into motion, the Tontos assuming screening positions on the wings.

They all kicked up a terrific clatter, and yet the Apaches appeared almost bemused, unmindful of any threat until the flying column pounded within carbine range. Then, suddenly, the three heeled away. If there was a lame horse among them, none looked so as they raced down the wide bed of the creek.

The Tontos opened up, joined by the carbines of the lead troopers. Kinman, reins between his teeth, was firing his revolver, though not yet in range.

At the first shots the Apaches scattered, riding low, two streaking in front, all fleeing downcreek. Unburdened, their mounts were outrunning the equipment-laden cavalry horses. As Ewing saw that, the mount of the trailing Apache broke stride, floundered, and went down. Its rider landed on his feet like a cat. He turned in appeal to his two companions racing on.

The Tontos rushed with yells for the dismounted man. He fired his rifle till empty, then raised it for a club. The Tontos closed like a pack, swirling about him. They leaped on him and threw him to the ground.

Kinman and the troop swept past the Tontos, hell-bent for the two fleeing Apaches. Ahead, the canyon suddenly pinched in, and the shine of the creek disappeared around the face of a jutting cliff. There the Apaches vanished.

For a hanging moment Ewing was conscious only of the excitement of the chase. And then a sudden wrongness smote him. He sensed, he knew: the decoy game. Ambush. He yelled at Kinman and waved him back and away, but his voice was lost in the thundering pursuit.

Nothing happened the moment the troopers tore around the base of the cliff. They were rods inside the narrowing passageway before shots crashed from the rocky walls. Kinman charged on, looking for targets. Only blooms of grayish powder smoke were visible.

Ewing kept yelling, "Back, back!" No need. Kinman was yanking rein and roaring a command. Troopers were piling up against the foremost riders. The Apaches fired into the mass. A trooper at Ewing's side slumped across his saddle. Ewing held him on, trying to steady the horses against the pressure of riders from the rear. A horse buckled. Kinman's unruffled voice rose above the din, bellowing his men into a rough order. They began pulling up and turning. Not until the last trooper wheeled back did Kinman spur after them.

The prisoner refused to talk. He was a Chiricahua, Archie said, probably just out of the Sierra Madre. Did Nantan want Archie to make him talk? Archie closed his hand over the handle of his knife.

"No," Ewing said. "Tie him up and stake him out tonight. That may loosen him up. If not, some time in the guardhouse will."

"Feed him?"

"Yes, feed him."

Disgust filled Archie's face.

"I know. You think I'm too easy on Chiricahuas," Ewing said, and raised a needling grin. "Reminds me. Believe the Warm Springs fooled the Tontos today with that ambush."

"Nantan wrong! Warm Springs fool *blancos*."

"You mean while the Tontos were busy capturing the Chiricahua?"

Archie smiled from the teeth.

Ewing walked across the bivouac, his mind heavily on the day's bitter price: one dead trooper, two with serious wounds.

Captain Kinman sat before a juniper fire. He appeared to be musing, his spare face thoughtfully set. Coming closer, Ewing saw that he was writing in an order book held on his knee. He looked up, his face changing.

"I fear my enthusiasm got the best of me today, Mr. Mackay."

"They were foxier than usual about the ambush, sir. Not the usual decoy into a side canyon. Too, it's difficult to halt a charge once it's under way."

"You are generous in your assessment. I am trying to set down the letter I'll send to the boy's people when we get back. Something more than the usual 'It is with deepest regret' . . . something what he was like as a soldier and a man. Trooper James Richardson. He was from Ohio. Just a boy

155

seeking adventure in the West. Reared on a farm. Good with horses. Liked by his fellow troopers. I might add that I've written a great many of these in my time." Somberly he laid the pad aside. "Any luck with the prisoner?"

"He won't talk, which doesn't surprise me. Sergeant Archie, my head scout, says he is a Chiricahua, probably fresh out of Mexico. Makes me wonder, since this is off the Chiricahuas' range."

"What significance, if any, do you attach to that?"

"That Victorio is getting reinforcements. That the call has gone out. Archie says this war party is heading for the Blacks."

"Sounds logical. A few more like this one today and we shall be calling for reinforcements ourselves. Major Thorn estimates that, despite the Warm Springs losses at Tres Castillos, Victorio has from fifty to seventy-five warriors of his own people. Men and teenage boys. To that, add the usual contingent from the Mescalero Reservation, war parties such as this one, and he'll have a fighting force of a hundred and fifty. Put them behind rocks and trees and you multiply their effectiveness several times their actual numbers." He stood and paced around the fire, his one good arm across his lean waist as if for balance. He said, "The longer this campaign is delayed, the stronger the hostiles will become. I see that now.

156

I did not before today. On our return I shall direct this to Major Thorn's attention."

"If the major had not been indisposed and the stage not attacked, the Tontos and I likely would be on our way now into the Blacks, looking for Victorio's *rancheria*."

"Ah, yes. Major Thorn's indisposition. It seems to strike him often." That was all. No amusement, no smirking, no oblique expression hinting at another's weakness for the bottle. Like Wirt Cooley, Captain Kinman was loyal to his commanding officer.

No more was said.

On his last round of the bivouac, Ewing stopped to check the prisoner. He was firmly staked, thongs around each arm and leg, spread-eagled as only the Tontos could tie him. Dingy firelight played across the dark face, ochered yellow and red for war.

Ewing squatted down beside him, poured a trickle of canteen water into the slash of the mouth. The man spat it out like poison.

"Maybe you used to be an Army scout at San Carlos . . . maybe Fort Bowie?" Ewing led off. He had hoped for a younger, more pliable-looking prisoner. This one's face, wild, hating, defiant, was a print of countless ambushes and waterless trails.

The Chiricahua didn't reply, but his eyes flashed.

"Maybe you savvy English?"

No answer. Just the silent hate.

"All Chiricahuas are cowards."

The prisoner struggled to free himself, spat at Ewing.

"So you do savvy English. *Enjuh*. Maybe you know where Victorio is camped?"

Silence.

"Maybe you will lead us to Victorio's *ranchería*?"

Silence.

"Maybe you would like to be a scout for Army again? It is a great honor to be an Army scout. You know that. Think back. Remember. The Army furnished you food and clothing, a good horse and a good rifle. Remember?"

Silence.

Ewing sat there for several minutes more without speaking, then said, "I will talk to you in the morning after you eat. You are brave. Very brave. A great warrior. I know that."

A scented night wind idled up the canyon, singing and sighing through the tall pines. Ewing lay down. For a few more moments he could feel the purring wind, could see the great arch of the star-studded sky. All at once his hard-muscled body let go and he dropped into deep sleep.

Was it a bad dream, those shouts, those stirrings? He bolted upright, his head clearing.

It wasn't a bad dream. The Tontos were yelling. Men were running. He snatched up his carbine and rushed there.

Archie was waving his arms, pointing at the stakes in the ground and the severed thongs. "Nantan, look!" Apologetically, as if the blame were his.

"He must have had a hidden knife," Ewing said.

"No! Nantan, that Chiricahua search we did. No knife. I tell you this thing, Nantan." His eyes said he wanted Ewing to know that he hadn't lied.

"I know you searched him," Ewing said.

Troopers were crowding around. Suddenly, Captain Kinman and Tisdale were there.

"We've lost our prisoner," Ewing said. "Cut loose somehow, though the scouts searched him."

"Maybe they just said they searched him," Tisdale put in. "They're all Apaches."

Ewing, getting angry by now, squared on Tisdale. "I can assure you, Mr. Tisdale, that the prisoner was thoroughly searched if the Tontos said he was. They don't lie."

"That will do," Kinman said. "The prisoner is gone. It will do no good to blame ourselves. At first light, Mr. Mackay, you will conduct a search of the area."

"Yes, sir."

Daylight was a brush stroke of pink in the east. Ewing turned away, his angry frustration vying with reason. The prisoner had not cut himself loose. It couldn't have happened that way. It could not.

CHAPTER 8

Search for the escaped prisoner ended at noon, fruitless as Ewing knew it would be when he started the Tontos looking. By this time the Chiricahua would be over the Mimbres Mountains and in the Blacks. No one among the Tontos had cut the man free because they were deadly enemies of the Chiricahuas. No trooper. No reason to. Somehow the warrior had concealed a knife. If so, he was the cleverest of Apaches.

Traveling slowly, with the wounded on improvised litters slung between gentle horses, the detachment arrived at Fort Cummings on the third day.

Two days of inactivity followed. Had Captain Kinman spoken to Major Thorn about the apparent concentration of the hostiles? He had, Adjutant Cooley told Ewing. The Old Man was feeling much better now, almost recovered from his "indisposition." But as yet there was no indication that Ewing and the Tontos would be heading into the Black Range. Ewing had expected otherwise. A summons about the coming campaign. Orders. Plans. Feverish preparations. A quick departure on scout to seek out the Warm Springs' camp.

Afternoon had come when Ewing saw the headquarters orderly, a corporal, riding up to the scouts' camp. The customary salutation and then, "Major and Mrs. Thorn request the pleasure of Lieutenant Mackay's company at dinner tonight. Six o'clock."

Just as he saw the trooper's beginning smirk, he sensed his own refusal. He said, "Express my regrets to the major and Mrs. Thorn. I am unable to accept the invitation. I am taking the Tonto scouts out on a night scout."

The orderly saluted and stepped to the saddle, not covering his amused surprise.

"Something bothering you, Corporal?" Ewing's voice slammed.

"Why, no, sir," the trooper said, turning his mount.

Now, Ewing thought, *I'll hear about this. Still more, if I decline a second time. What then?* He hoped that she would understand, and knew that she would not. His lips pinched together. Physical needs went too long unfilled on the frontier. Why enlisted men patronized the "hog ranches." Lust for life was hardly an excuse, however. He had made a damn-fool mistake. Still, in doing so, he had discovered something about himself and his true intentions. Recalling Wirt Cooley's warning, he also understood about the other bachelor officers. Their reassignments, their resignations. He could be in deep trouble.

He did not sleep well.

At nine o'clock next morning he saw a lone rider rapidly approaching the camp from the fort. It was Mrs. Thorn, attired in a gold-braided riding habit, a forage cap over her flowing hair. She was forcing her mount rather hard. He waited, expecting the worst.

Josephine Thorn pulled her mount to a sliding stop. Her violet eyes glinted. She flung a scathing look about the camp. "I will not talk in front of these . . . these heathens," she snapped, and rode off a way and halted, waiting. He read the maneuver: she was making him come to her.

He took his time, saying, "These heathens, as you call them, are enlisted Army scouts. By working in advance, they save a good many troopers' lives."

"Lieutenant," she said, ignoring that, "I'm not accustomed to having my dinner invitations spurned."

"It was not spurned. I was getting ready to go on scout."

Her furious eyes blazed even higher. "You *did not*. I checked on you. I asked Wirt Cooley."

My friend Wirt, Ewing thought, *who cannot tell a lie. But who would if he had known the particulars.* He had no extricating answer for her.

"Don't you have anything to say for your unforgivable behavior?" She was being most put-upon, most righteous, which colored the smooth

163

whiteness of her skin, which brought out her undeniable beauty. In that moment, feeling again their mutual wanting, he considered apologizing and renewing the liaison. But, instead, he said, "What happened, just happened. Why not leave it there?"

"Leave it! I refuse to be scorned."

"You are not being scorned, Josephine. You are a very beautiful woman. You will be, always. No man scorns beauty."

She softened perceptibly. "Will you accept, then, if I invite you again? You will find me as . . . amenable as before. Even more so."

His silence was his answer. He did not trust himself to speak, not realizing until now how difficult it was to back off.

She said, "Surely you found me interesting? Surely I didn't disappoint you? I found you most manly and pleasing."

He looked at her without speaking, not wishing to sound sanctimonious. There was a silence between them. It lasted only until he saw an intuitive suspicion take root in her mind and flash to her face, hardening there. Her voice cut at him. "It's that poor, homeless girl on the stage, isn't it? I happen to know that the Cooleys entertained you both."

The blood was rushing to his face. Womanlike, she had gleaned the truth. "You forget what's at stake here, Josephine," he said, at last finding his voice. "Your position. Major Thorn's. My career as an officer, such as it is. It could all come crashing down."

Her head tilted upward in that proud manner she had. "So you refuse? That is your decision?"

He was slow replying, nodding. "But in no way are you being scorned."

She jerked the horse's head so hard it fought the bit, its eyes walling. Her petulant voice reached a higher key. "It will be to your everlasting regret, Lieutenant. I do not hand out invitations with abandon. You shall see. That day shall come, I promise you."

She whirled her mount and lashed into a gallop, an unforgiving, vindictive figure. Yes, he knew, he was in trouble.

Another restless day went by. At headquarters a kind of lethargy seemed to have set in. Adjutant Cooley allowed only that Major Thorn was back on duty after recovering from the "gout," spoken with a loyal, straight face. There was, he said, nothing in the wind about further preparations for the campaign. No immediate plans to send the Tontos out again.

"Time's getting away from us," Ewing said. "Meanwhile, Old Vic's recruits keep coming in."

"I know."

"Captain Kinman has a good grasp of the

situation. He could get things moving in the field."

"But he is not the C.O. If the concept for this campaign were the Department's idea, we'd be getting nudges now from that direction. But it's all the Old Man's, to win or lose. Acclaim if it works, silence if it does not."

"Major General Willcox must know. He signed the order that assigned us here."

"So far as he knows, over there in the Department of Arizona, you and the Tontos are requested replacements for the Navajos we sent home. That is all. It's the Old Man's private show."

Ewing was in the adjutant's office when the sergeant of the guard reported. "There's a Mexican at the gate. Says he's got a message for Lieutenant Mackay. Looks like he's come a long way."

"Bring him in," Cooley said.

The Mexican, a small, leathery man, was dusty and weary, somewhat in awe of his military surroundings.

"I'm Lieutenant Mackay," Ewing said. "What is it?"

"A message from *Señor* Montoya. He said tell you Gómez, you better come at once."

"Did he say where Gómez is?"

The little man shrugged expressive shoulders. "He did not say. Only what I told you he said."

"Gómez," Ewing said to Cooley, "is the name of the Warm Springs captive who escaped at the Tres Castillos massacre with Victorio. Remember? Montoya must know where Gómez is. He didn't know—said he didn't—when we went on scout up that way."

They were both thinking of Major Thorn, Ewing saw, and what action, if any, he would take now. Ewing looked at the messenger. "Is that all Montoya said?"

"I have told you all he said. I rode all night. It is safer. I will go now."

Ewing thanked him.

Cooley said, "Wait," and instructed the clerk to take the man to the mess hall.

"I've got to see Major Thorn," Ewing said. "This can't wait. Gómez could lead us to Victorio. He's the only man who can. Our only alternative is to go in there blind, hoping the Tontos can smell out Victorio's camp. That could take days, maybe weeks."

"I understand fully," Cooley said, rising suddenly. "Wait here." He went out, striding to Thorn's office. Within a brief time he was back. "The Old Man will see you, Ewing. I warn you that he's in a foul mood," to which Ewing could not resist appending, "I know. His gout."

Major Thorn looked bloated and heavy, his lower jaws flaccid, but the pitted eyes were alert and aggressive. He said, "Mr. Cooley tells me

167

that you have received word on the whereabouts of the Warm Springs captive Gómez." He had made an effort to tidy his beard and thick hair. His blouse appeared clean. He was, Ewing thought, the picture of a man trying valiantly to climb back on the water wagon and finding the ascent, rung by rung, almost too steep.

"My guess is he's either at Montoya's ranch or in Hillsboro. The messenger didn't know. I respectfully suggest, sir, that I take the Tontos there immediately, in hopes Gómez will lead us to Victorio's *ranchería*. He's the best bet we have."

"The escaped prisoner on the Mimbres might have done the same," Thorn replied critically, his eyes accusing. "Mr. Tisdale agrees."

"He showed no signs of cooperation that night when I questioned him. An unreconstructed Apache. Neither do I have an explanation for his escape. He was thoroughly searched. Yet his thongs were cut."

"Mr. Tisdale reported the prisoner probably freed himself because the Tontos guarded him loosely."

Ewing's anger flared. "I do not agree with Mr. Tisdale's reported opinion, sir. The prisoner was staked out near the center of the bivouac, equally under surveillance by both troopers and Tontos. Neither did Mr. Tisdale interrogate the prisoner. Since he did not, there was no way he could conclude that the prisoner would have been receptive to helping us."

"That is of no matter now," Thorn said brusquely, his hand shunting it aside. "What if this Gómez refuses to oblige us?"

"I can take the Tontos into the Black Range. Lying doggo in the daytime, watching for smoke and movement. Ourselves moving only at night, which would be tedious and lengthy. Each day that we wait the hostiles could be gaining strength."

"Captain Kinman is of the same opinion. I'd have sent you into the Blacks days ago had I been able to take the field. I am now able to do so, the surgeon tells me. Recurrence of my gout, plus this ever damnable hernia, has virtually invalided me."

"Sorry to hear that, sir."

"Very well, Mr. Mackay. It is time to go see the elephant, as we used to say early in the War. You will draw ten days' rations and proceed first to the Montoya ranch. You will send a courier back as developments dictate, keeping uppermost in mind that the command will require two days to reach the Hillsboro area and be in readiness to reach you in the Blacks. Meanwhile, preparations will get under way here for an extended campaign."

Ewing nodded, mentally projecting those phases.

"Once you come upon Victorio's trail—for that matter, any trail you think leads to a large *ranchería*—you will stick to it so long as a serviceable animal or scout is left. You will be operating under verbal orders, which gives you adequate leeway. I believe in letting a junior officer in the field act on his own judgment."

"Thank you, sir."

The gravel-pit eyes bored into Ewing's. "That," Thorn stressed, "also increases his responsibility within the framework of his orders. You are dismissed, Mr. Mackay. Good luck."

Ewing had taken but a few steps when he heard an arresting, "One final thing, Mr. Mackay." He turned. In his concentration, he had forgotten Mrs. Thorn. Had she spoken to her husband? Was he about to hear himself accused of conduct unbecoming an officer?

But the major merely sighed. His eyes lost their directness, his jowled face fell, evoking Ewing's sympathy and likewise his guilt. And Thorn said, "Don't ever let yourself get old. There's no rocking chair on the *ramada* for old soldiers—only duty—and duty it must be for all of us. Keep that in mind, Mr. Mackay."

"Yes, sir. I'm glad you're feeling better." He meant that, finding within himself understanding for an ailing older soldier that also furthered his growing sense of self-reproach.

• • •

Tim O'Boyle hurried, his anticipation mounting with each long stride. Catching the initial notes of guitar music, muted on the night wind, he felt an even lighter buoyancy. Again he rehearsed how he would tell her. Again he touched the ring in his breast pocket for strength. Everyone on the post knew a campaign was in the offing by the sudden flurry of preparations. Supply sergeants running around with detailed lists. Officers going and coming from Adjutant Cooley's office. Major Thorn, not seen for days on the parade ground, suddenly much in evidence. Ammunition drawn from the stone magazine, dry rations packed. Saddles being cleaned and oiled, side arms and carbines inspected. The constant din at the stables of farriers shoeing horses. Tempers on edge. Thus, he must get this done and decided tonight before the command pulled out, which could be any day.

He was close to trotting when he sighted the lights peeking over the fold of moon-washed desert. Forcing himself to slow down, he walked the remaining distance to the main shack.

Inwardly bracing himself, he entered. The hour was early and he saw only one lone trooper getting drunk at the plank bar, Gannon behind it as usual, thick arms folded like a Greek wrestler, the sad guitarist plunking away, and Teresa. Good! Wexler wasn't here. Tim had timed his arrival just right. Wexler usually came later.

Flashing her smile of recognition, Teresa showed him to a table. He removed his forage cap and regarded her without speaking, just enjoying the picture she made. He stared so long that she blushed. "Señor Tim, you are very quiet tonight. Has *el gato* got your tongue?"

"*El gato?*" he repeated absently.

"*El gato*—the cat."

"Guess so. You sure look mighty nice, Teresa," he managed to say when, instead, he had wished to come out with something flowery and romantic.

"You always say that."

"And I always mean it."

She lowered her eyes and looked away, faintly troubled.

Seeing Gannon watching him, Tim asked her, "Does he have anything besides that awful whiskey? Maybe some beer?"

"He has mescal. It is better than the whiskey. But both are bad." She made a dour face that brought his appreciative laughter. "I will bring you mescal," she said.

Tim paid and she took the money to Gannon and came back and sat close to him. He longed to tell her now, before the place filled up, before Wexler barged in, but the words seemed stuck in his throat. While he delayed, the trooper pushed away from the bar, came weaving over to their

172

table, swept off his cap with an exaggerated flourish, bowed ceremoniously, and said, thick of voice, "Señorita, may uh have th' honor o' this dance?"

"After we finish our drinks and dance," she said, putting him off but smiling. "You know *Señor* Gannon's rule: one drink, one dance."

"Slipped m' mind," he mumbled. "Uh beg your pardon." Another extravagant bow, a doff of his cap, more mumbled apologies, and, straightening, he set a precarious course for the gambling room. After a short while, Tim could hear the trooper's voice rising, another man's voice arguing.

"Let's dance," Tim asked her.

She rose and moved into his arms. The slim feel of her paralyzed him momentarily, drugging his senses. Like silk, he thought. Always like silk. He held her close and she did not resist, not keeping distance between them as he had seen her do with amorous troopers. When she rested her head on his shoulder, his mind spun. They danced like that to the end of the room. Turning, Tim met Gannon's scowling disapproval. Simultaneously, Gannon signaled the guitarist to stop playing.

"That was too short," Tim complained to her, escorting her back to the table. "Gannon did that to stop us. That's not right."

"Ramón is old and tired of playing the same tunes over and over," she said, skirting trouble.

"And I," she laughed, "am tired of hearing them. But that is better than no music at all."

Now, he decided to himself. Now. If he could just begin. Begin, he did, roundabout, "When my enlistment is up, I'm going back to the farm in Illinois. I like green fields . . . rolling hills . . . cool creeks."

"You don't like the desert?"

She was a child of the desert, this Mexican girl. Wishing to please her, he said, "Oh, I like it . . . it's clean and the sky out here is the bluest I've ever seen." He gave her an indulgent smile. "Only it's a little bit on the dry side for a farm boy from the Middle West. I'm a good farmer. Why, I can grow corn as tall as a juniper tree."

"Some junipers are very tall in the mountains," she humored, pursing her lips.

Unabashed, he went on. "My folks don't have a big farm, but it's big enough for another family. Good bottom land. Flip a seed and it'll sprout. They're getting on in years. I'll have to take it over before long. I've picked out a nice site for the house I aim to build. There's a limestone spring nearby and—" He paused at the outbreak of angry voices from the gambling room, one shouting, "Cheat!" Chairs scraped. A table crashed amid scuffling sounds.

Gannon charged in there like a mad bull. Tim heard whacking sounds. Two struggling figures filled the doorway, Gannon and the trooper.

Surprisingly, the latter seemed to be holding his own until Gannon locked him in a powerful bear hug and hustled him outside.

Tim supposed the fight was over then; however, the trooper must have broken loose, because the slugging sounded again.

"Let 'em fight," Tim said, and seized the moment, his pent-up words freed on a tide of emotion. "Listen to me, Teresa. I love you. I want to marry you. I want to take you away from this. We'll have the post chaplain marry us tomorrow. You can live at the post as an enlisted man's wife."

Astonished, she opened her smoky eyes wide. The softest of expressions overspread her face. Her eyes became misty, while he waited in silence, hoping.

"Listen," he said, when she didn't speak. "There's a big Apache campaign coming up. We'll pull out any day now for the mountains. Anything can happen. I want us to marry before I leave. That way you can live at the fort. I love you. I'll be good to you. You won't have to do this anymore."

"Oh, Tim." She was about to cry.

"You will marry me, then? You will leave here tonight. I'll wait for you on the path. Take you to the post. You'll be safe. Later, we'll go back to Illinois. I'll build you a big house."

Her glistening eyes lifted toward the doorway

and froze, fear immediately sharp upon her face. "I can't," she said, in a shaky voice. "No, Tim. It cannot be."

"But . . ."

"You don't understand," she said in a stricken voice and said no more.

Shock and crushing hurt caught him by the throat. She had refused him, when he thought . . . He followed her gaze to the doorway. Gannon stood there, wiping the back of one hand across his bloody mouth. He moved to their table. He spoke to her, nodding toward the gambling room. "Take care of our friend in there," and strode to the bar, nursing his mouth.

Tim sat frozen. Teresa rose like an obedient child, went woodenly to the doorway of the gambling room. For a fleeting moment she looked back at Tim, her eyes like great bruises, before she went quickly on.

Sick at heart, Tim rushed out into the night, stumbling blindly. He seemed to be lost in a choking fog. He was sobbing. He touched his face. His hand fell away, wet with tears. He reeled on, hardly aware of where he was.

Footsteps registered on his consciousness. A figure materialized on the path. A dim face. A baiting voice said, "If it ain't Boyle. Guess it's about your bedtime, early as you're leavin'. Time to be tucked in."

Boiling with rage and hurt, Tim swung wildly.

Wexler ducked away, laughing, "Can't spar you tonight, sonny boy. I'm in a hurry. Gonna have a drink with Teresa. Go on." He hurried past.

So it was Wexler. His breath hacking in ragged gulps, Tim glared after him. At that moment he could gladly have killed Kirk Wexler. *Next time,* Tim raged, *I'll be ready for him. Next time. Soon.*

CHAPTER 9

Ewing looked down from the stony hilltop at the outscatter of the Juan Montoya ranch. Only a few head of horses milled in the maze of corrals. No other movement. Reason and a deeper sense told him that something had happened to cause Montoya to change his mind about Gómez.

The Tontos trailing behind him, Ewing rode slowly down the long slope and up to the adobe house. The door was closed. He called. No one appeared. When he called a second time, a man opened the door and came out on the *ramada*. It was Montoya.

"I got your message," Ewing said.

"Dismount, my friend."

Shaking hands, Ewing was struck by Montoya's changed appearance. Normally an erect man, he looked stooped and broken, thin to emaciation, an engraved sadness overshadowing the piercing eyes, now like dark smudges.

"What's happened?" Ewing asked.

In a voice that shook, Montoya said, "I tried to be friends. I was a friend. I was always generous. I shared what I had. But now . . . this terrible thing. We are enemies. I cannot accept it when they killed my oldest son. My Manuel."

"My God, I'm sorry," Ewing said, stunned, and impulsively laid his hand on Montoya's shoulder.

Tears welling in his eyes, Montoya said, "This time they came to the house for horses. They saw Manuel's Steel Dust gelding, his favorite. A fine horse, only three years old, not yet in his prime. They wanted it. I pleaded with them. 'Take any of the others, take them all,' I said. 'But leave my son's favorite.' They paid no attention. They had been drinking mescal. It was a joke to them. They started to lead the Steel Dust away, my son's favorite. My son wouldn't listen to me. I said, 'Don't fight them. Give them the Steel Dust or they will kill you.' He wouldn't listen. He loved that Steel Dust. He ran after them. He fought them. They killed him before my eyes . . . shot my Manuel. I was helpless. I could do nothing. . . . My poor wife, Rosa. She will never be the same. Nor I. Nor Luis. Nor my little María." He broke down, weeping.

Ewing could only shake his head. He grasped Montoya's shoulder. "Was Victorio with them?" he asked after a moment.

"No. Victorio was not. Had he been, my Manuel would be alive. They were all young warriors. A war party. They had raided a mining camp and found the mescal. Had Victorio been along he would not have allowed the mescal."

"Were they all Warm Springs?"

Pressing a hand to his forehead, Montoya

thought for a very long moment and said, "No—a few Chiricahuas. I have to think hard. My mind is crazy."

"Any Mescaleros?"

Not hesitating, "Some Mescaleros—I know them. They raid sometimes with the Warm Springs."

"Was Gómez with them?"

"He was not."

"But your message said Gómez."

"Gómez stays in and around Hillsboro. He was there when you came here the first time. I did not tell you because I did not want to get involved." His head sank and he spread his hands, a gesture of retribution. "Look what it has brought upon us. Only sorrow. I am helpless."

"There is something you can do," Ewing said, not without sympathy.

Montoya's eyes bored into Ewing's. "I am only one man. What can I do?"

"You can take us to Gómez. Ask him to lead us to the Warm Springs' camp in the Black Range."

Montoya pulled back, an unwillingness upon him, gripped by his old impulse of non-involvement. Ewing saw it pass like a shadow across his sad eyes, saw Montoya harden. He started to speak and choked, suffering written in cruel marks upon his face. He threw out the words, "I will! I will take you to Gómez! I will do it now!"

• • •

They struck north through the foothills, the smoky masses of the Black Range rising far to the northwest.

Late afternoon brought them to the beginnings of Hillsboro, a clutter of tents, adobes, and cabins huddled along a wooded creek and studding the sides of the rolling hills.

Montoya said to Ewing, "I will leave you here. Gómez has been staying with a Mexican family. I think it wise if I approach him alone, so as not to alarm him. That he not see you and the Tontos—not yet. As I told you, he is more Warm Springs than Mexican, his wariness is that of an Apache." He gestured toward the west. "Ride around the town. Camp along the creek. I will come as soon as I find out something."

Ewing took the scouts around and they made camp under cool cottonwoods. He became more and more restless. Success or failure of the campaign could hang on what happened here the next twenty-four hours—on what luck Montoya had in finding Gómez, and after he found him. Even while military concerns occupied his mind, Ivy Shaw persisted in the background of his thoughts. His restlessness grew.

Evening was at hand, the Tontos' cooking fires going, when Montoya rode up. "Gómez," he said, "was not at the house. The people there are afraid. They look another way and shrug when you ask

181

about Gómez. They would not tell me where he is. You see, he comes and goes. Sometimes he disappears for a few days, but always he comes back."

"Where does he go?"

Montoya shrugged.

"Back to the Black Range, perhaps?"

"Nobody says. But he is around here somewhere."

"What makes you think so?"

"The way the people at the house acted. If Gómez was gone, they would have said so. If he was around town, they would be evasive—they were. So I will look some more, go to the saloons and stores. I know other people here. I will talk to them, and I will watch the house. I will see you in the morning."

In the morning, Ewing mulled! Watching Montoya ride away, he suddenly slapped his thigh and, leaving Archie in charge, headed for town.

Second adobe west of the post office, she had said in her letter. He found it, a house with a wooden fence enclosing the front yard. A light burned there. Tying his horse by the gate, he went to the door and knocked. Light footsteps within. The door opened and Ivy Shaw stood before him. Her eyes flew wide, her mouth fell, leaving her too astonished to speak.

"May I come in?"

She stepped back and he entered, aware of how the lamplight, falling across her face, touched the long-lashed eyes, the high cheekbones, and the full, even mouth, still wordless in surprise. Looking down at her, he noticed the brooch pinned high on her calico dress. He bent his head and gently kissed her lips. She looked too thunderstruck yet to respond. Then, all at once, she returned his kiss, closing her eyes, and her arms went around him. Afterward, they looked at each other for a long time without speaking until he said, "Dear Ivy," and kissed her again.

"How long can you stay?"

"Not long," he said and told her briefly what he was about.

"There's so little time," she said. Taking his hand, she led him into the tiny parlor. "You can stay for supper, can't you?"

"I think I can manage that."

She broke into rippling laughter, tinged with tenseness, and it occurred to him how seldom he had heard her laugh. He said, "It makes me feel good when you laugh. It's lovely to hear."

"Sometimes," she said, sobering, "it is just to hide my true feelings. I'm still afraid, Ewing."

"Of what?"

"Not afraid to love you. Afraid you'll be taken from me, like my folks were. That's terrible to say."

He drew her to him and smoothed her dark hair back from the porcelain white of her temples, feeling her trembling, sensing again what he had before. Hurt long ago as a child, she held back from happiness, always guarding her feelings, apprehensive lest she should be hurt again.

"I guess I'm a coward."

"You," he said, amused, "are no more a coward than my Tontos. They recognize and respect danger. So do you. That's merely being intelligent. Only a fool is insensible to danger. It is the brave who move against it, knowing it, the brave who endure, who go ahead and take their chances day by day. You're the bravest person I know, Ivy."

"Why, here I am acting like a bowed-down old woman," she said suddenly, favoring him a bright smile, "just when you need your supper." She freed herself from his arms and hastened determinedly to the kitchen, warmly redolent of baked bread, chatting as he followed her. "I've been making bread and selling it to the miners. They insist on paying me a dollar a loaf. That's way too much, but I try to make the loaves large. I must do something. I can't just sit in this house and do nothing. I have some for you to take to your Tontos."

"They'll like that. Sergeant Archie calls you 'that *blanco* woman.' He keeps telling me to take you for my wife."

"Why?" she asked curiously, while she set the table.

"Because you don't complain."

"Oh, I do. Not as much as I want to sometimes."

"Why not?"

"What good would it do? Just make me weaker."

"That's practical. Well, it's time to tell you that I've decided to take Archie's advice. He's quite an authority on the subject of matrimony. Has several wives at San Carlos. When he was a hostile, not many years ago, he wasn't reluctant to stealing an extra one from the Chiricahuas."

He ceased speaking, his smile fading. She was holding herself in check again. Still resisting, still standing watch over her emotions.

She said, straightforward, "I'm no lady, Ewing. You can see that. I've slept more times in tents than I have in wagons or houses. This house . . . this little 'dobe . . . is like a palace to me. I'm not educated. Eddie and I went to school when and where we could. Wasn't often. For practice, he would read to me and I would read to him. Anything we could get our hands on: old newspapers, magazines. Once in a while a book. Even read the labels on baking powder cans. We used to memorize what was on whiskey bottles. Sam Thompson: the World's Finest Bourbon . . . Golden Wedding: Fit for Any Occasion. Made and Aged in the Old-Fashioned Way . . . Old Green River: the Whiskey that Made Kentucky

Famous. . . . We always had trouble spelling Guggenheimer. . . . I can cuss like a freighter. You ought to hear me. I can stagger a mule at thirty paces. . . . I don't like to ride sidesaddle. Britches are more sensible. I can rope and throw a calf. I can handle a rifle. No, I'm no lady." She stopped in breathless confusion.

He said, gently, "You are only endearing yourself to me, Ivy. I wouldn't change you if I could. Like you said, there's so little time. When I come back off this campaign, I want you to be my wife. We'll be married right away."

Her face seemed to go blank, freezing her emotions beneath its tight surface.

As well as he thought he knew her, he was unprepared when, without a word, she busied herself preparing supper. He watched her in concerned silence, wrung by an enormous wish to make her happy. When the food was on the table, he seated her. Save for an occasional polite word when she passed him something, they ate in silence. When he complimented her on the dinner, he saw the same tight little smile he had seen at the San Simon Stage Station, when he had tried to encourage her. Later, she washed the dishes and he dried them. In all, he guessed not a dozen words had been exchanged between them since he had blurted out his feelings and hopes, causing her to retreat into her childhood fears.

In the parlor, they talked of mundane things:

brother Eddie working in the Ready Pay Mine north of town, of reported rich silver strikes to the south and west, of the fortune seekers streaming into the region, and of the inevitable changes settlement would bring. She was thoughtful, almost pensive at times, and he avoided any references to the campaign. Soon it would be time to go. He dreaded the thought of leaving her.

Glancing into the purpling darkness of the street, she said suddenly, "Your poor horse. He's still tied out there. Why don't you take him to the shed behind the house? There's feed and water."

When he returned, she was waiting in the center of the room. Her face had smoothed, free of doubt, free of the past, he thought. Her eyes were shining as she met his, and with that touching honesty she possessed, she said, "I don't want you to leave here tonight. I want us to be together here tonight. Have what we can have together, this night. Who knows what tomorrow may bring? You are so right, Ewing. Life is to be lived day by day as we go along, not in the past or looking only toward the future. Today was yesterday's tomorrow. No other woman could ever love you as I do, because you are as life itself to me."

They lay locked in each other's arms. A consciousness of time nagged at Ewing, woke him.

The night was passing much too swiftly. Ivy was sleeping. Gently disengaging his arms, he left the bed to look out the window at the starry night. Past midnight, he judged, and turned back. Ivy had let down her hair. In the room's tallow light, it was not unlike a dark veil across the paleness of her breasts down to her hips. She slept like a child: face turned on the pillow, one arm flung up, breathing evenly and softly. In reality, he thought, her childhood had ended that dreadful day in the Bradshaw Mountains.

As he lay down beside her, trying not to wake her, he felt stealthy arms stealing around him. "You were gone too long," she said.

"I thought you were asleep."

"I was, but I knew when you got up. I sensed it. I did because you are part of me and that part left me."

He kissed her.

She seemed to fall into a reflective mood; presently, she said, "What was she like, Ewing?"

He turned his head to look at her.

"Your wife. You were married. Something tells me. Your courtesies. Little things."

"You're sensing again," he said, a stir of laughter in his throat.

"I'm a woman—that's why. But don't tell me if you don't want to, if it brings up too much of the past. I know how that is. No, Ewing. Please don't. I'm wrong to ask. Forgive me. I'm sorry."

Instantly, she followed up with an apologetic kiss and caressed his forehead.

"I don't mind," he said, holding her while he lay on his back. "She was an eastern girl from a well-to-do family, far more than mine. My father was an Indiana farmer. Poor, but honest, as they say. We were married soon after I was graduated from West Point. Our first and only home was at Fort Bowie, my first post. In all fairness, it was hard living for her, accustomed to the many comforts of home. After a few months, she went back East. I never saw her again. Never heard from her again, except through her lawyers. No letters. It was finished. She has since remarried— well, I understand."

"Didn't you try to talk her out of leaving?"

"Why should I? She wanted to go. She wasn't happy. Neither was I. It was over."

"Didn't that leave you sad?"

"Ivy, you are a little pry. However, I'll tell you the truth. My ego suffered for a while, but I soon got over it. I began to see that it was all for the best."

"Would you mind telling me her name?"

"Elinor."

She took his hand. "A pretty name. I almost feel sorry for Elinor. I mean, losing you."

He gave a low chuckle. "I don't think she looked at it exactly that way. She was relieved to get out. The final straw, as far as I was concerned, was when she insisted I resign my commission and clerk in her father's dry-goods emporium. I refused."

She kissed him again. "So you took charge of the Tontos, lived like a Tonto?"

"How did you know that?"

"Horse sense. You had to make a change."

"Yes," he said, impressed with her insight, "I did that. Also, Army people are very caste-conscious—something I've never liked, growing up among rural folks. The Tontos, for all their violent ways, are very democratic. To them, the most important aspect of life is to be brave. They are the firmest of friends, friends to the death. But God help their enemies. They show no mercy."

"I know Elinor was a lady," Ivy persisted in his ear, her voice brushing wistfulness. "She was educated to be one. Manners and such. How to dress. How to look nice. . . . The latest Butterick patterns . . . glycerin soap . . . cucumber cream . . . English lavender water. How to set a proper table. How to be polite. How to talk to people. Somewhere I think I read the word for it." She groped in silence.

"Etiquette, maybe?"

"Yes. I remember now. Eddie and I found it in a magazine we picked up behind a hotel in Prescott. Etiquette. Why, it's as hard to spell as Guggenheimer." He listened with a drowsy smile as her sweet voice murmured on. "Elinor was used to nice things back East. I know she was pretty, too. Wasn't she?"

"She was. But you are beautiful."

"I want to be honest, Ewing. I have to tell you I'm almost jealous she ever had you."

"You needn't be, because she never had me. Now, don't ask any more foolish questions. That's all past. All rubbed out, as the Tontos say."

Long moments slipped by. He dozed, lost in contentment. Her voice, conveying the softest of tones, broke the silence. "Ewing?"

"Uh-huh."

"Was . . . she better in bed than me?"

He let out a burst of startled laughter and pulled her tighter to him.

Montoya did not come to the camp until midmorning, but he arrived on the gallop. "I've found Gómez," he reported. "He came back to the house, just as I thought he would. I was watching. He's there now, waiting. He will talk to you, Lieutenant. But don't expect him to do as you want. He's a Warm Springs at heart. Leave the Tontos here. Hurry."

They rode around behind the house, where an unsaddled roan gelding was haltered, and dismounted. When Montoya knocked at the back door, a silent Mexican woman let them in, walked ahead of them to the front room.

Gómez was standing. A stocky man of

indeterminate age, full through the chest and shoulders, like an Apache, his dominant feature darting black eyes more hawkish than friendly. The stern mouth set like stone in the watchful face. Hair cut long, like an Apache but minus the usual headband. Intricate gold chains trailed from each ear. A silver necklace encircled the strong neck, a silver bracelet on his left wrist. He wore a calico shirt, the long tails out, Apache style, gray pants, and black boots. A silver-buckled belt cinched his lean middle, a long knife at his belt.

He bowed and courteously gestured for them to be seated, took a chair by the door, and spoke in Spanish to Montoya, who, in turn, said to Ewing, "He says he wants peace. No trouble. He is tired of war."

"Good. Tell him we want the same."

Montoya did so. Gómez replied, smiling, and Montoya said, "He wants to know who you are?"

"Tell him I am flattered that he would ask. I am Second Lieutenant Mackay, Sixth Cavalry, on detached duty at Fort Cummings from the Department of Arizona."

Gómez smiled, his teeth small and white and as even as piano keys, and spoke, and Montoya said, "He says he can tell you are a second lieutenant by your shoulder straps without bars. He has fought many blue coats."

"His eyes are sharp, tell him."

Gómez launched into a staccato exchange,

blustering, gesturing, glancing derisively now and then at Ewing, and Montoya said, "He says he has fought blue coats with single bars and twin bars. Once he fought a blue coat with silver eagles on each shoulder. He wants to know what kind of soldier chief that man was?"

"A colonel," Ewing explained wryly. "Did he kill the colonel?"

Gómez's reply was a vague laugh and moderating shrugs and words. "He reminds you," Montoya followed, "that he is a man of peace now. The war-trail days are gone."

"I am glad to hear that."

"He wants to know where your blue coats are and why you are here?"

"Tell him I have no blue coats with me, only a few scouts, and I want him to lead me to Victorio's camp. Since he desires peace, surely he will do that," Ewing said, and saw Gómez stiffen at Montoya's word, shrug, and move his hands. Ewing could almost read his evasive reply before Montoya interpreted. "He says Victorio changes camp often because the soldiers keep looking for him."

"Is Victorio still in the Black Range?"

"An Apache, he says, is like the wind. One moment in plain sight, gone the next, like smoke."

Ewing had to smile at that evasion. He said, "Ask him how many warriors Victorio has."

Gómez pondered at length. He resorted to signs.

"The chief's strength varies from day to day," Montoya passed on. "Warriors come and go."

"Ask him to confirm what you told me. About Chiricahuas and Mescaleros with the Warm Springs."

"There are always Mescaleros, he says."

"How many?" Ewing persevered.

"Maybe ten. Maybe fifty. They come and go."

"What about the Chiricahuas? How many?"

"Some, he says. They move around much of the time. Sometimes they are in Mexico, killing Mexicans like flies."

"Pin him down, if you can. Ask him again how many warriors Victorio has most of the time. His average strength."

Gómez looked up at the ceiling and folded his arms. After which he spoke slowly to Montoya, his guttural voice rising and falling.

Montoya said, "He says he cannot tell you exactly. If the camp is low on food and the men are out hunting, there will be as few as a handful left, mostly old men. Other times there will be many warriors if there is plenty of food."

"Ask him what he means by 'many'."

Irritation plaited Gómez's face. He chopped off his reply.

"It is only a guess," Montoya interpreted, "since he says he left the Warm Springs some time ago.

Seventy-five warriors. Maybe a hundred. Maybe less."

"He's not telling us much. I think he is purposely misleading us. Ask him again if he will lead us to Victorio's camp."

Once more Gómez shrugged. He pushed out his thin lips expressively, cut fluid signs with his hands.

"He says Victorio will be one place today, another place tomorrow. The Black Range is vast. There are many places to hide. He says if he led you into the mountains and you did not find Victorio, then you would blame him. You would say he was lying, and he doesn't want that name. He is a truthful man, tired of the war trail. A peaceful man now. A man of honor."

"He is beating around the bush. Tell him I know he is a great man, a great warrior. Ask him point-blank if he will lead us to the general area of Victorio's camp."

For the first time Gómez showed other than impassive control. Anger leaped to his face, just briefly, however, as he curbed the feeling and forced a smile, speaking with ease.

"He says his first words will stand," Montoya said. "He doesn't want to disappoint the soldier chief by leading him into the mountains and finding dead campfires. Besides, he says, you forget that he has quit the war trail. He wants no more of that. He wants to follow the white-eyes' peace road. He will live like a white-eye from now on."

They were getting nowhere, Ewing saw. But he nodded agreement and said, "Tell him that as a soldier I understand his talk. He speaks from the heart of a warrior."

Upon that, Gómez inclined his head and half smiled.

"Now," Ewing said, "ask him if Victorio was killed at Tres Castillos."

The black eyes blinked surprise. Gómez answered rapidly, emphatically, and Montoya said, "Victorio will die an old man, an honored warrior, and leader of his people. His medicine is too strong for any mere Mexican ever to kill him." Gómez came to his feet. The parley was over.

"Guess it's time to go," Ewing said flatly. "Thank him for talking to us. Tell him it was a great honor for me, a blue coat."

Gómez nodded in recognition.

"Peace," Ewing said, looking at him, and walked out.

"You're right," Ewing said as they rode toward camp. "He's still a Warm Springs, about as peaceful as a rattler. I wouldn't trust him if he said he would lead us into the Blacks."

"You must remember," Montoya said thoughtfully, "that he was taken captive as a child, raised as an Apache. His blood is Mexican, but his mind is Warm Springs. A man becomes what he is taught."

"You said that he comes and goes a good deal."

"They say that in town. Sometimes he is not seen for days. Not long ago he rode east and was gone a week or more."

"What does he do for a living? Work in the mines?"

"He does not work. But he always has money—gold, which he trades at the stores."

"So . . . ?"

"I wonder," Montoya speculated, staring ahead, "I wonder if Gómez could be a spy? He talked to us, but he was always evasive. He was courteous in the beginning—almost too courteous. Then he would flare out at you. He told us nothing, yet he wanted to know all about you and where the blue coats are. I wonder . . ."

"If he is a spy," Ewing said, "he will leave again for the Warm Springs' camp. This time to report the presence of an Army officer and some Indian scouts in Hillsboro. If so, wouldn't he leave soon, possibly this morning?"

Ewing pulled up sharply, seeing his rough guess register in the other's face. Of one accord, they swung off the road to circle back to the house. "Wait," Ewing said, after they had gone a short distance. "Maybe we'd better keep everybody together." And they rode on to the camp. With the scouts trailing them in close order, they angled around to a hill that sat back from the house, overlooking it, tied their horses in the brush, climbed the hill, and flattened out to watch. The roan was still tethered behind the house.

An hour or more passed.

"Maybe I'm wrong," Ewing said.

"An Apache has more patience than a white-eye," Montoya said. "Maybe he is waiting until dark. Look!"

The Mexican woman left by the rear door, took a path to a well below the house, drew a bucket of water, and returned. Coming out again, she went to the woodpile, chopped an armful, and took it into the house. Presently, smoke rose from the chimney.

"He will eat and then have a siesta before he leaves," Montoya predicted.

"We'll see," Ewing said.

The sun was commencing its westward slide when a hatless Gómez stepped out the rear door into the yard. He fiddled with the roan's halter, took a casual but long look around, turned, and walked to the front of the house, gazing up and down the street. There he rolled a cigarette, and while he smoked, he watched westward, in the direction Ewing and Montoya had ridden from the house. As if satisfied, he threw down the cigarette and disappeared toward the front of the house.

"He is coming in the front way," Montoya said. "I believe he has made up his mind."

Half an hour more. An hour.

"Maybe I am wrong, Lieutenant. Maybe he is not a spy."

"On the contrary, I am beginning to believe what you said more than you do."

Hardly had Ewing spoken when a hatted Gómez opened the back door, carrying saddle, blanket, and bridle. While he saddled, the woman brought forth a pack and rifle. Gómez tied the pack behind the cantle, slipped the rifle into a long scabbard alongside the saddle, and mounted. With a wave and yet another sweeping look around, he reined for the street, crossed it, and rode into the deep tree shadows of the creek, gone in moments.

"We'd better keep him in sight," Montoya said, getting to his feet.

"There's time for this," Ewing said. Taking an order book and pencil from his blouse, he wrote rapidly:

Major Thorn, sir: I have the honor to report that at this moment Gómez is leaving Hillsboro for the Black Range. I will follow immediately with the scouts and Montoya. Montoya and I parleyed with Gómez this morning. He was evasive, refused to guide us into the

Blacks. Montoya believes, as I do, that Gómez is a spy for the Warm Springs. I respectfully suggest that the command proceed to Hillsboro as soon as possible.

In accordance with your instructions, I will drop back couriers to keep you informed. I firmly believe this is our best chance to locate Victorio.

Respectfully,
2nd Lt. E. H. Mackay

Ewing handed the report to Archie. "Give this to Rowdy. Tell him to take it to Major Thorn with all haste."

Tim O'Boyle could see figures, singly and in groups, making quietly for C Troop's stables set behind the barracks. He turned nervously to Corporal Duffy. "Wexler's already there. Let's go."

"Not yet, lad. Make him wait. Make him fret a little. It's an old wrinkle, makin' an opponent wait and sweat."

"Waiting won't bother him. Odds are five to one on him."

"Odds? What are odds, but some fool John's notion on the past. Wexler ain't had a fight in months. He's fat and slow. They don't know you been workin' out. They don't know how fast you be with your mitts. Nor the footwork I been schoolin' you on, nor the punch you developed on the heavy bag."

"Tell you the truth, Pat, I've never been so scared in all my life. I'd rather fight 'Paches any day than Wexler."

"Scared? That's only natural, lad. Means you're ready. Just the way a man ought to feel right before a fight. I was shakin' scared right before I whipped Tom Finney for the New England belt. Knocked him out in the twenty-third round with a right cross to the jaw, the same punch I been schoolin' you on after you feint with your left. Only tonight you'll be aimin' for Wexler's big gut. The right cross, with your shoulder behind it. . . . Bareknuckle, them days, lad. A round continued till a fighter was down. His corner had half a minute to revive 'im and return 'im to the scratch line. If they didn't, the fight was over." Duffy sniffed. "The game's got considerable softer, if you ask me. That Marquis of Queensberry an' his pussyfoot rules."

"Well, I'm glad we're using gloves."

"Oh, sure, lad. I meant no reflection on your grit."

The dark figures dwindled until no more came from the barracks.

"I reckon we can go now," Duffy said, picking up the bucket of water, sponge, and towel. "That Dutchman's had time enough to think about what you're gonna give 'im."

A sickness knotted Tim's stomach. Swallowing against the dryness in his throat, he went ahead in a cold sweat. His mind strayed inevitably to Teresa, seeing her, dimly at first, then with sharpening clarity, as if she moved toward him through the mists of his thoughts. He hadn't seen her since that devastating night, unable to bring himself to go back. Wexler, however, had gone to Little Chihuahua every night. Tim had seen him leave the barracks and heard him return late each time, noisy and profane. With the command pulling out tomorrow morning, Tim wished now that he had seen her just once more. He ached with memories of her. What if he was killed, never to see her again?

Ahead, sallow light seeped from the stables' cracks. They passed the first lookout. Tim could hear the hum of expectant voices, could sense the waiting inside. He paused before the curtained entrance; breathing deeply, he drew it aside and went in.

"Good luck, Tim," the second lookout said as he passed. "Knock that Dutchy's ears down."

He turned along the lantern-lit runway, through the eager crowd, some troopers slapping him on the back, voicing encouragement, while he made his way to the makeshift ring, two ropes strung around four barrels, which could be dismantled at a moment's notice should the lookout give the alarm of an officer's approach.

Wexler sat on a stool in the ring, naked to the waist, muscular arms folded across his broad chest, stolid, unconcerned, confident, exchanging jesting remarks with his backers. Private Hoch, his second, deferred to him.

Tim eased through the ropes, went to the opposite corner from Wexler, removed his blouse, handed it to Duffy, and looked across at Wexler, who ignored him.

"Ain't he the bully boy," Duffy breathed in Tim's ear. "He won't be so cocky after you work on that gut."

Sergeant Larkin, tonight's referee, stepped to the center of the ring and held up both hands for quiet. The chattering dropped to an undertone. He said, "Remember to keep your voices down. No shouting or hollering. Or the fight will end before it's over and we'll all be on report, myself busted. . . . This bout will be conducted under Queensberry rules till one man can't continue. Be three-minute rounds, a minute between rounds. Seconds will stay out of the ring during the rounds. The timekeeper will clang two horseshoes together to start and end a round— that should be distinct enough for all to hear. And now . . . to introduce tonight's contestants. In this corner," Larkin barked, pointing, "the challenger . . . Private Tim O'Boyle—a good Irish lad who loves his dear old mother and writes her at least once a year." There was such an outburst of clapping that Larkin motioned for quiet. Tim stood and waved, nodded, and sat down, feeling embarrassed and weak-kneed.

"They're all for you, lad," Daffy chimed in Tim's ear. "It's the best tonic a man can have."

"In this corner," Larkin was announcing, "the heavyweight champion of Fort Cummings . . . a man who fears no man—Private Kirk Wexler!" Grinning, Larkin added, "Formerly Corporal Wexler," which kindled raucous laughter and a smattering of applause. Wexler got up and bowed all around to the crowd, flexing his thick arms, and sat down.

"Eight to one on Wexler!" Tim heard a man call out. There were no takers.

Larkin motioned both fighters to the middle of the ring and said, "There will be no wrestling or hugging. No gouging—no kicking—no hitting below the belt—no hitting a man when he is down. I can disqualify a man if he does that, declare the other the winner. If a man goes down to one knee, he is considered down and the ten-count will start. When a man is down, the other must go to a neutral corner. The down man must be up by ten seconds or he loses by a knockout. Now, go to your corners and come out fighting."

"Ten to one on Wexler!" a man chanted. "Where's all that Mick money?" There were no takers.

Duffy's battered face—the broken nose, the

scarred forehead and chin, the gray hair receding around the temples, the patch over the sightless left eye, shot out at Antietam, which gave him a fierce appearance—wore a look of fatherly concern as he put his arm around Tim's shoulder and said, fast and low, "Remember now, box him. Bob and weave. Stay low. When he swings, duck under and move inside. Work on his gut. Keep workin' on it. Make him chase you. Move away when he tries to corner you. We want to wear him down. Footwork will do it, lad. Footwork. Now, go to it."

The horseshoes clanged.

Tim's confidence sank when he saw Wexler's brawny shape barging out from the opposite corner, the mighty right arm cocked for the knockout. Tim seemed to freeze, until he heard Duffy's urgent, "Move, lad! Move!"

Wexler grinned and advanced closer. Suddenly he threw the right. Tim, ducking low, saw it swish by like a flying brick. He danced away, almost too late, missing the chance to punish Wexler's open middle. He kept backpedaling, bobbing and weaving, as Wexler plodded after him. All at once Wexler stopped and called, "Fight, you damned Mick!" He stood flatfooted, arms hanging, glaring.

Tim feinted left, then threw the right to Wexler's jaw. Wexler's head barely moved with the blow. It was like pounding rock. Pain shot up

Tim's gloved hand to his elbow. Wexler attacked again, displaying the same mirthless grin of promised destruction. Tim tried a tentative left to the nose. Wexler brushed it aside like a fly. Tim sped away. Now, Wexler took an uncertain stance, refusing to chase, his guard down.

The round clanged to an end.

"He's tryin' to lure you inside," Duffy said, sponging Tim's chest. "Keep dancin'. His middle is wide open."

When the round opened, Wexler stood and motioned for Tim to come to him. Instead, Tim waited in the center of the ring, waving his gloves, and continued to dance. Both fighters dallied so long that the crowd began to boo.

"Afraid to come outa your corner, champ?" That was Duffy's baiting voice.

His face reddening, Wexler charged. He would have crashed into Tim had Tim not sidestepped. As Wexler bulled past, Tim pounded him twice in the ribs. Wexler whirled, fast for a big man, faster than Tim had expected. Wexler threw a wild punch. Under it, Tim drilled a left and right to Wexler's paunch and bobbed out of range.

"You jiggin' Mick!"

Suddenly Wexler closed, both fists swinging. Tim was caught off guard. A looping right took him on the shoulder, sent him careening off balance. When he regained his footing, the ropes were against his back. At that moment Wexler, overeager for the kill, rushed in, his right cocked like a bludgeon.

Tim danced aside.

Wexler, unable to stop, shot through the ropes as if catapulted, landing face down on straw. He lay there, stunned, while the crowd roared. Larkin, at the ring's edge, began the count, but stopped when he saw Tim watching beside him. He waved Tim to a corner. By then, Wexler was up. He climbed through the ropes, murder filling his eyes, as the round ended.

The troopers were still full of voice. Larkin held up his arms and waved for them to quiet down.

Round three. Tim sensed the change at once. Wexler advanced purposefully, his stance lower, more balanced. Tim circled him warily. His confidence growing, he bobbed in, feinting, and found his adversary's nose with a flicking left. The blow brought blood, seemed to infuriate Wexler. He closed, swinging wildly. Tim pretended to back away, but instead suddenly stepped in, landing twice to Wexler's ample middle. The last punch, the Duffy-schooled right cross, drew a grunt of pain. Wexler's face sagged. Great rivulets of sweat poured down the hairy matting of his thick chest. He was hacking for wind as the round closed.

"Where's all that Wexler money now?" a man howled, jumping up and down.

"Keep on just like you're doin'," Duffy coached while he sponged Tim's face and chest. "In and out. Always movin'. You've got him worried. But watch his right!"

Next round Wexler walked out instead of moving immediately to the attack, a smirk on his face. He was still winded. He made no attempt to throw his right, content to spar while Tim danced in and out, landing light jabs. In between dry-throated grunts, Wexler began to talk, his voice taunting and suggestive. "Teresa an' me . . . we had us a time other night. . . . Gannon wasn't there. . . . She asked me to take her outside. . . . Had us a real time. . . . Best I ever had. . . . That little Mex is some dish. . . . Wouldn't even take my money."

Tim quit moving. His anger was instantaneous, surprising even him, an erupting emotion, terrible to feel, uncontrollable. He attacked furiously, raging. Wexler's taunting face just a reddish blur before him. Distantly, above the constant din of the crowd, Duffy's warning cries registered once. After that, he heard only the thud of gloves on flesh. Wexler let him punch, warding off most of the wild swings. Tim ached to hurt that face. He crowded the big man. His engulfing fury drove him closer. He was coming in too high, careless of his guard. Too late, he saw Wexler plant his feet. At almost the same time he glimpsed the blur of Wexler's right. Too late, he tried to weave and duck under. The left side of his face seemed to explode. His whole body went numb. He felt himself knocked sideways, the lantern-light spinning, spinning, growing dimmer and dimmer.

He had the sensation of emerging out of splintering darkness into unreal light. His reeling senses slowly righted. He blinked. Over him, he heard a voice tolling "Seven," then "Eight." On the count of nine, the horseshoes clanged, ending the round. Quickly, Tim felt Duffy's powerful arms lifting him to his feet, dragging him to the stool, Duffy sponging his face and chest. Duffy stuck a little bottle under his nose. Tim sniffed, grimaced at the pungent ammoniac smell. He could see better now.

"Footwork, lad. Footwork," Duffy breathed, his anxious face up close. "Stay away from him till your head clears. Can you come out for the round?"

Seeing Wexler leering at him across the ring, Tim said, "I'll try."

"Footwork, now. He'll come at you like a mad bull."

Duffy lifted Tim to his feet, held him up, giving him strength. At the clanging sound Tim went forth on rubbery legs and raised his gloves as Wexler fairly bolted toward him for the knockout. On instinct alone, Tim feinted as to meet him, then held up.

"Fight, you yellow Mick!" Wexler fumed as

Tim slid away, avoiding the roundhouse right.

Tim faked a punch and danced out of range again. Wexler gave chase, mouthing frustrations. The round ended in that futile vein, neither fighter having landed an effective blow. Tim's head had finally cleared.

Round six. This time Wexler waited for Tim to come to him. The big man was heaving for wind, too weary to taunt, his perspiring face an open target. Tim danced around him, jabbing Wexler's right eye time and again, while Wexler threw wild punches. The eye was closing. There were marks on Wexler's face. His mouth looked pulpy. He spat blood.

Tim, feeling stronger, evaded a violent rush and pummeled the soft middle, forcing Wexler to back up. The troopers yelled at the flurry. Tim put two more shots to Wexler's belly, then raised his sights to the damaged eye, now a lump of blue flesh. For an indecisive moment Wexler appeared to ponder what he must do next, with his wind going fast. He made as if to retreat. Tim, overanxious, bored after him. Wexler pivoted suddenly, his quickness unsettling, lashing out with left and right.

Though the second punch didn't land solidly on Tim's jaw, he could feel its raw power. He staggered and slipped to one knee, momentarily hurt.

Before Larkin could wave Wexler to a corner

and start the count, Wexler loosed another knockout swing. Tim, still down, saw it coming and swayed away from it. It missed, and Wexler's momentum carried him past.

Wexler was wheeling to come in again, ignoring Larkin's protests, when Duffy shouted, "Foul!" and climbed through the ropes. Charging up to Wexler, he threw the Duffy right cross, his burly shoulder behind it, to the point of Wexler's jaw.

The big man dropped like an axed steer and did not move. Shouting troopers surged into the ring.

Amid the bedlam the second lookout ran to ringside, waving his arms in alarm, signaling for quiet. As the uproar gradually lessened, he cried, "Lieutenant Cooley's comin'!"

In moments the troopers dismantled the ring and pushed the barrels to one side and dispersed along the runway. They became busy grooming horses, oiling and polishing equipment.

When Cooley walked in seconds later, Tim had his blouse around his shoulders. Wexler was just sitting up, still groggy, left to his own resources.

"What's going on here?" Cooley demanded. "Sounded like a circus."

When Larkin didn't answer, Duffy said politely, "Why, nothin' much, sir. Just tidyin' up. Last minute details. Gettin' ready for tomorrow."

Seeing Wexler, Cooley asked, "What happened to him?"

"Why, sir, he happened to hit his head on a stanchion. Just about knocked him out, it did, sir. Most unfortunate. A terrible hard blow. Caused quite a hubbub, sir."

"So I heard." Then, straight of face, "Of course, Wexler would happen to have his shirt off, sweating like a farrier, as he went about this . . . ah . . . tidying up, while the rest of you did not. Wouldn't he?"

Duffy's old-soldier countenance did not alter one whit. He said, without pause, "You see, sir, we took off his shirt to give 'im air an' revive 'im with that bucket of water there one of the boys ran an' fetched."

"I see," Cooley said thoughtfully. "Well—better get Private Wexler to the barracks at once. We pull out at five."

"Yes, sir."

"And keep down the hubbub, Corporal."

"Yes, sir!"

Cooley had to go out quickly before he gave himself away, thinking, *At last, somebody has given Wexler a long-overdue licking.*

CHAPTER 10

Once across the creek, Gómez took off galloping. Ewing sent Archie and Jim ahead to keep him in sight. Archie soon swung back. "Gómez has stopped. He watches if followed he is. Like Apache, that *hombre*."

"Did he see you?"

Scornfully, "Gómez stop, Tontos stop. We know what Warm Springs up to."

"He's a Mexican, remember?"

"Here," Archie said, tapping his head, "Warm Springs Gómez is."

The tracking continued at that broken pace, Gómez pausing often to check his back trail before riding on, no faster than a walk. He was traveling north into stony foothills cut by small canyons and draws.

Late in the afternoon Archie hurried back, his dark face glittering excitement. He and Jim had come upon a dead Mexican sheepherder. Sheep were scattered everywhere, some grazing, some dead.

When the detail reached the place, Montoya crossed himself and looked down at the herder's body, clad poorly in white cotton pantaloons and shirt, rawhide sandals fastened with thongs. He said, "It was not like this in the old days. The

Apaches depended on herders and others like myself for supplies and communication with the settlements. Now no one is spared. This poor man was killed like a little rabbit, too frightened to lift a hand in his defense. What harm could he have done to them?"

Montoya started to ride on when Ewing, looking closer, said, "This man was scalped. Apaches usually don't take scalps." He turned to Archie. "Do Warm Springs scalp?"

Archie shook his head in denial.

"That means," Ewing reasoned, "we have warriors from another tribe joining the Warm Springs. Mescaleros might do this. I don't know. I know Plains tribes scalp."

As if their deliberating had given pause for solemn proprieties, they piled rocks around the victim, Montoya said a prayer, and they rode after Gómez.

When evening came, Gómez camped and made a big fire. The Tontos crept up to observe him.

"That *hombre* good tobacco smokes he does," Archie reported. "We smell it could. He ate like Mexican. Dried beef. *Pinole* with water he stir, sweeten with *panocha*."

"Why the big fire?" Ewing asked of Montoya.

"He's getting into Warm Springs country. He's safe."

"It strikes me as unusual. You or I would make a small fire, just enough to cook by."

"But he is Gómez."

The scouts bedded down a mile away behind a rocky ridge, boiled bitter black coffee, ate hardtack and bacon. Gómez, the inquisitive Tontos reported with interest, kept his fire high until late into the night, and he was still in camp when the sun stood hours high.

After breaking camp, Gómez kept to the foothills at an idling gait, stopping now and then, walking his horse, avoiding the high brokenness of the Black Range towering to his left, where eventually he would go.

"He rides like a man killing time," Montoya concluded.

Much of the morning had worn away when Jim reported that not only was Gómez stopping again, but he was making a fire and balling up green juniper branches in a blanket to put on the fire.

Before long Ewing saw a spiral of smoke curling up to the hot, windless sky. Apaches, he had learned from the Tontos, did not carry on conversations by smoke signals as many *blancos* believed—that was nonsense. A smoke signal was a simple message, often one of distress, such as "We need help" or "We are here" or "Enemy is near."

Ewing scowled. "Maybe he's spotted us."

No, Jim said. But the scouts would have to move with greater caution when Gómez turned into the mountains, where he could look down on everything below.

Gómez lingered on his hilltop long after he quit sending signals. He was yet there when the sun hung straight overhead. Then, as if impatient, he made another fire and sent more signals.

Into the afternoon Ewing sighted a streak of dust boiling up from the southeast. The dust became riders driving a bunch of horses. He looked through his field glasses. Indians, all right, but what tribe? He handed the glasses to Montoya, who studied the horsemen a long time. "Mescaleros," he said ominously. "I know them."

"How many?"

"Forty or so. The horses were probably stolen around Mesilla."

"Quite a war party. Could be that explains why Gómez rode east not long ago. If true, I have to give him credit. He's one hell of a recruiter. Having that much influence, though, would surprise me."

"It comes back to what I have told you. Though a Mexican, he is a Warm Springs and has to be a warrior of some standing if he can bring Mescaleros in."

For a better look, Montoya and Ewing crawled to a stand of bushy junipers studding a higher knob. From there they watched the Mescaleros wind through the rocky hills and join Gómez. A parley followed, after which Gómez led them away. By now the afternoon was about spent. Before dark the Mescaleros camped along a creek tumbling out of the Black Range.

The Mescaleros were careless, the Tontos reported with disdain. They did not attempt to hide their fires, were noisy, and did not put out guards. Archie gloated that the Tontos could kill many at daybreak and drive off all their horses, if Nantan ordered, he suggested hopefully. The Mescaleros rode good horses, he said, and the horses they drove were good. He could use a good horse, he pointed out. His own was tired.

"True," Ewing said, quirking his mouth at the rationalizing. "But we need Gómez to lead us to Victorio's *ranchería.* If we attack, Gómez might be killed. If not killed, he would run and we'd probably lose sight of him. True, you Tontos could do that. Later, when we find Victorio, there will be plenty of fighting and plenty of horses for you to take."

Afterward, listening to the faint sounds of his camp, the snuffle of a horse, the scuff of moccasined feet on gravel as a Tonto left to stand watch or returned, Ewing arrived at some reckonings how the loose ends of the campaign could be pulled together. Major Thorn and the command could be in Hillsboro about now. He would hurry because he thirsted to redeem his reputation. From Hillsboro into the Blacks would be much slower going. This place near the creek would make a likely bivouac for the command on the march into the mountains. Gómez was the key; otherwise, finding Victorio could take days on end, with the Tontos patiently working out trails and the mountains strange to them.

He thought of Ivy, reliving the closeness of her, her sweet giving, the gentleness of her nature, her lovely laughter, hidden from him until that night. Her openness, her candor. She had asked about Elinor and imagined to herself what Elinor was like, quite accurately, too. So young, yet wise beyond her years in living. "I will be here when you come back," she had told him, striving to conceal the fear she felt for him. That was the picture he took with him. Thinking of her, he fell asleep.

Gómez and the Mescaleros were late breaking camp next morning.

While following at a careful interval from the hostiles, who seemed to be seeking an easier way into the mountains with their stolen horses, one of the advance scouts reported and gestured excitedly to the east. Big dust, he said.

Ewing halted the detail. There it was, far off, another dust trail, this one coming fast. He raised the glasses, surprised to see these were not Indians, when he had expected another war party. These were Anglos and Mexicans, heavily armed. He passed the glasses to Montoya, saying, "What do you make of them?"

The rancher spoke while holding the glasses to his eyes. "I'd say it's a posse. Volunteers. Probably from Mesilla. On the prod to take back their horses. The way they're riding I believe they've seen the dust of the Mescaleros."

Ewing said, "They could ruin everything, if the Mescaleros scatter, Gómez with them. I don't dare send a scout down there to warn them off. They'd shoot him on sight."

"I will go," Montoya said.

"No," said Ewing, after a moment's thought, "we'd only give ourselves away to the Mescaleros. Just hope they don't spoil it for us. Reminds me of some barroom Indian fighters over in Arizona, called themselves the Globe Rangers. Went hunting for Apaches, primed with the best whiskey in town. When they stopped for a little siesta, the Apaches stole their horses and they had to walk back to town."

"We could not stop them now if we tried," Montoya said gravely. "Not enough time. Those men are foolish, reckless to rush in. They have spotted the Mescaleros." He handed back the glasses. "They are out of sight now, behind this hill."

Dismounting, they climbed to the crest and lay flat. Watching, Ewing felt like a spectator viewing a hair-raising melodrama. By now the Mescaleros had seen the posse. Leaving some loose horses behind in an arroyo, they drove the rest out of sight and soon reappeared on foot, taking cover along the boulder-cluttered sides of the arroyo.

A sick feeling went over Ewing, not relieved by the knowledge that he could not have stopped the posse had he tried. The stage was set, the actors in the wings.

On the possemen rode, already at the mouth of the arroyo. Sighting the loose horses, they charged with strident yells. As they approached the horses, shots cracked and the arroyo blossomed powder smoke. The possemen pulled up. Horsemen fell. The others wheeled and raced back the way they had come, firing wildly, not slowing for a wounded rider struggling to stay aboard his mount and keep up.

Now, the Mescaleros came down from their hiding places, finished off the wounded, took their arms, gathered up the loose horses, and disappeared.

The entire foolhardy scene had lasted but a few minutes. When Ewing looked again, the possemen were still riding frantically eastward, trailed by the wounded rider.

"I guess," Montoya said, "they ran out of whiskey."

As the morning gave way to afternoon, the scouts crossed new and numerous unshod tracks coming in on what was now a well-traveled trail angling into the massive Blacks.

"Looks like another war party," Ewing observed to Montoya. "Archie says these tracks are days old. He's puzzled. Everything comes in from the northeast. Wouldn't be more Mescaleros. Not from that direction."

Montoya said tiredly, "I've quit thinking. Nothing seems to make sense anymore. Victorio once told me the Warm Springs had allies besides the Mescaleros and Chiricahuas."

These past few days, Ewing realized, he had almost forgotten Montoya's great sorrow. He said, feeling guilty sympathy, "Juan, why don't you go back to be with your family? You don't have to ride on with us. You've already located Gómez for us—more than we could have done. We can follow him on, I think."

Montoya's face hardened. "I must avenge my son. My heart is like stone."

Evidently feeling safe from any pursuit, the Mescaleros camped early along the banks of a broad creek that flowed eastward toward the Rio Grande.

"They're on the Animas," Montoya told Ewing.

"Would make a nice base camp. Wood, water, and forage. No wonder Victorio prefers these haunts."

"Not here—this is too accessible. His *ranchería* is up there somewhere. His favorite place is said to be like a park. Very hard to reach. I expect

221

Gómez will head in that direction tomorrow, for I think it is on the headwaters of the Animas. You don't know what rough country is, Lieutenant, until you have ridden the Black Range. The ridges are like knives."

True to Montoya's prediction, the trail started climbing the following morning, through stands of stately yellow pine, spruce, and fir, whose dark density, viewed from afar, gave the range its name; through tenacious scrub oaks, junipers, and piñons, the way always rocky and steep. Sometimes they led their horses over windfalls. Archie reported he could no longer keep the Mescaleros in sight.

Well into the afternoon, to the now-and-then rumble of summer thunderheads, Ewing halted and sent Archie and Jim ahead on foot. He had begun to feel concern for them by the time they came in shortly before dark. The Mescaleros, Archie said, had entered a big, rough canyon and posted lookouts. Strange, when last night they had not in the foothills. Why here, deeper into Warm Springs country?

Montoya showed a quick interest. "They are nervous about something," he said.

"Maybe us," Ewing worried.

Also, Archie said, he had noticed some strange Indians coming down with some Warm Springs to meet the Mescaleros.

"Strange?" Ewing asked. "How do you mean?"

There was much sign talk, Archie went on. The Mescaleros made the sign for snakes, which puzzled Archie and Jim. These strange warriors were thickset and stout, though taller than most Apaches, and very proud of bearing. They wore their hair long without headbands; instead, they ornamented their hair with beads and stringers of silver. They rode fine horses. They were well armed. They carried shields fastened on their arms near the elbow. Some carried lances and war clubs, bows and arrows. All had rifles.

Ewing glanced at Montoya for further explanation, but the rancher just looked intent.

Archie had no more to say, though his eyes held unanswered questions. They camped below a high ridge that led to still higher country, chewed hardtack, and made no fires. A dim game trail ran up the ridge. Archie went up it. Darkness had settled when he came down. He sat facing the trail, troubled in his silent way.

A light shower fell during the early night hours, releasing the sweet pungency of pine and piñon. Ewing catnapped, Archie's unrest about the hostiles' lookouts drumming through his mind. A man never slept soundly, anyway, on scout. Over in Arizona, General Crook's tactic of night marches and dawn attacks had been markedly successful because the hostiles did not put out sentinels. Their lack of discipline and lie-abed habits had cost them hundreds of lives.

A keen observer, Archie knew the change in the Mescaleros' camp meant something. Had they spotted the trailing scouts? Ewing couldn't sleep.

Sometime after three o'clock he sat up, took his carbine, and on moccasined feet crossed the few steps to Archie. The Apache was already sitting up.

"Get Jim," Ewing said.

"*Enjuh*, Nantan."

In silence, no words passing among them because talk was unneeded, the three left the bivouac and turned up the game trail. Here milky light broke through the pines, outlining the dim trace. The damp timber and earth smelled like incense to Ewing, clearing his senses. The trail zigzagged around a shoulder of rock, swung back, and climbed sharply; as the pines thinned, the light grew stronger. They walked silently for some minutes, until Archie stopped, on the backbone of the ridge. Here they would wait and watch, several hundred yards above the bivouac.

Wailing, drawn out, a coyote's falsetto voice reached them from higher up. Another answered, more distinct, nearer the three watchers. The singing ceased.

At that, Archie took position by the trail behind a scrub oak.

If there was a wrongness in those wailings, Ewing reflected, remembering that the human voice echoes more than any other in broken country, he couldn't tell. If Archie or Jim did, they gave no sign. Yet, he judged, suspicious of any deviation, waiting for the familiar chorus that did not come, it occurred to him as unusual that the coyotes, which the Apaches called "medicine dogs," had cut short their singing. For coyotes, like choir singers, fancied the sound of their own voices and would carry on and on.

Now, Jim moved to the opposite side of the trail from Archie. Ewing hunched his shoulders against the chill and searched the leaden light along the ridgetop.

A tedium of waiting now. A great deal later, yet not as long as it seemed to Ewing, a whippoorwill cried *prrrip, purr-rill* on the other side of the ridge and another repeated the rolling call. These sounds also died prematurely and likewise were not renewed.

Archie rose to a listening attitude, held it awhile, then sat back on his haunches.

Streaks of dull light pinked the eastern sky. If they're coming, Ewing knew from the past, it has to be soon. Before long there would be too much light for a surprise attack. He relaxed when a nighthawk swooped low over the trail, emitting sharp *peents*.

Daylight was only minutes away when Ewing caught a turkey's *put, put, put*. It seemed to come from down the ridge to his left, on Archie's side of the trail. Ewing faced that direction, more curious than alarmed. Another moment and, late coming, meaning traveled through him: never had he heard a turkey gobble in midsummer. It wasn't the season. His whole body tensed.

Archie and Jim were likewise shifting that way. *They know, too,* Ewing thought. With the same awareness, he made out a figure through the misty light. Archie let the man come in on the trail. When he was a step past the scrub oak, Archie lunged, knife held high.

Ewing heard the knife's *thunk,* the man's startled grunt of pain as he crashed down, moccasins scuffing gravel, arms flailing. Something clattered; his rifle.

Footsteps pounding up. Jim was there, anticipating. The two collided, grunting. Ewing ran forward to help, seeing Jim's knife arm whipping up and down twice. The second hostile cried out and tore away, lurching blindly down the game trail toward Ewing. With the blur of a pain-twisted face framed by long hair before him, Ewing drove his knife into the naked chest. The blow sent the man reeling. Jim was after him like a cat, pouncing, knife arm whipping. The man went limp, jerking convulsively.

A rifle blasted not thirty yards away. Ewing hit the gravel and grabbed his carbine, keyed for more shots and more Apaches. Instead, he heard feet running down the ridge, but he couldn't see the man. The pounding *slap, slap*

of moccasins pinched out. The forest fell silent again.

When daylight soon came, Montoya and the other scouts examined the dead hostiles. The first, the one Archie had killed, was a Warm Springs. The second puzzled the curious Tontos. This man was stout and broad-chested, of medium height, his broad face a bright copper color, his black, straight hair waist length. He wore a breechclout of blue cloth, fringed buckskin leggings, and moccasins of a design unknown to the Tontos, distinguished by fringes that ran from the lace to the toe and along the seam at the heel.

Montoya, gazing down, said, "When I was a boy living far north of here on the Rio Grande, I hired out to a merchant who went way out on the Plains to trade with the buffalo Indians. I remember moccasins like this. Besides the fringes, sometimes the moccasins were decorated with beads and small silver jinglers." He turned to face Ewing. "Comanches wore such moccasins. Lieutenant, this man is a Comanche."

Ewing nodded. "So another big war party has joined the Warm Springs. Guess we know, too, who scalped that poor sheepherder— Comanches." Thumbs hooked in belt, he paced out a tight little circle, head bent. "Now they know where we are. Next time they'll come like a swarm. I estimate, with the Comanches, Victorio's strength is approaching two hundred

and fifty warriors. Maybe more. Maybe three hundred." He paced to the crest of the ridge and looked northwest where the riddle of the campaign lay, masked by the roughest terrain a cavalryman could travel. In his mind's eye he saw the rise and fall of the mountains from where he stood down to the lower Animas, the streams, the canyons, the few trails—saw those features as if on a map, while he made some calculations to sort matters out. Assessing and projecting, figuring the scouts' choices, how and where Thorn could best bring up the command, how long it would take, where Ewing might link up with Thorn before the major moved into the higher reaches of the Black Range.

Going back down, Ewing told Archie, "I want to give that Indian plenty of time to reach Victorio and for Victorio to think about where our camp is. When we figure the Indian has had time to carry back the news, the main detail will pull out for Hillsboro and deliver my report to Major Thorn. You and Jim will stay with me. But we won't be here if the Warm Springs get suspicious and decide to see if all of us have gone. I want you to make clear to the scouts how important it is for the Warm Springs to see them leaving. Tell them to ride across the open places. To take their time going down. To string out. Stir up some dust. Halt awhile. If they do that, the Warm Springs will see them. Once the scouts get in the

foothills, tell them to ride fast to Major Thorn."

Archie turned to the scouts, speaking to them in choppy, emphatic Tonto.

Ewing thought a moment and walked over to Montoya, sensing in advance the answer he would get. "Juan," he said, "I should like for you to return with the detail to Hillsboro. In addition to my report to Major Thorn, you can explain the general situation to him. Tell him I'll send another courier back the moment we locate the *rancheria*. You can—"

"Lieutenant," Montoya said, his tone over-riding, "I could not live with myself or face my family if I left now, when danger is upon us. You forget that I know the Black Range. Not as well as a Warm Springs. But I can help. You need me."

"No doubt about that. I just want you to think about it some more." He waited, and when Montoya's face did not change, Ewing said, "All right. With you, we won't be groping about so much. First thing, I'd like for you to draw me a map, showing about where we are and the hostiles are."

Taking a stick, Montoya sketched a rough map on the graveled earth, naming the courses of the main streams, marking particular peaks here and there, jabbing with the stick to punctuate his words. "About here," he said, "is where I think Victorio is. It is very rough, very steep, getting there, cut by canyons and arroyos and a number

of small creeks. But there is also cover for cavalry laying over in the daytime. From the surrounding peaks, Victorio can see all movements of riders below. That is your main worry, Lieutenant. You cannot surprise Victorio."

"Unless . . . unless we move up on him at night. About how far do you estimate it is to Victorio's *rancheria* from here?"

"Five to eight miles as a crow flies or as a Warm Springs travels afoot, up and down. Fifteen or twenty miles the way cavalry would have to go around." He tossed the stick away, his motion deliberate and remembering, and continued, "Victorio ambushed the Ninth Cavalry and a company of Navajo scouts in these mountains back in the early fall of seventy-nine. A bunch of townsmen from Hillsboro rode to the rescue— they thought. Victorio whipped them all. Even captured the officers' personal baggage. Took many government horses and mules. You cannot surprise Victorio, Lieutenant."

In camp, Ewing drew a map corresponding to Montoya's on a piece of paper; ready to write his report, he reconsidered, Montoya's family pressing in on his thoughts, and said, "Juan, you can still change your mind and go back with the detail. Frankly, I think you have done enough."

"Finish your report, Lieutenant." He walked away.

Ewing then wrote:

230

Major Thorn, sir: I am sending most of my scouts back in order to draw the hostiles' attention away from our remaining party of four, which includes Montoya, who has volunteered to stay, as he knows the Black Range. It is my recommendation that you follow the trail to the lower Animas and bivouac there until I send another courier. I will do so as soon as we locate Victorio's ranchería. Montoya thinks it is between the headwaters of the Animas and the North Fork of Seco Creek. The enclosed map shows these salient features and where we are at this writing. I have also written in the estimated distances from Hillsboro on your line of march.

However, we must move from here at once, likely northwest, since our location is known. At dawn this morning three hostiles approached our camp. We killed two, one escaped. One of the dead warriors was a Comanche, which confirms that Comanches in addition to Mescalero war parties have recently joined Victorio. I now estimate his strength around 300 warriors.

Respectfully,
2nd Lt. E. H. Mackay

Ewing watched the scouts mount and trail off single file through the pines, soon dipping downgrade, soon lost from sight, the clack of shod hooves on rock lingering after he no longer saw the riders. He climbed the ridge with Montoya to watch. Save for a scattered band of thunderheads off in the west, the morning was bright and clear. He could see eastward for mile upon mile. Presently, far below, a feather of dust spiraled up. Good. If he could see it, so could the Warm Springs.

"I think," Montoya then said, "it is time I found us a new hiding place, Lieutenant."

CHAPTER 11

Keeping to the cover of the forest, Montoya rode hard on the scouts' tracks for half a mile or more. At a rocky wash he cut away and followed that broken course to a rough arroyo. There he took them on a winding, horse-grunting climb, halting again and again to check his bearings, constantly swiveling his head. No word was said. To Ewing, he seemed to be wandering, no definite destination in mind. Yet, coming to a rushing stream, he unhesitatingly rode in and up it a long way. Reaching a low shelf of reddish rock, he reined out and across, on another sharp ascent, switching back and forth through the pines and rock clutter, over windfalls. About another hour had passed when he pulled up and pointed below.

"See where we camped, Lieutenant?"

Ewing had to search a bit to find the ridge, some two thousand feet below, he figured. It appeared near, but by the roundabout way Montoya had taken them, Ewing knew they had covered not a few miles. Here they were high on the flank of a narrow, wooded ridge, its crest not unlike the cutting edge of a knife blade.

"We stay here till moonrise," Montoya said. "Where we go depends on what we see today. I want a peak where we can see better. Farther

in and higher up. Maybe that peak over there."
He pointed northwest, to a cone-shaped summit.
"That's about five miles, down and around,
before we start climbing." He loosened his saddle
girth, tied his horse where it could nibble oak
leaves, and settled down to watch. Archie and
Jim posted themselves along the upper ridge.

Ewing uncased his field glasses and slowly
scanned around. Nothing moved anywhere to his
eye. The shaggy peaks and steep ridges seemed to
ride a gently swaying sea under the benign blue
eye of the great sky. A purring breeze whimpered
about his face. The deceptive tranquillity brought
its all-too-familiar reminder. The old waiting
game was in force—lying doggo through the
daylight hours, squinting for blurs of movement
that could mean a deer or an Indian, moving at
night on stumbling, brutal marches, the Tontos
leading the advance, literally feeling the trail.
But the only way to whip Apaches. *Nothing has
changed,* he thought. *Nothing will for a long
time.* It was a wearying reflection.

Already Ewing could feel the coming ache in
his body. He rose and, staying low, made his way
higher up, to glass the other side of the ridge.
That was when he saw the dark rope of smoke
rising from another conelike peak, nearer than the
one Montoya wanted to reach, uncoiling strand
by strand, twisting and thinning as the capricious
wind played with it.

Everybody converged on Ewing at the same time.

"What does it say?" Ewing asked Archie.

Archie studied for a full minute before he answered. "They saw enemy leave . . . that dust, Nantan. Other Apaches they tell."

"Hell, that means there's another *ranchería* out there somewhere," Ewing said, irked at the new complication.

Archie did not say.

The smoke was drifting and breaking up when a series of sudden puffs shot up from the peak.

"Now, what are they saying?"

"They say, 'Come. Come in.' "

"We don't know where those other Apaches are," Ewing said.

Montoya said, "We will, when we find Victorio. The hostiles were split up till now. Many mouths to feed, many horses to find grass for. Three hundred warriors are too many for one *ranchería*, even though the Comanches and Mescaleros did not bring their families. They will all band together now, expecting a big fight. I don't like it, Lieutenant."

The signals were not repeated, the smoke tailed off, and in a short while the mountains were as deceiving as before. Noontime sun dazzled the ridgetop. The breeze ceased. Within the coolness of the pines a sense of ease had descended, likewise make-believe. Ewing rested, they all rested, preparing for the night's march. Time seemed not to pass.

It was Jim who grunted the alarm, crouched down to watch. Ewing's blood jumped when he saw a file of riders and warriors on foot emerging from the dark depths of a canyon. They crossed an open place as they climbed the bony ridge overlooking last night's camp.

Ewing handed the glasses to Jim. "What are they?"

"Warm Springs . . . Some Comanches . . . Some Mescaleros . . . Some Chiricahuas. Big war party, Nantan."

The naked eye told that alone. After the warriors had passed the clearing, Ewing's rough count tallied fifty-odd.

It was, he thought, after a long span of time, as if the brokenness down there had swallowed the hostiles. He glanced in question at Montoya, who said, "By now they have buried the dead warriors in the rocks and gone over our camp like sniffing dogs. They see where the scouts rode off. They see where we rode off, our tracks mingling with the scouts'. If they did pick up our tracks, they have lost them at the wash. If they did not there, they lost them at the creek. That is the puzzle I tried to leave them, Lieutenant. But it is hard to fool an Apache."

A flutter of movement below. A mounted

warrior took form. Another. Now more. From habit, Ewing started counting.

Montoya sighed his relief. "They're going back."

Ewing watched until the last warrior passed through the clearing. He felt his throat tighten as it came to him, a delayed alarm. He said, "Juan, something's wrong. Fifty-odd warriors passed the first time. Only forty-some came back. They either sent a party after the scouts—which I doubt, with the lead the scouts had—or . . . ?" He waited no longer, waving Archie and Jim over. "Not all their warriors came back. Let's move the horses farther out of sight along the ridge."

That was done swiftly.

They were thus between the main body of the war party and those unaccounted for, if indeed there were and he had not miscounted, Ewing reckoned. In that case, it also occurred to him, the main party could be playing the same game the scouts had earlier, pretending all had departed, while leaving a smaller force behind to search the vicinity of the camp. The stratagem was not new.

The four squatted down to wait. Archie on Ewing's left, Jim left of Archie, Montoya on Ewing's right. The horses were well-hidden behind them, near enough, however, that Ewing could hear when one stamped.

A jay squawked raucously. Ewing looked, but couldn't see it. Archie, head cocked, got up after a wait and prowled down the ridge. Long minutes had passed when he drifted back, shaking his head.

Midafternoon. The wind had quit and the forest drowsed. Ewing was on the point of deciding his fears were groundless, when Jim suddenly raised a warning hand. He had heard something that Ewing, even Montoya, had not. Jim pointed down-slope and somewhat to their left, and shifted that way, as did Archie. Ewing eared back the hammer of his carbine.

Not very long after this, Ewing saw an Indian clad in a red calico shirt step around a juniper, rifle at the ready. He had, Ewing thought, crawled all the way up the ridge to the tree. Figure by figure, now, the forest seemed to grow Indians, until eight or ten formed an irregular line, their attention fixed in the direction of the horses. So they had heard the horses. They moved on, stalking faster toward the horses.

Archie looked at Ewing, who nodded. They couldn't wait much longer. Ewing raised his carbine, sighted on the center of the red calico shirt. A fraction after he pulled the trigger, Archie and Jim let go, then Montoya. The .45-caliber slug drove Ewing's man backward, astonishment crashing across his paint-streaked face. He collapsed. There were yells. Ewing reloaded. Through the acrid powder smoke he saw three hostiles down, a fourth dragging himself away.

The rest flung about, preparing to charge. The second volley hit them before they could. That broke them. The survivors scattered downridge. All but one. He ran screaming up the ridge.

Deliberately, Montoya dropped the man ten yards away.

The ridge fell silent. Lingering powder smoke made a bitter stink. From below came the rattle of loose rocks. After a little run of time, Ewing heard horses going off.

He got up, said, "The main bunch will be swarming up here pretty quick. I don't think they went very far. That was all show. Too plain. Where do we go from here, Juan?"

"They will expect us to run like that posse—to go down," Montoya said. He kept fingering the tobacco sack in his shirt pocket.

"Do that, we'll play hell ever making it back up here again without being seen. Be like starting over, only harder."

Montoya looked down in deep reckoning. The muscles in his dark face worked, settled. "They will come straight to where they heard the shots. They are coming now." He gestured with his right hand. "We," he said, pointing with his left hand, "can go along the ridge on this side. That way we will pass them. They will be behind us. They will look for us here and down below. That and what they find here will hold them, here for a while."

239

"Then what?"

"We can go on—go higher—work around to that peak. If they trail us, we can spot them, because they will be below us. It's either that or run for it, Lieutenant."

Ewing moved that through his mind, back and forth. Actually, there wasn't much choice. The objective of the whole campaign could hinge on which way they rode. You couldn't get fancy, fighting Apaches; but neither did you have to do the obvious, which now would be getting the hell out of here and running to lower country. If they did, it wasn't likely they could get back, even with the full unit of Tontos. Going deeper into the heart of the Black Range would provide a small cushion of precious time—time to locate what they had come after—time—maybe—before the Warm Springs caught on.

"Lead off, Juan," he said.

As they ran for their horses, Archie and Jim, ever on the lookout for loot, legged down to the fallen hostiles. When they caught up, each had a brand-new Winchester and a belt of ammunition.

A new and grim realization flashed across Ewing's mind as they rode off. Instead of being the hunters, they had become the hunted. From now on it would be that way.

Adjutant Wirt Cooley, riding at the head of the column with Major Thorn and Captain B. B.

Kinman, acting as second in command, had learned the first morning out from Fort Cummings that this was going to be no book campaign, such as when they had gone into Chihuahua after Victorio in early October last year. Unexpectedly disdaining wagons, even pack mules, the major had taken on ten days' rations and struck for Hillsboro, there to await impatiently another courier from Lieutenant Mackay. When the detail of Tontos arrived in afternoon, he had ordered an immediate march and made dry camp that night. On this second day from Hillsboro, the command was approaching the lower Animas for evening bivouac.

It annoyed Cooley to see Luke Tisdale, the fringes of his buckskin suit flapping, dashing out to the advance and back, when he wasn't at Thorn's elbow. Without Mackay and no one else who could communicate with them, though Cooley knew that Private Rowdy spoke some English, the Tontos kept to themselves, content to ride as part of the advance screen. Rowdy's concealment, Cooley suspected, was tied to dislike of Tisdale.

Yesterday's tableau between the two kept evoking Cooley's grin:

"You big chief Apache. Me big chief Army scout. You speak um white man's talk, maybe so?" Tisdale asked.

Rowdy, who had conversed in passable

English when he delivered Mackay's report to the adjutant's office, appeared to have lost his power of speech and comprehension. He merely stared at Tisdale, who, exasperated, tried again. "Me"—pointing—"me big chief scout for Army. You"—pointing—"big chief for Apaches. You savvy?"

Rowdy's stony expression did not change in the slightest.

"You savvy some English," Tisdale insisted. "I've heard Mackay use it around you."

Rowdy broke into a torrent of Apache, pointing to the sky, pointing here, pointing there, pointing everywhere. He talked on, his style oratorical. Pleased with himself, he beamed on Tisdale and stood back, arms folded, his manner saying the scout not only understood, but was impressed.

It was Tisdale's turn to look blank. Frustrated, but determined, he started over, this time more slowly. "Me—scout—you—Apache. You—me—make—um—friends. Good friends. Heap good friends." He paused for that to register. "You savvy now?"

Silence. Rowdy's face impassive.

Tisdale turned his head and winked at Cooley, saying, "Betcha he'll savvy this," and facing Rowdy, he grunted, "You—take—um—*mucho* horses—*mucho* mules? Shoot—*mucho* Mexicans?" He simulated raising a rifle and firing and pointed toward Mexico.

Rowdy stared straight at Tisdale, his face expressionless.

Baffled, Tisdale resorted to a flurry of signs, waving his arms like a country preacher, making air pictures, pointing to his heart, to Rowdy's heart. Finished, he made the sign for "Done."

Rowdy simply regarded him in silence.

Tisdale muttered aside, "That dumb Tonto don't understand a thing about signs," and walked off, shaking his head.

When Tisdale was out of earshot, Rowdy raised the shadow of a smile and, slightly aloof, remarked to Cooley, "Such bad English him speak. How you *blancos* understand him?"

After supper, Major Thorn sent an orderly to fetch Cooley and Kinman. His mood was plainly dark, as it had been since departing Cummings. His jowled face looked slack, his eyes bloodshot, his unruly black hair like tumbled sheaves. He was drinking again, Cooley could tell. Thorn lumbered back and forth as he talked. "I want double sentries tonight, Mr. Cooley."

"Yes, sir. They're posted."

"Captain Kinman, there was some straggling this afternoon."

"That was A Troop, General. They've got some lame mounts."

"And we aren't even into the Blacks yet," Thorn growled, glaring at him. "If A Troop can't keep up, we shall dismount them as infantry. See

243

how they like that." He made a gesture of futility. "Some of the remounts we've been getting of late couldn't pull a sutler's wagon. Why they keep sending us the overlarge, long-coupled type of horse is a mystery to me. But persist they must, when it's been proven in campaign after campaign since the War that the short-coupled Western type is far superior in mountains and desert country."

"I think it is chiefly because we are at the tail end of the supply line, General," Kinman said, his voice as tolerating as Thorn's was not.

Kinman, Cooley thought anew, was one officer who could address the Old Man by his brevet rank without making it sound favor-seeking. With him, it was professional courtesy and no more.

Thorn was saying, scowling as he spoke, "We may be here only a few hours tomorrow, or possibly several days. At any rate, I want this command ready to move at any hour, day or night. Therefore, first thing after breakfast, troop commanders and first sergeants will inspect each and every mount for fitness. Meantime, there will be no bugle calls, and once we reach the mountains, no fires." He glared at both officers.

Kinman and Cooley nodded together.

Thorn stopped his rapid pacing and swung around, his official bearing shifting to one of hesitancy. "I should like your judgments on a matter of importance." He faltered, as if groping for words, and said, "It concerns Lieutenant Mackay."

Cooley was startled, thinking, *Mackay—so that's what's been chewing on him.* Yet was at loss to fathom the reason, unless the Old Man thought Mackay was negligent in not sending more frequent couriers. He saw Kinman stiffen, controlling his surprise.

"Captain Kinman," Thorn said, "since you are the senior officer present, I shall ask you first. What is your opinion of Lieutenant Mackay as a field officer?"

"Why, sir, I've found him first-rate. Capable. Experienced. Exceptionally so with Indian scouts. An officer of judgment, which enables him to evaluate what is happening and what may happen. Evaluations made without delay. I enjoyed my scout with him and the Tontos when we went up the Mimbres."

"Do you consider him a gentleman?"

"I do—yes. I have no reason not to. He is considerate of the opinions of other officers, so I found, and shows concern for those serving under him. Gets along quite well with the Tontos. He respects them, they respect him." Kinman's correct manner loosened and his austere face let in a condoning smile. "By saying he's a gentleman, I do not mean that I would categorize him as the parlor type—no indeed, though women likely would find him a congenial companion. I would say he's a man's gentleman."

Major Thorn, not sharing Kinman's humor, inclined his head and asked, "And you, Mr. Cooley?"

"As you know, sir, I haven't served with Mr. Mackay in the field; however, from all reports and based on my acquaintanceship with him, I can state unequivocally that he is a gentleman, based on visiting with him in our quarters."

"In your quarters?"

"At dinner, sir, when Miss Ivy Shaw was our house guest."

"Miss Shaw?"

"She was on the stage with Mrs. Thorn when it was attacked in Cooke's Canyon. You will recall that Mr. Mackay was in charge of the Indian scouts escorting the stage through, and earlier, when they made it from Stein's Peak to the Mimbres River."

"Oh, yes, the stage," Thorn said, his tone preoccupied. "I . . . I believe that is all, gentlemen. Good-night."

"Now what was all that about?" Cooley pondered when they had walked away.

"I wonder the same. I'd say the major is concerned whether Mackay can pull it off. Whether he can locate Old Vic and get a courier back to us and not get hemmed in up there, and whether we can wriggle up through these awesome mountains without alarming every hostile within a hundred miles. I've never seen such abominable terrain for cavalry."

"But what's that got to do with Mackay's being a gentleman?"

"Nothing," said Kinman and took his departure.

In C Troop's bivouac, Tim O'Boyle lay back and let his mind drift to Teresa, wanting to, yet not wanting to, because of the pain it brought upon him. He forced the memory down and spoke across to Duffy, "Think we're in for a big fight?"

"You can bet on it, lad. Or we wouldn't be here and that Lieutenant Mackay and his other Tontos wouldn't be up there in the Blacks, lookin' for Old Vic's stronghold. When the next courier rides in, up we go into them devil mountains. That's the word I hear along the line."

"Guess you've fought 'Paches?"

"More times than I like to tell about."

"What he means is," Wexler butted in, "he did most of his fightin' behind a big boulder."

"Which is the only dependable way," Duffy retorted, "when all you can see of them red devils is a puff of smoke bloomin' up behind another boulder on a canyon wall."

"There are other ways," Wexler said, sounding wise.

"Just how would you Dutchies suggest a man go about it?"

"You Paddies could put your evil eye on 'em."

"There's just one drawback," Duffy snorted. "It works better on Dutchies than 'Paches."

"Like your right cross?" a trooper asked, and the nearby men broke into laughter.

Wexler shut up. Despite his knockout at the hands of Duffy, he had lost none of his mocking belligerence that Tim could see. No words had been spoken between them since the fight. There was scant opportunity for talk on the march— during the first day Wexler had nursed his swollen jaw in silence—and on bivouac troopers were busy on the picket lines, hustling wood and cooking and standing guard.

The fire dulled to a cherry-red glow. Tired voices stilled. The hour came for Tim, on guard duty, to relieve the sentry on Post Number One. He paced back and forth, tensed for the slightest suspicious sound. Looking off toward the mass of the Black Range, he could sense its rugged vastness, its mystery alien to him, a farm boy from the midlands, and felt a mingling dread and awe. Something in him wanted to cry out. A cold loneliness clutched at his heart, and he was afraid.

CHAPTER 12

They were climbing again, the punished horses puffing and blowing. They topped a sunbaked ridge and clattered down it, twisting, angling, sometimes sliding. At the foot of the ridge rushed a small stream. They watered the horses, drank, and filled canteens, and Montoya hastened on through a park of wind-singing pines. In the green meadow beyond, he drew rein and pointed.

The cone-shaped peak loomed high above them. Ewing's distant illusion of gentle slopes didn't fit. Broken, timbered, gashed with rock slides, it squatted there like an ill-tempered watchdog, daring them to come closer. Down one rough flank, Ewing noticed a swaybacked depression, heavily wooded.

"We might picket the horses in that saddle," he said.

Nodding, Montoya rode to the peak's base, dismounted, and led his horse up a steep wash slippery with loose gravel. Going up was hot, hacking work as Montoya took a zigzag course; they left the horses on picket in the saddle's juniper thicket and resumed climbing.

The sun was dropping, evening's early coolness enveloping the peak, when they scaled a nest of boulders the size of huts and reached the summit.

Easing down, Ewing found a natural bowl, ringed by the boulders and dwarf oaks. An unexpected satisfaction occurred to him. Here they could build a cooking fire tonight.

He sank down, pulling for wind, and felt the strain ebb from his legs and thighs. Soon the restless Tontos rose to gather wood. Montoya rested, eyes half closed, hat on his lap, sweat beading his forehead, the wind ruffling his thinning, gray-black hair, exposing a beginning bald spot. Understanding and respect spread through Ewing. Montoya was well into his forties, a horseman not accustomed to climbing mountains afoot, and his short body was drained. But he would go on and on, not sparing himself, driven by the terrible wrong, the senseless wrong, inflicted on his family. A tough little man. A brave little man.

"We'll have us some coffee pretty quick," Ewing encouraged him, and got up to look. Through the field glasses he could see higher peaks far to the north. This one, however, commanded the view for miles around, a lofty aerie. Rough access and lack of water barred its choice for an Indian camp. Montoya had chosen the right one for a lookout. North and west, the precipitous land plunged and rose, a tangled maze of wooded canyons and small creeks that left sobering thoughts. The *rancheria* was in there somewhere. They were seven or eight thousand feet up, he reckoned, visualizing the punishment of moving cavalry through there.

When darkness rolled in, they dug a hole for the fire and cooked salt pork, fried hardtack in the grease, and boiled strong coffee. Seeing the comfort smoothing the three faces, Montoya's as dark as the Tontos', Ewing was reminded of how little food and coffee it took to restore a man's well-being in the field. A little was a great deal tonight, and you were damned grateful for it and the company of the men around you.

Afterward, Archie took his watch from a buckskin pouch and admired the gold-filled hunting case, turning it this way and that to catch the stag leaping across the golden firelight. Jim was stretched out like a dozing cat, his lean body soaking up strength for tomorrow. Montoya rolled a cigarette. His sad eyes, staring into the flames, could be seeing remembered images.

Ewing slept.

Waking abruptly, troubled, he saw the fire was out and the others were sleeping. He sensed that much of the night had gone. Rising, he flexed the stiffness out of arms and legs and stepped quietly away, drawn to the north side of the bowl. Standing in a gap between two boulders, feeling the air, sharp and clean, redolent of pine and juniper, he looked down and across.

Somewhere down there was the *rancheria*. That

was what had prodded him into wakefulness—the not knowing, the having to know.

He turned to go back, when a pinpoint of light caught his eye. He jerked around, so suddenly that he lost it. Leaning forward, he tracked his gaze across and back, up and down. There, now, it was again, a tiny spire of light. He was in that watchful attitude when he heard a scuff of sound behind him, and Archie said, "What, Nantan?"

"There's a light off there. You look."

Archie, standing beside him, looked and did not speak.

"Don't you see it? Look far out. Not straight down."

"Archie see. One campfire."

Jim and Montoya came over. "What is it, Lieutenant?" the rancher asked.

"We've spotted a campfire."

"Just one?"

"Just one. Doesn't tell us much."

"Could mean much. We could go down there and find out."

"Too near daybreak, Juan, or I'd say go. We'll start tomorrow evening. Gives us a day to observe what's going and coming around here." By the same token, he thought to himself, it also gives the Warm Springs another day to find us.

Just before daybreak they took the horses to water, picketed them again in the juniper grove, and climbed back up to the bowl.

In the middle of the morning, they saw mounted Indians stringing in from the southeast, to fade into the labyrinth of canyons.

"Our big war party is coming back," Montoya said. "They have scouted out everything below us. I hope they think we went southwest to the Mimbres River. But it is hard to fool an Apache, Lieutenant."

In preparation for the night's scout, Archie and Jim spent considerable time studying the northwest canyons and lower peaks and how they would all go. They would point and discuss, differing or nodding, jabbering, gesturing.

"We've seen no smoke signals today," Ewing reminded Archie. "What does that mean, if anything?"

Archie tendered him a tolerant grin. He said, "All warriors down there now, Nantan," and made coming-in motions from the four great directions. "No more warriors out there," he said, motioning away.

Before midday, with the boulders reflecting the heat, the bowl had become an oven. The resourceful Tontos cut oak branches and constructed a crude wickiup for the four of them.

So far, Montoya had seldom talked about his murdered son. While resting and smoking in the wickiup's shade, he grew thoughtful and said, "I cannot understand, Lieutenant, why my Manuel was murdered. Victorio's warriors had always spared my family. Victorio had always protected me—was my friend. I will never understand why my Manuel was killed." He kept shaking his head.

"These are mean times, Juan. Worst I've ever seen." He told Montoya about the teamsters found in Doubtful Canyon. About other trains where the Chiricahuas had burned the vehicles and pitched the wounded and dying into the flames. "But the worst," Ewing said, "was last spring south of Tucson, when we came upon a Mexican woodcutter's hut. The whole family had been rubbed out. One of the kids hung on a meat hook."

"When will the killing stop, Lieutenant?"

"When the last hostile Apache is dead."

"When can that be?"

"Years."

"Archie and Jim are Apaches—yet you trust them?"

"I think you have to take Apaches as individuals. You have to with any race. I wouldn't trust all Tontos anymore than I would trust all white men or Mexicans. I trust Archie and Jim and the rest of the detail because we are friends. We have suffered and shared together—that makes friends."

"And I thought Victorio was my friend."

While the Tontos took turns dozing and prowling the peak to watch around and Montoya smoked and nursed his bitter grief, Ewing reviewed their situation and objective. Once again the element of time pressed upon him. In the eye of his mind he saw again the map of the mountains: the lower Animas, where Major Thorn should be bivouacked by now; the distance from there to the camp where the Tontos had ambushed the hostile scouts; the up-and-down terrain to the lookout peak, and northwest, the pristine but frightful brokenness which they must penetrate tonight.

Evening stillness. Purple shadows laced the peak and darkened the canyons and ridges. Time to go. Archie started down, followed by Jim and Ewing and Montoya. Ewing had considered urging Montoya to stay behind and rest; on thinking it over, he had not, knowing the rancher would not, that there could be no rest for Juan Montoya.

The slope pitched steeply, the Tontos swinging down it faster than a horse could travel and more surefooted, skirting brush thickets, outcrops of rock, and strewn boulders, weaving through stubby timber, never stopping. At the bottom Archie paused, waiting while Ewing and Montoya caught up. Jim grunted something, whereupon Archie struck off. Soon they were following a narrow canyon, above them the guiding dimness of fast-fading twilight. They worked out of the canyon along an ever-climbing ridge, down it into another canyon.

Sweat was dripping down Ewing's chest when Archie stopped again. Jim, at his shoulder, whispered a sibilant word. Archie spoke briefly, a differing to his tone, a questioning. Ewing could hear Montoya's rapid breathing as he closed up, could sense the older man's unspoken relief. Up ahead Archie and Jim conversed in low tones.

They went on, down and up, helped by the fugitive light. Moonrise would be late tonight. After a long while, Archie slowed the pace, his caution greater.

We're getting close, Ewing thought.

About four hours after they had left the peak, Archie led them to the mouth of a wide gap and halted. "Wait, Nantan," he said, and he and Jim faded out ahead.

Long later, it seemed, the two became visible through the gloom, moving like wraiths. "Warm Springs back there," Archie hissed and touched Ewing's arm to follow, circling left of the gap. After some distance, Archie stopped. Before them rose the dark line of a wooded ridge. He said no word and, alone, disappeared into the ridge's blackness.

An interminable waiting clamped down. Still, Archie did not come back. When Ewing stirred, deciding he should send Jim to see about him, Jim placed a quieting hand on his arm.

Later, Ewing heard a faint scuffling on the

ridge. Brush snapped. A choked cry floated down. That was all. When the chirrup of a cricket followed from up there, Jim chirruped back and touched Ewing to go ahead.

They started climbing through mealy darkness. Minutes of this and Jim halted, as if waiting. The cricket's call came again. Jim gave a low *tweet* and, guided by the call, angled to the ridgetop.

Archie rose to meet them, hissing caution.

At that moment Ewing stumbled over something soft and heavy against his foot—a body—and jerked back, understanding instantly. Archie had killed a sentry.

"Look, Nantan," Archie whispered.

With a sense of surprise, Ewing stared at the campfires below. Many campfires. A scattering of fires near the mouth of the gap. It was one of those that he had spotted last night from the peak. A noisy camp. A big camp. He could hear voices. Down the gap he saw the bulky outline of the horse herd.

"Big *ranchería*, Nantan. Victorio's *ranchería*."

The dead sentry worried Ewing as they started back. Come morning, he would be missed and found and scouts would go out, and the factor of fleeting time would take on even greater importance. But they had found the *ranchería*.

Moving faster once beyond the gap, they reached the foot of the peak not long before first

257

light. While they rested and ate cold rations, Ewing told Archie, "We don't have much time. They will discover the dead sentry in the morning and come looking. I want you to go find Major Thorn. Tell him we've found Victorio's *ranchería*. Tell him it's a big one—tell him to come fast. The command should be on the lower Animas by now. If not there, it will be on the trail from Hillsboro." Ewing left off, figuring the distance from the lower Animas. "Bring Major Thorn to the stream there in the pines. We'll meet there."

Turning to Montoya, Ewing said, "Yesterday I thought when the major got into the mountains, he should lay over in daytime and march at night. Now, there's not that much time left. Scouting parties will be swarming around here today. Do you think Victorio will break camp and scatter if he sees the command coming up?"

"With three hundred warriors? He can defend the mouth of that gap with a handful. He won't run, Lieutenant. He will fight."

"*If* he can set an ambush," Ewing said, and thinking of the day ahead, "Let's bring the horses down to water."

Now the four of them were at the stream. Archie mounted and spoke to Jim in Apache. Something passed between them. Archie was older than Jim and thus had experienced more on the war trails, and his tone carried an older warrior's instructive tone. That and Archie looked at Ewing and Montoya, ready to leave.

Ewing walked out a way with him, saying, "Watch out for any war parties coming in to join the Warm Springs. Good luck."

"You watch, Nantan," Archie said and rode off through the timber, heading for the high ridge.

Reaching the juniper grove where they picketed the horses once more, Ewing turned to look back at the breaking light swimming with colors. For a space the threat of the present seemed to fall away. His face relaxed. Any other time, he thought, such a sunrise would be like a benediction: the friendly eye of the sun, the clearing sky, changing from gray wool to soft pink, the promise of another good day. He crushed out the thought and said aloud, "Think we can get these horses inside the rocks up there? They'll be found here."

Jim said he thought they could and led to a cleft on the west side of the bowl; by scraping saddles and horse flesh, they worked the mounts through and unsaddled.

Montoya and Jim stretched out at once to sleep.

For Ewing, sleep wouldn't come. He kept thinking, *Time, time.* By hard riding, Archie would reach the lower Animas today. Ewing could depend on that. If Major Thorn broke bivouac this afternoon late and marched throughout the night, he might arrive before noon tomorrow or early afternoon. If Thorn wasn't on the Animas, he couldn't possibly get up here until late tomorrow or the day after—and that, Ewing reasoned, if he knew Apaches, would be too late for them on the peak. Yet, for this, they had come here. He slept, then, on those hard reckonings.

The morning passed without change, not a cloud in the great sweep of the sky. That wasn't the sun blazing down at them, it was a merciless golden ornament taunting them. Seldom still, Jim cut oak branches for the horses to feed on. He produced a deck of Spanish playing cards and soon he and Montoya were gambling, while Ewing watched and roamed the rock-ribbed fortress. In doing so, he found on the floor of the bowl some curious pieces of broken pottery with geometric designs—black-on-white, red-on-white. Gazing at the shards, speculating, he could imagine the presence of those Ancient Ones— lean, small-bodied people, blackened by the sun, their straight black hair cut in bangs, the stoical men in squatting postures, arms over their knees, their enduring women nursing naked babies— who had known about this aerie so long ago. A refuge then, with wood and water and game below. A refuge now. But the hostiles, if they searched as only Apaches could, would discover where the horses had stood in the juniper grove and the tracks leading up to the peak. Simple. Only a matter of time.

Time became a laggard companion, unbearably dull, always straggling. Ewing's thoughts wandered: Ivy Shaw, waiting for him with the fears of childhood relived, seemed far away and unreal. Likewise, Major Thorn and his command, stumbling through the rocky wilderness below. To bring himself back to quick reality, Ewing had only to look off where the *rancheria* lay hidden in the tangle of canyons.

He saw the first rider about the middle of the afternoon. An advance scout, obviously, by the cautious way he rode his mouse-colored horse. After him, riders coming like a string of ants. At first sight he observed them almost objectively, without a rush of alarm—some thirty-odd—and felt only a mild surprise when they rode on to the timbered stream, instead of turning their attention to the peak as he had expected. He saw them no more for a long while, and therefore he knew they were mulling over the tracks coming this way and Archie's horse tracks going away. But when they rode back, appraising the ground, when the sun was behind the peak, coating everything down there in shadows, his pulse quickened and he clamped his lips together. Again it was simple. They would see where the horse tracks came down from the peak, then follow the tracks to the trampled juniper grove. But, wait. It was getting late; soon it would be dark, and Apaches, so many whites believed, never attacked at night. But not Ewing Hall Mackay, who knew better.

They were still down there, milling around, off their horses, nosing the cluttered tracks, when darkness blotted them from Ewing's view. Would they wait till daybreak?

Ewing decided to take no chances. You assumed nothing when fighting Apaches. Each man would stand short watches; that way each would get some sleep.

There wasn't much wind, but as the night advanced he felt chilled. Below, everything was like a black sea; above, the dimness awaiting the late-rising moon. In the direction of the *rancheria* he saw no campfire lights, not one; perhaps that meant something, a precaution. Once he heard the faintest of sounds at the rock wall, a scratching and then a pattering and an inquisitive mewling. When he whirled to see, a skunk waddled across the bowl. Ewing stayed motionless with relief as the visitor tailed out the other side.

The night was hours old when Jim touched Ewing awake and whispered that he was going outside to scout below. He would give the cricket signal before he showed himself so Nantan would not shoot him like a Warm Springs.

Dawn wasn't far away when Ewing heard the chirruping signal and Jim crawled over a boulder like some night creature. The hostiles, Jim reported, were in the juniper grove. Some were sleeping, some not. He had heard their voices.

"They will come soon, Nantan," he said and stripped for battle. Removing his calico shirt, he folded and placed it under his belt and tied his long hair behind his head.

Ewing roused Montoya and they posted themselves on the side of the bowl facing the juniper grove.

An owl's cry sent Jim into whispered warnings. Within moments, Ewing saw shapes, one by one, crawling over the rocky humps and running to cover behind the dwarf oaks and scrubby junipers. They seemed to melt into the rough slope. The next seconds felt endless, soundless until the owl's cry reached Ewing again and again the figures scurried uphill, spaced like skirmishers, and took cover.

By now Ewing could distinguish their pale shirts and leggings and headbands. He eared back the Springfield's hammer, overcoming the impulse to fire hurriedly.

Just as amber light was touching the peak's top, the owl's cry hooted again. At that signal, with shrieks and howls, the hostiles charged, moccasined feet pounding.

Ewing's shot was low, but it spun a man down—a thigh shot. Reloading, he saw Jim's warrior sprawling. Montoya's sat down and clutched his middle.

The element of surprise now lay with the defenders, who poured rapid shots into the confused line. It broke as a wave breaks on rocks, all at once, lapping back as suddenly as it had surged.

"Nantan—watch!"

Ewing sighted the painted face at the same instant that Jim shouted. Suddenly there it was, looming over the boulder. Ewing ducked. The warrior's rifle roared, but Ewing felt only the hot blast of the charge, tasted its acrid powder. He swung his carbine there, firing, and the face disappeared in a cloud of smoke. He dropped back and reloaded, seeing the broken line fading out of sight below a shelf of rocks thick with underbrush. It was over, for the moment.

While Jim and Montoya faced down the slope, pumping shots here and there, Ewing pulled away to check his flank, up which the warrior had crawled. Nothing there. He ran to the far side of the bowl. It likewise was clear.

He went slowly back, feeling the drum of his pounding chest, the letdown after the attack. On impulse, he began making a fire for coffee.

Time seemed fixed, but the sun read close to midmorning. Nothing moved except a red-tailed hawk. Ewing watched it glide by, swooping, then rising, riding the wind currents, watching below, hunting.

Occasionally shots cracked from below and ricocheting slugs whined off the boulders. Minutes would go by without gunfire, and then there would be a scattering of shots. Where, Ewing asked himself again, was Major Thorn? If the command didn't come up by late afternoon, that meant Archie had gone on to Hillsboro. Or worse, that Archie hadn't made it through. Ewing took a sip of tepid water.

Now, the sun stood straight overhead. Jim reported more warriors were moving around down there. He thought they were preparing for another charge. As he finished, a taunting voice called up from below, "Aaaaiiah! Aaaaiiah!" followed by a torrent of what sounded like abusive Apache. Jim's face hardened. He went to the rocks, shouted back a string of harsh Apache, and stood there glaring.

"What're they saying?" Ewing asked him.

"He say Warm Springs say Tontos big cowards. Say come down and fight."

"What did you say?"

"I say, 'You Warm Springs are women, not warriors. Come up here and Jim kill you all."

"We may have to break out of here," Ewing said. "Let's saddle the horses."

Nothing happened. The taunting died, as did the spasmodic firing to remind them they were still under siege. Ewing slouched, waiting, the sun hot on the brim of his pulled-down hat.

Not long after, Jim's shout yanked him up. Jim was pointing. Hostiles were crawling up from the juniper grove, hugging the broken face of the peak. As Ewing watched, Montoya called that warriors were moving up on the east side. Running to the north side, Ewing saw Indians advancing there as well. Only the west face of the bowl was clear; it sheered off sharply a short distance from the top.

Montoya's rifle banged. Quickly, all three were firing. Ewing shot at a running shape, which flattened just as he fired and missed. He caught another warrior rising to make his rush. A yell drifted back. The man did not get up.

"Nantan—over here!"

Ewing ran to Jim's side.

They were bunching down there. When Ewing and Jim opened up, Montoya ran across to help. Together they stalled the charge before it had covered three rods, the hostiles dropping flat or scattering. Some lay where they fell. After that the three would rush from side to side, whichever was most threatened. One Apache, running like a deer, sprinted for the back side of the bowl. Ewing and Jim both snapped shots, both missed. Before Ewing could reload, the Apache had leaped atop a boulder, outlined against the sky. Montoya blasted away. The Apache jerked, started falling over the edge. He appeared to hang suspended for many moments before plummeting from sight.

Of a sudden silence overhung the peak, and the slopes no longer squirmed with fleeting shapes.

While this respite held, Ewing grimly assessed their situation. The brunt of the charge had come up the side above the junipers, the south side. Warriors were still thick there, flattened down, biding their time. They were so close it was doubtful that three men could stop their next charge. The hostiles looked thinnest on the north and east slopes. The north side broke away toward the *ranchería* and likely more Apaches. The east let down to the meadow and the stream, into the pines, away from the Apaches. Only the sheer west side was safe. They would have to go out that way, come around, then break down the east slope.

"Let's get out of here," he said, making his tone hearty, and told them how it looked to him. Montoya inclined his head and cinched his saddle a trifle tighter. Jim untied his mount. At the cramped opening of the bowl, Ewing said, "Try not to string out. Stick together. If anybody goes down, the others pick him up."

Mounting with an eye for the straight drop to the rocks far below, they rode single file a short way. The silence continued as they came around on the north flank of the peak. Ewing had the prickly feeling of being a sitting target. When a shot greeted them, he dug heels and jumped his horse away. Swinging around to the east, they formed a quick front, Montoya in the center, and charged straight down the broken slope at a clattering run.

Close before them crawling figures sprang up, raising startled yells. "Aaaaiiah! Aaaaiiah!"

Brush tore at Ewing's face and arms. He snapped off shots with his revolver. A warrior bulked, barring the way, rifle tilted. There wasn't time for Ewing to fire. He flung himself aside as the rifle blasted and felt his horse and the man collide with a fleshy thump, felt his horse stagger, hump up, ride over the man and smash ahead. Conscious of a gap on his right, he glanced and saw Montoya's horse hesitating before an outcrop of slanting rock. Montoya dug spurs. The horse balked, took off, stumbled and slid to its knees, bringing a clatter of loose rocks. Montoya yanked its head up and they rushed on. Jim was beyond, clinging crablike to the side of his horse.

Behind them Ewing heard the scattered firing. But they had broken through. Nothing to hinder them now but more rocks and brush and scrub timber.

It was then that Ewing heard the clear notes of a bugle soaring up from below and realized it had been blowing some seconds before registering on his senses. The bugler was sounding officers' call, a cavalry signal of recognition.

They plunged down the last of the long slope

and hit the bottom running. Past the green meadow and the stream, in the cool pine forest, Ewing sighted a cavalry column of fours coming hard on the gallop.

CHAPTER 13

To Ewing's puzzlement, Major Thorn was coldly formal and awaited Ewing's salute before saying, "At last, Lieutenant, we have caught up with you." Lieutenant Cooley and Captain Kinman had extended eager handshakes. Thorn had not offered. After hearing Ewing's report, including locating the *rancheria*, Thorn said reproachfully, "That leaves us no chance of surprise as I had hoped."

"No, sir. I regret it does not. We've been fighting here since daybreak. By now, the war party has no doubt spotted the command and reported to Victorio."

Thorn studied the back of his gloved left hand. "Then we have but the one choice: attack at once or Victorio will slip away from us, and all this will have been for naught."

"I don't think he will run, sir. We estimate he has three hundred warriors, more or less."

"Did you count them?" Thorn demanded curtly.

"Only one party of Mescaleros, sir. In excess of forty, when they drove in horses stolen on the Rio Grande. There are also Comanches."

"How many?" Once more the critical interrogation.

"We saw where a big war party had come

in from the northeast. Wasn't likely more Mescaleros from that direction. *Señor* Montoya figured Plains Indians. After that, we killed a Comanche when scouts jumped our camp in the mountains."

"How do you know it was a Comanche?"

"*Señor* Montoya identified him as such. I believe that was in my report, sir. Later, we counted some fifty warriors—Warm Springs, Chiricahuas, Comanches, and Mescaleros—making for our old camp where we had killed the Comanche."

"That hardly adds up to three hundred warriors."

Ewing was straining for patience as he replied, "Well, sir, the night the Tontos led us to the *ranchería*, we saw many campfires in the gap."

"How many?" Thorn barked, unconvinced.

"I didn't count them, sir, but there were many. A big camp. I'd like to say that if not for *Señor* Montoya and the Tontos, the *ranchería* could not have been located."

Thorn nodded in recognition to Montoya. "I understand that without being reminded by a junior officer, Mr. Mackay. Now, I ask you again. In your opinion, do you think Victorio will pull out on us?"

"I do not, sir. I believe *Señor* Montoya is of the same opinion," Ewing said, turning to Montoya, who said, "Victorio's position in the gap is very strong, Major. He will wait for us to attack him. That is the Apache way. Expect an ambush."

"You don't think he will come out and fight?"

"No, Major. Why should he give up a strong position for an open fight? That is not the Apache way."

"In which case I am prone to think that you and Mr. Mackay have greatly overestimated the hostiles' strength. It is an established rule of warfare that an inferior force will hold back and not come out when strongly fortified." He slapped his thigh. "If that's what Victorio wants, then by Jupiter we shall accommodate him! Adjutant Cooley, we'll noon here for half an hour, then move right out with the Tontos in advance. Meantime, there is another matter that can be kept in abeyance no longer. Mr. Mackay, I will speak to you aside."

Thorn reined away, and as Ewing rode after him he could not fail to see Cooley's look of dire warning.

"Mr. Mackay," Thorn said, wheeling his mount, "it has been brought to my attention by Mrs. Thorn that your conduct after dinner in our quarters was unbecoming an officer and gentleman." The jowled face broke, reddening, on the brink of wildness. "Mrs. Thorn informed me that you tried to assault her sexually."

So that's what it's all about, Ewing's mind raced. She waited till just before the command moved out to tell him. He thought, *A woman scorned . . .*

"Speak up, Mr. Mackay."

"Sir, I did not assault Mrs. Thorn. I would not do that."

"You deny it? You question her veracity?"

"I do, sir."

"I remind you, Mr. Mackay, of the extreme gravity of this charge. I also remind you that it was only with the utmost reluctance, and after much soul-searching and self-examination of the effects of such a charge against a junior officer, that Mrs. Thorn could bring herself to inform me of what happened. Now, for the last time, sir, did you attempt to assault Mrs. Thorn?"

"I did not, sir." *Attempt . . . attempt.* So she had used that subtle wording, omitting that any forcible intimacy had occurred, thereby saving her exalted virtue as the lady of the commanding officer.

"I should hardly expect you to admit guilt, Mr. Mackay. But I remind you that in addition to the first charge, there will be a second—conduct to the prejudice of good order and military discipline. What is your reply to that?"

"I have nothing further to say, sir."

"Don't flank the question, Mr. Mackay."

"I have nothing further to say, sir."

Suddenly Thorn exploded with, "Then what did happen that evening while I napped?" He leaned toward Ewing, one gloved fist raised. "Did—?" He withheld the rest, as if fearful what he might hear, and slowly settled back in the saddle.

Ewing faced him without speaking.

"Well, then, Mr. Mackay, you are hereby relieved of command of the Tontos and placed under arrest. You will remain at the rear of the column. Mr. Tisdale will take charge of the scouts. An indictment will be drawn up on your return to Fort Cummings. I shall request the departmental commander to authorize a general court-martial." Upon that, Major Thorn rode back to his staff, his face set like flint.

The volley of unexpected accusations, coming hard and fast, left Ewing shocked and dazed. The first charge—conduct unbecoming an officer and gentleman—of course, was that general catchall that covered any variety of situations, particularly when a ranking officer had little evidence to go on when punishing a junior officer. There would have to be a specification brought before the court. Beyond that, he could not think, unless it was total ruin of his Army career. Looking around, he found Tisdale watching him. Ewing rode over to him.

"You got your wish, Tisdale. At last you're in charge of the Tontos. Guess you saw this coming, judging by the major's mood?"

Tisdale's acknowledgment was a cat-ate-the-mouse nod.

"I believe now," Ewing said, angering by the moment, "I can figure out who cut that Chiricahua prisoner loose on the Mimbres."

Tisdale's head snapped up in a huff. He rode across to Thorn.

The conniving s.o.b., Ewing muttered to himself. He watered his mount and led it back under the pines, wondering what could happen next and feeling strangely isolated.

Montoya came up, his eyes full of inquiry. "What is wrong, Lieutenant?"

"I'm under arrest, Juan, for something I can't very well explain. Tisdale has been placed in charge of the scouts."

"Tisdale! That is bad. He is a man of small judgment."

"Juan, get out of this. Go back. Go home. It's going to be bad at the gap. The major doesn't believe there's a big force of hostiles in there."

"Why does he not believe us?"

Ewing shrugged. "Go back to your family, Juan. You've done enough."

"I cannot. I have to see this to the end, Lieutenant."

Soon, Archie and Rowdy and Jim were there, their fierce faces upset. Ewing explained briefly about the change in command.

"That *blanco* man him say him scout," Archie said, instantly furious, his thin lips curling. "I

275

tell you this thing, Nantan. Back to San Carlos Tontos go will."

"You are enlisted Army scouts. You will be expected to lead the advance to the *ranchería*. That will be an order from Major Thorn. If you don't do that, you will be disobeying orders and subject to arrest."

Archie spoke to Rowdy and Jim and much heated Apache talk followed, after which Archie said, "Nantan, you see," and they rode to the other scouts and talked to them. On that outcome, they all drew apart to themselves, glaring at the staff officers, sitting their horses like so many copper images.

While the troopers finished watering their horses and filling canteens, Ewing saw Tisdale go over to the Tontos, speak, and point northwest in the direction of the *ranchería*. Ewing flinched at his manner: patronizing, the new *blanco* commander taking charge of inferior, heathen Apaches. No Tonto spoke. They just looked at him; or rather, Ewing perceived, through and beyond him. Tisdale said something more. Nothing changed. He tried wheedling words and crude signs. *Me— friend—you—friend.* The Tontos ignored him. He cursed them then, but if they understood, which Ewing knew they did, they did not let on. They continued to insult him by pretending he did not exist, a mere *blanco*, which, next to shaking the breechclout, was the supreme Apache insult.

Meantime, the staff officers observed the stalemate.

Tisdale talked on and on, his voice kiting higher and higher. Suddenly he ran out of words. Rigid with rage, shouting abuse and threats, he spurred back to Major Thorn.

A staff conference ensued. Thorn, Kinman, Cooley, and Tisdale. The scout kept shaking his fist; apparently, he wanted the Tontos arrested. Kinman pointed to the sun: time was passing. Cooley spoke, always the peacemaker. Thorn then looked at the sun; as if counter to his judgment, he addressed Cooley at length and made a curt get-on-with-it motion.

Cooley galloped across to Ewing. "There's been a change in orders, Lieutenant. The Tontos won't budge under Tisdale. The Old Man is roaring mad and called them Navajos. He says for you to take over the scouts, but said to remind you that technically you are still under arrest." In a changed and concerned tone, "Ewing, what the hell's going on? The Old Man won't say, other than your conduct has been unbecoming an officer and gentleman—the old hogwash."

"Maybe you've already guessed what happened the night I went to dinner at the Thorns," Ewing said. "That was my first mistake." He managed to muster the ghost of a twisted smile. "The second one was when I wouldn't go back. She—well . . ."

Mounting, he left Cooley and saddled over to

the Tontos. "Let's go," he said, and they formed behind him as he reported to Major Thorn. "We're ready to move out, sir."

Thorn said, "You will cover the advance to the gap. When it comes in sight, you will report for further orders." The gravel-pit eyes dismissed Ewing by looking straight ahead.

Montoya rode up beside Ewing as he led the scouts off.

"Go back, Juan."

"You will need a tough Mexican where you're going."

They crossed the stream and left the cool meadow. Beyond, there was no sign of the war party in the vicinity of the peak. Archie spoke an order and the scouts fanned out ahead.

Shortly, Jim reported finding a dim trail. It took them deeper into broken country, devoid of movement and much too quiet to Ewing's notion. They worked past numerous places offering concealment for ambushes. The steep, wooded slopes and brushy canyons and arroyos seemed empty of life. Looking back, Ewing saw the dark snake of the command following in a column of twos.

While the advance continued unopposed, Ewing asked Montoya, "What do you make of this, Juan?"

"Victorio is a wise general. He has chosen his own battlefield. His warriors and allies are already counting how many blue coats they will kill. How many rifles and horses they will take. How much ammunition they will gather up. After all, he whipped the blue coats once before in the Black Range. Victorio is waiting, Lieutenant."

As the sun marched on to midafternoon, Ewing saw the V-shaped gap cleaving a passage through the forested ridge. Telling the scouts to hold up, he reported to Major Thorn. "There it is, sir. The *ranchería* is beyond that gap."

Thorn uncased his glasses and stopped for a long look. "I observe no movement," he said, his tone critical.

"I doubt that they would show themselves now, sir. They are waiting for us to attack."

"We shall see." Thorn brought down the glasses. "You will take the scouts and feel out the gap. Pitch into 'em. Stir 'em up. I want them to expose their positions—if they are in there—if they haven't flown the coop."

Ewing's face flamed at the order, sensing its hidden intent. Ten Tontos and one officer taking on the whole camp without support. The sides of the gap would be studded with warriors. A deadly outcome of an attack by them on the scouts was far more certain than a guilty verdict by a military tribunal, besides making unnecessary the embarrassment of a commanding officer's wife having to testify about the intimate details of a seduction.

Captain Kinman reined in closer. "May I suggest, General, that we dismount a troop and move them up in support of the scouts?"

"Your suggestion is well taken, Captain. However, Mr. Mackay has assured me the scouts are quite capable at this sort of work. Proceed, Mr. Mackay."

Ewing was wheeling his horse when Thorn's voice cut at him, "I believe you forgot to salute, Mr. Mackay. Must I remind you that military courtesy is not dispensed with in the field?"

Ewing could feel the blood surging up his neck and face. But when he turned and saluted, he had himself under control. He reached the Tontos and passed the order. They would all advance on foot except the youngest scout, left with the horses. And then he told them, "Once they start firing and show their positions, we halt and pull back. Understand?" Seeing Montoya dismounting, he said, "Juan, the major's order was for the scout detail alone. Not you."

Montoya's answer was to hand the reins to the young horse-holder. "I have come this far with you and the Tontos, Lieutenant. I will go on with you."

After the Tontos had stripped for battle, Ewing formed a line of spaced skirmishers and they started walking, naked to breechclouts. Approaching the mouth of the defile, they broke into a run and took cover along both sides of the rough slopes. A pause and they advanced a short distance again and sought cover among the rocks and brush. Again, they repeated the maneuver.

Archie's eyes on Ewing as they crouched together said, *Do not be fooled, Nantan. They are up there.*

A blur of motion high on the right-hand slope pinned Ewing's gaze.

The bullet struck as he watched through the field glasses. Above him there was a *splat* of shattered rock, followed by the sound of the shot, and Ewing flattened out instinctively. As if that were a signal, the jaws of the ridge puffed with smoke and the gap reverberated with the rapid firing. Bits of rock and brush rained around the scouts. There was nothing visible to fire at, only the smoke puffs. For a while, Ewing let the scouts trade volleys; then he shouted at Archie and waved him back, and Archie shouted to those on the other slope and motioned back.

By the time Ewing reached the staff officers a discussion was in progress. Major Thorn was doing most of the talking. Ewing had to wait an interval before Thorn took notice of him. "Well, Mr. Mackay—"

"They're on both sides of the gap, sir. They've thrown up stone rifle pits."

"I b'lieve that was observable from here." Thorn's eyes were bloodshot. His overly correct voice conveyed a faint slur, and his pugnacious features looked more pronounced than usual. He wallowed a bit in the saddle. Turning his back, he said to Kinman, "I agree, Captain . . . uh . . . charge through th' gap would be foolhardy at this juncture . . . though th' element of surprise can produce uh smashing blow, sir."

"True, General, at the proper time. But to dislodge them from the pits, we'd have to go in on foot. From their field of fire high on the slopes, they would soon pin us down."

"You have uh alternative, Captain?"

"A flanking movement, General. There is no other way I see, without placing the command at a disadvantage that would cost many casualties."

"A flankin' movement, here?" Thorn swiveled his gaze about. "Th' terrain does not lend itself to that."

Ewing, feeling he had to speak up, said, "Sir, there's a side door to this gap. The Tontos found it the night they located the *rancheria*."

"I was about to ask the lieutenant's opinion," Kinman said, pressing for more.

"It's to our left," Ewing said, speaking faster. "Down the ridge about a quarter of a mile, maybe farther. A sort of low saddle. From there that night we could see the entire camp below us. That should place us above the rifle pits on that side."

"A page from Cooke's *Tactics,* Mr. Mackay?" Thorn broke in. "This is not Virginia."

"I realize, sir, we'd have to mask our intentions some way."

Kinman's brisk voice joined in. "A demonstration in front of the gap might do it, General, while the scouts and one dismounted troop slipped off behind us." He paused to test Thorn's reaction.

"Go on, Captain," Thorn said. Suddenly he looked quite weary. "At th' moment I see no other alternative."

"I would suggest that we bring the command up and form a broad front, as though we are preparing to charge. That should hold the enemy's attention and raise sufficient dust to conceal our purpose. At the same time send another troop on foot to flank the right ridge. Once the enemy is forced from the rifle pits, we charge the gap—but not till then."

"Very well, Captain. I jus' hope Victorio won't break off an' run before we can smash him. Apaches can't stand close quarters." He swayed a little. To Ewing, he looked depressed and drunk.

"Sir," said Lieutenant Cooley, anxiously eyeing the major, "would you like to pull back to the shade over there? I have an extra canteen."

The bloodshot eyes hardened. Thorn became erect, his mood gone. His voice thickened. "I need no suggestion from m' adjutant as to where I m' view th' operation. Bring up th' command, Mr. Cooley."

CHAPTER 14

Waiting with the Tontos and Montoya, Ewing heard the commands come fast. "Left front into line! Guide right!" As dust enveloped the flat before the gap, C Troop rode into the timber and left its mounts with horse-holders. At that, Cooley galloped over to a troop commander and the troop swept to the left and back to the center, raising clouds of yellow dust. Behind that concealment C Troop double-timed over to the Tontos, and Ewing moved the scouts off at a dogtrot along the base of the left ridge, C's men on the scouts' heels. A like movement was going on to the right, covering the other flanking troop.

Archie went swinging ahead with Jim. When the low saddle slid into focus, a swaybacked dip on the long shoulder of the wooded ridge, they halted and pointed. The scouts caught up and the panting troopers followed by straggling twos, the low-voiced noncoms urging, "Close up! Close up!"

Private Wexler was blowing like a stud horse, sweat runneling down his scarred face, dropping off the tip of his broken nose. "All the time I thought I'd jined the U. S. Cav-va-ree—an' it was the infantry," he mocked.

"It's that Little Chihuahua belly-wash oozin' out through your mean hide," Corporal Duffy said.

Wexler wiped his face. "You Micks an' your saintly ways."

"You Dutchies and your foul-fightin' ways."

"Cut out the talk," warned Sergeant Larkin, going along the line. "Want the 'Paches to hear you? Not another word when we start up the ridge."

Tim O'Boyle considered the forbidding ridge, dreading what might be up there and what awaited them, for certain, on the other side. He was afraid, of course he was afraid; but when he looked at Private Otto Hoch, a surge of sympathy replaced his own fear. Hoch was even greener than Tim was. He looked ill. "Buck up, Otto," Tim said. "I'll be right alongside you."

Hoch swallowed and wet his cracked lips.

The young second lieutenant hastening forward Ewing remembered as officer of the day when the eastbound stage, attacked in Cooke's Canyon in daylight, limped into Fort Cummings. Very young. Bold mustachio flaring on the sun-baked, boyish face. They shook hands. Arthur Nolan, Ewing Mackay. "I understand we're to follow you up," Nolan said, much as if they were on maneuvers.

Ewing nodded. "We're ready when you are, Lieutenant."

285

"We are. I won't deploy skirmishers till we get on top."

If not before, Ewing thought silently. *If the hostiles haven't anticipated us.*

He started working up the rough slope with the scouts, squeezed by the afternoon's banked heat. The sounds of the toiling troopers reached him as grunts and stumbles, brush snappings and boots scraping on rocks. He felt the prod of haste. That ridgetop. That high ground. Even the Tontos were too slow for his thinking. Above him, finally, he saw bright sunlight breaking through the timber where the ridge shelved off to form the saddle. And then there, quite suddenly, he saw with shock the heads and shoulders of advancing hostiles.

The lead Tontos opened up at once. They had, Ewing knew, run head on into a flanking party hurrying to fall upon the command's flank.

Ewing wheeled and bawled, "Come on, Nolan! Come on! Quick!"

Going on, he sensed as well as saw a slowing down of the advance as the scouts, meeting fire, scattered and took cover and fought back. But the hostiles held the saddle above them and yelled reminding taunts at the scouts, who yelled back. Bitter smoke drifted through the woods like rolls of cotton. Ewing fired at low white puffs. Before long he heard a rush of new sounds coming in on his right: troopers crashing through brush on the

286

double, noncoms roaring men into some kind of order. Next he saw skirmishers deploying. There was young Nolan as if on the parade ground. And afterward troopers swept along the crest of the ridge, firing and shouting as they came.

Flanked, the warriors holding the saddle began bunching and milling in confusion. Some dropped.

The scouts charged up the ridge, their screeching high above the voices of the troopers. In moments the saddle was cleared.

There, Ewing and Nolan met. "Much obliged, Lieutenant. They had us pinned down. Now, let's go after those goddamned rifle pits."

With the scouts in advance of C Troop, everybody double-timed along the uneven backbone of the ridge. Ewing, looking ahead, halted abruptly. Mounted Indians were massing near the mouth of the gap. His jaw fell slack. He said in a thunderstruck voice, "See that paint horse, Nolan? That's Victorio's war horse. I never believed the story till now, but there it is."

"That's not all," Nolan said. "Look beyond the gap. I believe the command is forming for a real charge this time."

"Not till the rifle pits are cleared—that was understood. I've heard no firing from the other flanking party, have you?"

"None at all. Just the same, the command is going to charge."

The staccato notes of charge were sounding before Nolan finished speaking.

Ewing was dumbfounded to see the lead troop galloping forward by fours, then another and another, troop guidons whipping in the wind. He thought he made out Major Thorn near the point of the column. The mounted Indians danced and whirled their agile mounts until the command entered the gap, then the rider on the paint wheeled and all the Indians turned and dashed into the pines. The charging troopers pressed the pursuit.

"It's the old decoy trick," Ewing said, dry-voiced. "Thorn took the bait. All we can do now is clean out the pits and support the charge."

But when they reached them, some two hundred yards on, the pits were empty and Ewing saw the last of the ridge's warriors streaming into the pines, no doubt to help close the jaws of the ambush.

Nolan didn't hesitate. He formed his skirmishers on the left and downgrade they plunged, a ragged wave, stumbling past the abandoned rifle pits.

Ewing kept glancing at the gap. For a time, Thorn's charge looked unchecked. When Ewing next looked, it had slackened. Riders piling up before the pines. Saddles empty. Horses down, others galloping riderless. As Ewing watched, the column broke, shattered, and suddenly its pieces went flying back toward the mouth of the gap.

At the foot of the ridge Nolan re-formed his troop. The Tontos, scattered coming down, pulled in tight, urged by Ewing and Archie. These hurry-up closings made as a volley crashed like a mighty shout from the other ridge. Ewing stopped. A second volley clapped. That meant the other flanking troop had made contact and was driving ahead. He waved at Nolan, who waved in understanding.

Scouts and troopers stalked into the pines, a parklike forest now casting afternoon shadows, dotted with deserted brush wickiups. Broken sunlight laid down a terrazzo of speckled shade.

Hostiles turned to meet this threat. A volley knocked some down, but many more, apparently freed after turning back Major Thorn's charge, rushed up. The forest swarmed with them. The air hummed and zipped. Pieces of twigs and bark flew like gravel. Powder smoke drifted in dirty globs.

"Aim for the sweat on their bellies!" Duffy roared. There were shouts of "Stay down! Stay down!"

Tim and Hoch, crouched side by side, fired at the elusive shapes darting from tree to tree. Closer, still closer they came. Seeing that unnerving sight, Tim suddenly discovered there was nobody on his left, that the platoon had fallen back. He and Hoch were in danger of being cut off. When he turned to yell Hoch back, he saw Hoch lurch with a stricken cry and fall, grabbing his head with both hands, his carbine flopping beside him. He jerked convulsively for moments and then lay still.

Tim stared in horror at Hoch's bloody face. "Get up!" he pleaded and shook him. "Otto, get up!" Tim reached for his canteen, then paused, stilled by an awful certainty. His hand fell. Hoch didn't move. He couldn't, Tim saw. He was already past any aid. He was dead.

As Tim picked up his own carbine to fall back, something seared his thigh and smashed him down. He tried to get up and run, furious at his incapacity, but could not. Shock rode over him. Everything went black.

A long time seemed to pass before Tim stirred. But around him the forest still shrieked of gunfire and the high-pitched "Aaaaiiah! Aaaaiiah!" of the hostiles and the deep-toned shouts of the troopers. He stirred and moved his arms. His left side felt numb from the waist down. He struggled to rise, fell back; inch by inch, he started crawling. The effort was too much. The forest became fearfully dark again. Sounds dimmed. He ebbed in and out of consciousness.

A little while later he felt powerful arms scooping under him. Tim protested, flailed out weakly, thinking of Indians.

A voice ground in his ear, "You damn Mick!

You was crawlin' right for the 'Paches. Now, quit fightin' me. I'm takin' you back to our line."

Tim felt himself lifted with ease, and soon the forest was rushing by, and patches of blue sky. How fast they moved! There was a flurry of shots behind them. Without warning, he felt the muscled arms give a jerk, felt a faltering in their zigzagging course; even so, they were going on, slower now . . . but going on, now down to a staggering walk. They fell and rolled. In the dim forest Tim heard friendly voices, felt friendly hands about him before the blackness rode him down again.

Ewing and Lieutenant Nolan anchored their thin line in the shallow run of a dry arroyo. Troopers and scouts lay on their carbines, keyed for the next charge, content to catch their wind after two head-on fights within an hour. Their wounded lay in the bottom of the arroyo. Their blue-clad dead lay scattered in the deepening gloom of the forest, among them two Tontos. Now and again a scout would wail.

Never had Ewing seen Archie so reckless as he had been today: daring and taunting, needlessly exposing himself to get a good shot. At this moment he was moaning and chanting while he rocked back and forth on his haunches, about him the damnable primitive fatalism that Ewing hated. Apaches. What white man could know them? Also, never had he seen hostiles stand and fight as these had, when usually they would break off to fight another day.

Except for sporadic shots, a false lull pervaded the forest. Ewing hadn't heard a volley in some time from the other flanking party. *They've been checked like us,* he thought. *A stalemate.* The hostiles were likewise regrouping, licking their wounds and making medicine; when they were ready, the battle would resume. The forest off through there pulsed with them.

Nolan had voiced Ewing's own view of their choices when he said, "If we pull back over the ridge to the command, it strikes me that would leave the other flankers in an extremely bad position."

"It would," Ewing agreed. "Same for us, if they pulled back and left us hanging." He looked at Montoya. These past days had worn him down to the very frame of his compact body. The skin across his leathery face was like parchment. But his dark eyes, while sunken, were still sharp and moved quickly. He went to the rim of the arroyo, settled himself, rolled and smoked a cigarette, and watched the forest.

Ewing judged the sun at about five o'clock, hanging like a gory red shield in the cloudless sky, and still the forest was hushed.

It was in the silence that followed, in the growing dimness, when they came—there, suddenly materializing, almost before Ewing knew it, so quietly they seemed a part of the forest.

He saw the single muzzle flash. It set off a storm of gunfire. He heard Nolan's young voice and, quickly, the rattle of carbines. The hostiles hurled taunts at the scouts. Archie replied with like insults and furiously worked his Springfield.

Through the din Ewing picked up a faraway sound. It seemed to reach him by degrees, rising from the gap, ever clearer, the scrambling rat-a-tat-tat of a bugle sounding the charge. He could hardly believe it. At the same time the hostiles' fire dropped off. Ewing saw them facing toward the gap, listening, intent on the unexpected threat, now backed by steady carbine fire.

Now, Ewing's mind raced. *Now. While they're turned.* He yelled at the Tontos. Archie yelled, understanding. Nolan yelled. And out of the arroyo the whooping scouts and shouting troopers erupted in a wave, driving straight ahead.

Ewing saw warriors dropping, others shrinking from the sudden charge. In moments the rest broke. The bugle was blowing again. Volleys crashed where the second flanking troop fought. Meaning flashed through Ewing. The center of the fight was shifting toward the gap. That meant the hostiles were being pinched from three sides.

Onward it was like shooting at fugitive shadows, shadows that suddenly became warriors turning to make a stand, then slipping back through the forest, still taunting the Tontos.

Ewing, hearing an answering yell nearby, spotted Archie dodging from tree to tree, firing as fast as he could while screeching his own challenges. There was a rattle of carbines to Ewing's left. Jerking that way, he saw a platoon coming up; when he looked again for Archie, the scout was lost from sight. Pine needles peppered down on Ewing's hat. He was soaked with sweat. He hacked for wind.

A bent-over young trooper stumbled up to him, left hand clutching the right side of his chest. "Sir," he heaved, "I'm hit—what can I do?"

Ewing sat him gently down behind a pine, gave the boy his own canteen and went back into the bloodletting, seeing that in those few moments the fight had swung away from him, closer to the gap. There was the hub of the battle now, being pushed to its final throes.

Plunging ahead, firing at the flashing shapes, he caught sight of horses through the smoky haze. A shuddering volley shook the woods. On that, the gunfire dropped off, and he saw fewer warriors in front of him, and then he saw none. He became conscious of a settling stillness, in the distance the falsetto cries of warriors breaking off from the fight and the cries of the wounded behind him. The shivering notes of recall sounded. It was finished.

He came to a heavy-bodied halt, the brunt of all this slugging through him. He felt used up and grim, down to the very last of himself. His ears rang. The hush was unreal. He tasted powder smoke, harsh, bitter, the dregs of the day itself.

"Nantan!"

It was Jim running up.

"What is it?"

"Come—Archie."

Ewing groaned and followed, dreading what he would find.

Archie lay under a tree, quieter than Ewing could remember seeing him. Archie tried to smile, "Get them will we, Nantan. You watch, Nantan."

Ewing crouched beside him, opened Archie's shirt, and averted his eyes.

The thin lips moved. "Archie . . . Big Sleep go."

"Like hell you are! You're not going to Big Sleep. You listen to me. You're not going to Big Sleep. Hear me! You're not!"

"No. Archie know. Big Sleep come." One hand moved. "You keep, Nantan," and he laid his watch in the buckskin pouch on Ewing's hand.

It was intolerable. He would not permit it. Ewing sprang to his feet, raging, his composure broken the first time today, calling, "Surgeon! Surgeon!" and cursing. Where was the god-damned surgeon? Of course, as usual, there was only one for the entire command, and of course troopers lay piled like cordwood along the path of the two charges up the gap, and more lay in the woods, and of course there could be no surgeon for a mere Indian, a bloody Apache, a heathen to boot, a primitive Apache who knew only how to be a trusted friend and brave and true to his oath as an enlisted soldier in the United States Army, which would soon forget him.

Ewing, taking Archie in his arms, had not wept in a long time. He wept now, without restraint. He thought Archie's back was broken; he could almost tell. He continued to hold Archie even after he had crossed over to Big Sleep, and then, miserable and wretched and grieving, Ewing rose and walked across the floor of the forest toward the command, behind him Jim and Rowdy, who let down their hair and bent their heads over their chests and wept and wailed like children.

In the arroyo Private Kirk Wexler was going fast. Tim O'Boyle lay next to him. Wexler said, "Boyle, it's gettin' dark."

"Good light left yet. And the name is O'Boyle."

"Looks dark to me." Wexler's breath came raggedly. He said, "Listen, there's something you ought to know. I didn't take Teresa out that night. I said that to get you mad . . . so you'd lose your temper and I'd win the fight. Damn near did till Duffy stepped in."

"You're lying. You're just saying that."

"She asked about you that night. Why you hadn't come back to see her."

"I asked her to marry me. She refused."

"Proves you know nothin' about women. She's afraid of Gannon—that's why."

"I can see things now I couldn't before. She . . . she's lived with Gannon. I see that now. His woman."

"Don't judge her. She was poor. Had to make it any way she could. She's young."

"She turned me down."

With straining effort, Wexler raised up to glare at Tim. "You high an' mighty Mick! Go back for her. Get her outa there. She's a good kid." He crumpled back.

Tim said, "It's not that I don't love her . . . I do. Only—" He fell silent, letting his mind dwell on Teresa and what he would say to her; off and on the fading battle sounds drifted back. Gradually, he realized that Wexler hadn't said anything for a while, and he turned as pain would permit and looked.

Wexler didn't move. His eyes were open and he was staring straight up at the sky.

Recall had sounded again and they converged at the edge of the forest in the gap, Ewing, Captain Kinman, Adjutant Cooley, Lieutenant Nolan, and Montoya, and a first lieutenant from the other flanking party.

Cooley said matter-of-factly, "First, I regret to report that Major Thorn was killed in the first charge."

"He charged too soon," Ewing said bluntly, refusing to bestow false accolades on a dead man bent on self-glory. "We hadn't cleared the rifle pits yet."

"I know," Cooley replied loyally. "But he saw Victorio on the paint horse."

"It was a decoy, a trap."

Cooley coughed discreetly. "At the time it didn't appear so. He was afraid Victorio would get away."

Ewing tiredly let that pass unchallenged, knowing those here were aware of the old story: Brice's Cross Roads. N. B. Forrest. Defeat. The volatile Sherman's banishment of Thorn to the Texas frontier. And Thorn's consuming obsession to wipe out his disgrace.

In his tactful way, Kinman said, "Paint horse and rider are down over there. I think that was when the fight turned for us and the other people broke off. Now, I suggest that we go see what the legendary Old Vic looked like."

They went there. The dead rider was pinned under the paint stallion.

Ewing, seeing the silver-encrusted saddle, the lance, the shield, the rider's face, called suddenly to Montoya, who was trailing the officers. "Juan, I wish you'd look!"

Montoya came slowly over. His reluctance was evident. His attention centered first in a remembering way on the paint, which Ewing recalled the rancher had given the Apache chieftain, and then on the rider. Montoya's interest sharpened. His eyes bored. He gave a start and, seizing the long hair below the calico headband, pulled the head back to look at the face. He gasped, "It's Gómez—" and stepped back.

Kinman and Cooley traded incredulous stares. Kinman barked, "You mean that is not Victorio?"

"It is not," Montoya said. "It is Gómez."

Troopers were passing with a captured Indian woman under guard. Montoya spoke to her in rapid, questioning Spanish. She answered and pointed to Gómez.

Montoya needed a moment to collect his thoughts. "She says Gómez was Victorio's adopted son—born a Mexican, raised as a Warm Springs to hate all Mexicans. When Victorio was killed at Tres Castillos, Gómez took his Apache father's war trophies, including his paint horse, and became the war chief." Montoya's eyes moved to Ewing; in them Ewing read something akin to reprieve, like faith renewed, and Montoya said, "I know now that Victorio would not have let them kill my Manuel. Victorio was my friend." Tears came. Head bowed, he walked suddenly away.

"There is another aspect of all this, gentlemen," Kinman said, his tone reasoning. "Major Thorn died gallantly. No man can refute that. There is no nobler way for a cavalryman to die than leading a charge against superior numbers. A decision made in the heat of battle often suffers unfairly from hindsight. Whatever, we have to agree that Major Thorn's conception of this campaign proved successful. Historians will probably call it the Second Victorio War." His eyes roamed the officers and paused on Ewing. "Would you like to say something, Lieutenant Mackay? Speak your mind. You have that right, you know. Certainly, you have earned it."

Ewing's first impulse was to voice what they all knew: Thorn's glory-serving charge had very nearly brought disaster to the entire command. In effect, Kinman was giving it the old Army whitewash and asking his officers to support it. Yet, what was to be gained by not? Why not leave matters there? Let Thorn go down as a hero. Leave him that. Ewing then said, "Why, yes, Captain. I do have something to say. I should like to know who led the second charge. It took the pressure off us."

"Captain Kinman," Cooley supplied when Kinman did not speak. "He rallied the command."

There was nothing more to be said at this time. They broke up to go to their respective units. Walking off, Ewing found Lieutenant Nolan alongside him and said, "There's a boy in your troop lying against a tree back there. I'm afraid he's badly wounded."

He went on, alone, thinking of what was gone and what was left. On second thought, there was a great deal waiting for him.

ABOUT THE AUTHOR

Fred Grove has written extensively in the Western field, both in fiction and nonfiction. He has received the Western Writers of America Spur Award four times—for his novels *Comanche Captives* (which also won the Oklahoma Writing Award and the Levi Strauss Golden Saddleman Award) and *The Great Horse Race* and for his short stories "Comanche Woman" and "When the Caballos Came." His novel *The Buffalo Runners* was awarded the Western Heritage Award by the National Cowboy Hall of Fame, as was the short story "Comanche Son." Mr. Grove has also contributed short stories to many anthologies, among them *Spurs West* and *They Opened the West*.

For a number of years, Mr. Grove worked on various newspapers in Oklahoma. It was while interviewing Oklahoma pioneers that he became interested in Western fiction. He now resides in Silver City, New Mexico.

Center Point Large Print
600 Brooks Road / PO Box 1
Thorndike, ME 04986-0001 USA

(207) 568-3717

US & Canada:
1 800 929-9108
www.centerpointlargeprint.com